The Makeup Artist

Coffee Book 2

Sophie Sinclair

THE MAKEUP ARTIST

Copyright © 2020 by Sophie Sinclair
Print Edition

Editor: Michelle Morgan, www.fictionedit.com
Proofreading: Michelle Morgan
Book Cover: Carrie Guy, Shawna Montague, Julie Troutman
Book Design: BB eBooks

All Rights Reserved

To JRG,
A little rain, a little sun, a little laughter makes everything
right when I'm with you.

The way I see it, if you want the rainbow,
you gotta put up with the rain.
– Dolly Parton

Will you dance with me in the dark?
Take this trip to Never Neverland?
Will you expose my heart?
Do a damn fine job of tearing it apart?

Take my hand, let's dance in the dark
Ooh yeah, let's dance in the dark
This isn't a love song, baby, it's a whole lot of heartbreak.

Not sure how I got here, all you do is take
I'm a closed-off man, unwilling to be a part of your plan
I can't trust you, baby, but I'm a trusting man.
This isn't a love song, it's a whole lot of heartbreak.

Will you expose my heart?
Do a damn fine job of tearing it apart?
Will you dance with me in the dark?
Take my hand, let's dance in the dark
Ooh yeah, let's dance in the dark
This isn't a love song, baby, it's a whole lot of heartbreak.

"This Isn't a Love Song" written by Lex Ryan, Tatum Reed

Prologue

Lex

"I HAD THE same dream again last night. I'm standing in the middle of an empty stage. It's dark, but I know she's there. I can feel her. My guitar is slung on my back, and I reach for it. I don't need light to strum the chords. I know this song by heart. I can play it with my eyes closed. It's the same song every time. I play a few chords and hum. The sounds echo through the small venue. I'm frustrated because the words won't come to me. Just the melody. I'm filled with so much dread and sadness, I want to cry.

"I just want it to end, and that's when I hear the voice. It's a woman's voice, but I don't recognize it and I can't see her. She asks me to come back. It's strange to me because it's the same thing every time. I don't understand what she wants or who she is. I get frustrated and shout, 'What the fuck do you want?' but all she whispers is to come back. And then I wake up drenched in sweat."

"I think you know who this woman is."

"I don't."

"You do. You just don't want to see her."

"Is it even a woman? Maybe it's the song whispering to me."

"I don't think so. You know who it is, Lex."

"I don't, Doc."

Sigh. "You do, Lex. She's trying to get your attention."

Chapter 1

Sarah

2 Years Earlier

"Hi, welcome to Gerry's Coffee House. What can I get you?"

"Well, hi there, beautiful. I haven't seen you in here before. Are you new?"

I hold my bright smile steady as I do a quick sweep of the clean-cut businessman in front of me.

"No, I usually work a different shift. What can I get you?" I continue to smile politely even though I want to scowl as I retrieve a paper cup.

I deal with jerks like him at least once a day. The kind of guy who thinks he's so charming by calling me dollface, beautiful, or babycakes. Although some might be flattered by the terms of endearment, I, for one, am not. Especially when they give me that smarmy smile or a wink as they stare at my boobs while I take their order.

As I stand, I notice someone else has come in behind Mr. Business Suit. He's looking down at his phone. A ballcap pulled low hides his face. He's wearing a fitted, long-sleeved t-shirt, which is kind of strange because it's, like, a zillion degrees outside. He's got a killer body—that much I can tell. Muscular arms strain against the material of his shirt. Jeans mold to his perfect muscular thighs. Not an ounce of fat anywhere.

Waiter? Yes, I'll take number two, please. Ugh, but first I have to deal with number one. My eyes cut back to the guy giving me a creepy smile.

"Uh…" He looks at my boobs as he pretends to look for my nametag on my apron. "Sare-ah. That's a beautiful name for a beautiful girl."

I internally gag. Where the hell is my coworker Neil? He's ten minutes late for his shift. "Eyes up here, Chuck. What can I get you?"

The hot guy behind Mr. Suit snorts.

"How about your number?"

Real smooth, Asswipe. It's all I can do not to roll my eyes at him. My smile starts to hurt as I hold it in place. "I don't give out numbers. Just coffee. So, what'll it be?"

"A date?"

And there goes my smile. Well, I tried.

I blow the bangs I'm trying to grow out in irritation. I'm going to kill Neil for being late, causing me to deal with this wiener-head.

"Dude, can you just fuckin' order and leave the poor lass alone? I'm in a hurry," the hot guy says behind the jackass. I hear an accent, but I can't place where it's from.

Jackass looks over his shoulder at Hot Stranger. "*Excuse me*, do you mind?"

Hot Guy looks up from his phone, and my mouth goes dry. Holy moly, this guy is sinfully good-looking. Dark, rugged, and dangerous. His sharp jawline with a hint of scruff ticks with annoyance. His dark hair curls at the edges under his ballcap. His aqua-blue eyes quickly connect with mine before they return to Mr. Wannabe-Wall Street.

"Actually, I do mind. I have a meeting I'm going to be late for if you don't order. And I'm pretty sure Sarah here would have given you her number already if she wanted to. If you're not ready to order, then please step aside."

Oh my god, his accent is to die for. It sounds Scottish, or something in that region.

"Asshole," Mr. Business Suit says under his breath as he turns back to me. "Can you *believe* this guy?" He gives me an incredulous look as he points his thumb over his shoulder.

I stare at him blankly as he continues.

"Sare-ah, I'd like a large, skinny latte with extra foam, and a light swirl of caramel with a hint of shaken salt. Two and a half pumps of vanilla with a splash of extra-hot water and one and a half packets of Splenda. Did you get all that, sweetheart?" He winks at me as he pulls his wallet out.

I want to reach across the counter and punch him in the nose, but I'm a lover, not a fighter. My eyes slide back to Hot Accent Guy and once again they collide with his aqua-blues. He arches a dark eyebrow at me. I think he wants to pummel this dude as much as I do.

"Got it," I bite out as I write his ridiculous order on the cup in shorthand. "Name?"

He leans on the counter with his elbow, invading my personal space. "This is going to sound silly, but I've got a super-important business meeting and I want everyone at the meeting table to know I'm in charge. Can you write down 'Captain Amazing'?"

"For real?" I look up at him, my pen poised as I bite my cheek hard to keep from laughing. Hot Accent Guy coughs as he hides his smile.

"Yes, that's my nickname around the office." He winks at me. "And my nickname with the ladies, if you know what I mean," he whispers seductively and chuckles. "Why don't you put your number on there while you're at it?"

Ew, ew, ew.

"Right." I smile at him then roll my eyes as I turn away from his penetrating stare. I write down a name and take his debit card.

Neil rushes in at that very moment. "Sorry, so sorry, Sarah. Oh my gosh, I'm sorry. I hope you're not late for your appointment." He ties his apron, washes his hands, and starts to make the drink I set to the side. I really need to go, but I'm intrigued by the gorgeous guy with the sexy accent.

"I've got one more minute. I'll ring this customer up and then I've got to jet."

"Yes, yes, of course. Again, I'm so sorry. Dang tourists on Music Row stopping to take pictures every two steps had me running late."

"No worries, Neil, it's okay."

I whirl around and come face to face with the most intriguing aqua-blues. They remind me of the clear Caribbean ocean I've only seen in pictures—the ones with the white sand, the palm trees holding up a hammock, and that incredible blue-green water.

"Hi," I say shyly, biting my lip. "Sorry for your wait. What can I get you?" He looks so familiar to me, but I can't quite place where I've seen him before.

He stares at my lips before pulling his cap a little lower like he's trying to hide his face. "I'll have a large black coffee, but can you leave a little bit of room for cream? Thanks." He hands me a crisp twenty-dollar bill. He leans in closer and I grab the counter, because it's all I can do not to pull him to me and sniff the incredible smell emanating from him. "You okay?"

I look up from his sensuous lips and meet his eyes, his question surprising me. I let go of the counter and busy myself with getting his change out of the till. "You mean because of the captain over there?"

He nods and gives me the most breathtaking, dimpled smile. "Yeah, Captain Wanker."

I laugh and smile. "I eat guys like him for breakfast."

"Ah, so you're a man-eater. Got it."

"I, um, did *not* say that. Definitely not a man-eater. I mean, I date guys, but I don't chew them up and spit them out."

Jesus, just shut up, Sarah! Agh! I quickly close my mouth and hand him his change as I stare at his megawatt smile.

"Keep the change, Love." He winks at me and grabs the coffee Neil places on the counter. A wink from the captain would make me queasy. A wink from him has my blood humming with pleasure. I'm so bummed I didn't even get a chance to write down his name. I watch his amazing butt in his Levi's as he walks toward the counter that houses the cream and sugar.

"Captain Poopy Underpants?" Neil calls out, looking shocked, realizing what he just yelled out across the coffee bar. "Uh…867-5309!" Neil looks over at me, thoroughly confused. "Isn't that an eighties song?"

Hot Guy nearly spits out his coffee as he opens the door, laughing.

"Order ready for Captain Poopy Underpants!" Neil shouts over the din of the coffee shop. I bite my laughter back as I untie my apron.

"Gotta run, Neil! Oh, and that coffee belongs to that goober over there on his phone. But since he has his head up his ass, just slip a heat shield on it and hand it to him. It'll be a nice surprise for his *very* important meeting." I smile gleefully as I slip out the back door, hoping for one more glimpse of Hot Accent Guy. My phone buzzes in my pocket as I look out across the street. I'm disappointed when I don't see him. I dig it out and answer it.

"Where are you?" my cousin Heather yells into my ear.

"I'm on my way. Keep your pants on. I had a little incident at the coffee shop. Oh my god, Heather, wait until I tell you—"

"Yeah, yeah. You're going to be working at the coffee shop for the rest of your life if you don't get your butt down here. I'm putting my neck out on the line for you to get this job."

"Okay, I'm sorry. I'll be there in five minutes. It's not even four. Plenty of time."

"Just hurry. Dragon Princess is pacing and being a bitch."

I hang up with my cousin and quickly get into my dependable Subaru. Heather is a makeup artist for Savannah Edwards, an up-and-coming country singer. Her boyfriend is Tatum Reed, another rising star, and he needs someone to go on tour with him and the band to do their makeup and maybe some styling. Even though I'm about to graduate cosmetology school, Heather has been my mentor and is a major influencer. She's been in the industry for five years and said this could be my big break, the one thousands would cut a bitch for. I don't want to cut any bitches, but I do really need this job.

I race over to the Sony studios off Demonbreun Street in downtown Nashville and find an hourly parking lot. I stuff a bunch of quarters into the meter and run down the block to the studio doors. It's hot and I'm slightly sweaty, so I pull my long blonde hair up into a topknot and secure it with an elastic band. Not the most professional look, but better than sweaty-head hair. I immediately text Heather once I arrive in the downstairs lobby. She tells me to take the left-bank elevators up to the twelfth floor. I nervously check my teeth in the mirrored doors as I wait to go up.

As I walk into the sleek reception area on the twelfth floor with ultra-plush cream carpeting and dark wood furniture, I'm finally hit with a case of nervous butterflies. What if I blow this, my one chance? I'll be stuck serving coffees to Captain Assholes for the rest of my life. I swallow back my nerves as I let the receptionist know why I'm here and quickly sit down in a comfortable leather chair. Just as I'm relaxing into the soft, buttery leather, Heather rushes out and grabs my arm.

"Okay, whatever you do, don't gush over Savannah. I

mean, answer her questions if she talks to you, but don't be overly eager. She hates that. But don't totally ignore her, either. That will bruise her ego."

"Wait, I thought I was meeting Tatum?"

"You are, but Savannah wants you to do her makeup to see if you're really up for the job. I mean, guys are easy."

"What? Heather! You never told me I would be doing Savannah's makeup. Now I really am going to throw up."

"Oh god, whatever you do, don't puke on Savannah. Trust me, I was just as surprised to see her as you are. I have my makeup case all set up, so just use that."

We reach a door and she opens it, pulling me behind her by my hand. "Hey, guys, this is my cousin, Sarah."

She motions me into a large dressing room with couches and a vanity set up with lights and a mirror. Four large guys with their backs to me are lounging on a sectional laughing and bantering back and forth as they watch a soccer game on the TV mounted to the wall. A beautiful but pissed-off-looking redhead stands next to the couch with her arms crossed.

"Hey guys, my cousin is here." They all turn their heads and stand up, except for the dark-haired one who keeps his back to me as he turns off the TV. "Sarah, this is Savannah Edwards, Tatum Reed, Matt Ingles—Tatum's bass player, Will Grady—his drummer, and Lex Ryan—his lead guitarist."

I nod to each person in the room as Heather goes down the line, introducing them, until I get to Lex.

No way.

It's Hot Accent Guy from the coffee shop—Lex Ryan.

No wonder I thought he looked familiar. He's changed into a tight, black t-shirt and now I get why he was wearing a long-sleeved tee before. Bright tattoos cover both his arms and are all-too-familiar to all of his fans.

"It's you," I blurt before I can catch myself.

Tatum coughs into his hand and Matt rolls his eyes. "Oh great, Ryan. Did you screw this one too?"

My eyes widen in disbelief that he just said that as Lex punches Matt in the arm.

"Shut the fuck up, Asswipe." Lex grins as he sizes me up. "Sarah, good to see you so soon. I apologize for my mate's crass words."

He remembers my name? I think I'm going to pass out.

"Do you two know each other?" Savannah looks like she swallowed a frog.

"No," we both say, causing everyone to look bewildered.

"We, um…"

"Sarah works at Gerry's. I just got me a cup of coffee." He lifts his paper cup in the air and takes a sip.

"He tried to pick you up, didn't he?" Will sighs.

I grin as my gaze slides to Lex. We share a moment, soaking each other in, before I shake my head.

"Actually, just the opposite. He came to my rescue."

Tatum scoffs and gets up from the couch. "You must have the wrong guy. The only thing Lex tries to rescue is his dignity after a night of debauchery." He reaches his hand out to me. "Nice to meet you, Sarah. Heather's told us great things about you."

"Thanks," I say shyly, suddenly starstruck by the gorgeous Tatum Reed as I shake his hand.

"Well, shall we get started?" My cousin claps her hands, breaking the spell I'm under. "Savannah, who would you like Sarah to style first?"

"Me, obviously, then Tatum." Savannah's voice goes a pitch higher as she talks to Lex in a baby voice. "Lex, do you want her to do your hair and makeup?" She scrunches up her nose at him and smirks.

Lex scowls at Savannah. "No."

Awkward silence descends on the room.

"Aw, come on, Lex. It'll be fun," I say in my best "go get 'em, tiger" voice. It usually makes people feel more at ease with me.

He looks at me and our eyes collide. I give him my best megawatt smile. He stares at me for a second that feels like a full minute. He grimaces as he gets up and punches Matt and Will in the arm to follow him.

"She's like fucking sunshine on crack," he grumbles on his way out.

Okay, then.

"Don't let him bother you. He's always a surly Irish bastard." Tatum smiles warmly at me. I smile weakly at Tatum's comment.

I try not to let Lex's sudden mood swing get under my skin, but it does. I don't want him to not like me, and I'm not sure what I did wrong. I mentally shake myself. I can't think about him right now. I have a job to do.

"Okay, let's get started," I say brightly.

Savannah sits down in her chair. "I want my hair up, but I have extensions, so obviously hide that fact. I want light makeup, but I want my eyes to pop. Got it?"

Yikes, no pressure. It would help if she could at least give me an encouraging smile instead of the perma-resting-bitch-face.

"Got it." I hide my discomfort behind a smile.

"Ow! You're pulling my hair," Savannah snaps as I brush out her long hair.

"Sorry, I'm nervous. I'll try to be gentler."

"Well, get your nerves in check or else I'll be bald."

Geesh. She's not as friendly as she appears to be in the tabloids. How does Heather put up with this? I quickly braid her hair and pin it up into a pretty side twist, my nerves soothed by the low hum of Heather and Tatum talking. Once I get her hair done, I pop a mint in my mouth and start her makeup. She's beautiful, but I can tell she's had work done, which surprises me because she's not even thirty yet. Her collagen-injected lips are too full and her pert nose is too small for her face. The fillers in her cheeks make her look older than she really is.

I finish up by glossing her lips and spin her chair to face the mirror. I smile at her through the mirror as she looks at her profile and then turns her head to study the other side.

"First lesson. Always ask where the client is going, and second, what they'll be wearing. Luckily this is very natural. But what if I was going to a black-tie event and wearing a dark dress and wanted smoky eyes? Then what?"

"Oh my gosh, I'm so sorry. I didn't realize you were heading out somewhere. I'm so embarrassed. I thought this was just a practice run. You're right, I should've asked." I'm about to break down into tears.

Savannah waves her hand, dismissing me. "Tatum, what

do you think?" she asks with a hint of doubt in her voice.

"Great job, Sarah. But then again, she had a beautiful canvas to work on. You look beautiful, Vanny."

He leans down to kiss her lips, but she shoves him away. "Don't mess it up! What's wrong with you?"

I gape at Heather, then quickly mask my face into one of indifference when she widens her eyes and gives me a quick shake of her head. Her words from her pep talk this morning reverberate in my head. *Be friendly, be courteous, but most importantly, be invisible.* Still, I can't ever imagine pushing Tatum Reed away from giving me kisses or scolding him when he's trying to be affectionate.

"Okay, Tatum, you're up if you'd like." I smile shakily, swallowing my tears and trying to diffuse the sudden tension in the room.

He smiles sincerely at me as he sits. I spray his hair down after putting a cape over him.

"Can I give you a trim?"

"Uh…sure?" He looks at Heather, and she nods her approval. Savannah sits on the couch, looking at herself with a handheld mirror, ignoring the rest of us.

"Don't worry, I gotcha." I grin as I cut and style his hair. We chat like two old friends, and the easy flow of conversation puts me at ease. It takes a lot less time than Savannah, and he's really happy with the new look.

"When can you start?" He smiles at me through the mirror.

My heart does high-fives against my rib cage. "Well, I finish school at the end of the month. When do you go on tour?"

"Next month. I'll have my manager Lee call you and iron out the details, but welcome to the band, Sarah. And don't worry about the other guys—they'll be on board."

Savannah snorts as she gathers her purse. "Come on, Tatum, we're going to be late for the party. Hopefully Lex hasn't screwed the hostess yet." She grabs her purse as she sashays by me without saying a word. Not a "hey, it was nice to meet you" or a "thank you for doing my hair and makeup." She doesn't even glance at Tatum's new haircut. *God, what a diva.*

"Thanks again, Sarah. I'm really excited to have you on board with us." Tatum shakes my hand and waves goodbye to Heather. The door closes, and Heather and I start jumping up and down as we squeal.

"Oh my god, you did it!" She hugs me.

"*We* did it. I couldn't have gotten this without you. But geez, I'm sorry you have to work with Savannah over the guys. She's a real delight," I add sarcastically.

"Yeah, she can be a lot to handle at times, but she's not bad one on one. She gets really insecure when Tatum's around other girls. She and Lex don't get along, either. They were squabbling over something when you got here. But who cares about her because you're working for Tatum Reed. You've hit the big time, Cuz!"

I hug Heather and although I'm so excited about this new chapter in my life, my mind immediately pings to Lex Ryan and those bottomless blue eyes I could go skinny-dipping in. Being on tour with Tatum means I'll get to see Lex every single day. I'm seriously crushing on him, surly bad-boy attitude and all.

"So, Heather, what's the deal with Lex? Am I allowed to fraternize with the guys in the band?"

Heather laughs. "Come on, let's go celebrate." She packs up her makeup case. "Forget about Lex Ryan. I know he's nice eye-candy, but trust me, there are going to be a hundred more Lex Ryans in this industry. Stay away from the OG. He's sweet, but he likes the ladies, a lot."

My heart sinks as she loops her arm through mine and we head toward the elevators.

"But he's so gorgeous," I whine.

Heather smiles. "Cuz, you'll find the right guy for you. Lex Ryan is *not* it. Remember, you're a professional now, you don't want to screw it up." She winks at me as my heart deflates. Resigned, I sigh as the elevator opens into the lobby.

Heather is right. I can't mess this opportunity up. I'll just have to man up, be a professional, and crush on Lex from afar.

Chapter 2

Lex

Present Day

I LEAN BACK in my chair and open up an iced-down bottle of beer. I hand it to my best friend Tatum, then open another one for me. We sit in silence on my back patio overlooking the golden sunlit horse pastures. We just finished playing eighteen holes over at the country club with Will, Matt, Kiki's brother and dad, and Tate's brother and dad. The two of us came back here to relax before the rehearsal dinner.

Tate eases back into his chair and takes a pull on his beer. "I'm not gonna lie, man. I can't wait for this to be over. Don't get me wrong, I love Kiki so much, and I want this as much as she does, but that sister of hers and her husband are driving me fucking insane. He cornered me this morning over the omelet station at the hotel and demanded I draw a prenup. I had to have Brad politely remove him from the breakfast line when he started acting cagey."

I grimace thinking of Kiki's leggy blonde sister and her asshole husband. She's one of those complicated batshit crazy kind of women that I never allow myself to hook up with. What was the word? High-maintenance.

"Well, you can always elope." I chuckle.

"Dude, there's no way Kiki will go for that. The wedding's tomorrow!"

"Well, then here ye stay." I tap my bottle to his as I get up to stoke the fire. Even though it's almost June, the evenings have been unusually chilly. "Want a stogie?"

"Sure." Tatum takes his phone out of his back pocket and stares at it. "Crap."

"What's up?" I look over my shoulder at him as I take two Cuban cigars out of the humidifier behind my bar.

Tate sighs. "Brooke and TJ just got into a fight about seating arrangements for tomorrow."

I cut and light the cigars and hand Tatum his while I puff on mine. "Sounds like a serious situation." I smirk, thanking the heavens above I dodged *that* bullet. TJ is Kiki's eccentric gay best friend. He's a little kooky, but all in all a nice guy.

Tatum looks over at me and chuckles. "Dude, are you ever going to tell me why you're such a pussy when it comes to commitment?"

I stare off into the distance. It's not that I don't want to tell my best friend, it's just that I don't want to relive the memories. My ex Alana didn't just break my heart, she reached in and tore it from my chest, and then ground her stiletto into it.

"Because why on earth would I want to get involved with a woman and have her pretend to love me, then use me, and eventually leave me? It's just biscuits to bears."

"Jesus, I would leave you too if you used terms like biscuits to bears."

I chuckle. "Fuck off, you stook. Wait 'til we go on the European tour. You'll be beggin' me to know what the fuck they're sayin'."

Tatum smiles. "Yeah, you ready for it? Did you tell Connor we're coming?"

I nod and take a long pull of my beer. "I did. He's excited to see us. He's sorry he couldn't make it to the wedding."

Connor is my identical twin brother. He lives in Kinsale, Ireland, a quaint little seaside town in County Cork about three hours outside of Dublin. He owns a pub there that I used to run with him before I moved to the States. We're going to stop over for three nights to see him and my parents before we head to Glasgow for a show.

Although I'm excited to see my parents and brother, I'm dreading going back home. I haven't been back in ten years for a reason. It's going to bring up a lot of painful memories for me, but I haven't told any of my bandmates that. They want to see Connor, meet my parents and do some sightseeing. I'll just have to suck it up and suffer through it.

Tatum puffs his cigar and eyes me over it. "Hey Lex, thanks for everything, man. I get the feeling it's not easy for you to be hosting our wedding. I know someday you'll tell me, but I think I understand why you can't." He clears his throat. "It means a lot to Kiki and me, so thank you. I couldn't have asked for a better best man."

"I wouldn't have it any other way, you know that." I smile tightly as emotion clogs my throat. I tuck that shit down deep and take a swallow of my beer.

"How do you feel about walking down the aisle with Sarah tomorrow?"

I shrug and side-eye him. "Fine, why?"

"Are you going to dance with her?"

"I dunno. Is that protocol?"

"Jesus, when are you going to get your head out of your ass?" Tatum mumbles to himself.

"What was that, mate?"

"Nothing. Just do me a solid and dance with her."

"It's your day, you call the shots."

"Okay, and one other favor—don't have sex during the party. With anyone."

I chuff as I look over at him. "It's your wedding day, give me a little credit." I laugh and smile wryly at him. "But I can after, right? I mean after everyone leaves, of course."

Tatum shakes his head. His phone buzzes again. He quickly glances at it. "Dammit, Kiki is now crying. Something about pictures and red wine…I better call her."

"Hey mate, in all seriousness, no matter what happens between now and tomorrow just remember, you got your girl—the girl of your dreams, and I couldn't be happier for you. I love the both of you like family."

Tatum stands up and I follow suit. We thump each other's backs in a half-macho-man hug.

"Thanks, brother. That means a lot to me. You're our family too. I hope you get to find a girl that makes you want her for forever someday too. But a word of advice, if you get married, have a small quiet wedding."

I laugh quietly. "Ain't happenin', brother."

"Well, I guess we have to go get ready for a nice drama-filled dinner." Tatum sighs. "If Kiki is crying, you know shit's gone bad."

"I'll take one for the team and sit next to Kiki's gobshite brother-in-law." I smirk as I stub out my cigar. "We'll put Matt next to her sister."

Tatum and I fist-bump as we head out.

Chapter 3

Sarah

OH, I HATE Kiki's sister with a passion. And I don't hate anyone. But Brooke Parker? She is number one on my shit list. How can she be such a bitch to her sister the day before her wedding? It started with little comments throughout the week dismissing Kiki's taste in flowers and food and what *Brooke* would have done better. She made the wedding coordinator burst into tears this afternoon, so Kiki gave her the rest of the day off. What wedding coordinator takes the day off the day before the wedding? One harassed by Brooke Parker, that's who.

I'm currently watching her and TJ have a tug-of-war over the seating list. Brooke tried to switch her table so she could be seated next to Nicole Kidman and Keith Urban.

"Just give it up, Brooke! You are sitting next to your parents."

"No! I'm not! Clearly whoever made this stupid seating arrangement should know I'm sitting with Nicole!"

"You don't even know her!" TJ tugs her closer to him,

the list tearing.

Kiki, her mom, and I gasp as Brooke tries to turn, knocking over one of the hotel flower arrangements.

"Enough!" Kiki steps between them. "This is fucking ridiculous!"

"Sorry, Kiki, you're right…totes embarrassing." TJ runs his fingers through his hair looking ashamed, his cheeks red with exertion.

"Sorry Kiki, I can't believe I lost my composure. Your friends bring out the worst in me." Brooke's voice drips with disdain as she eyes TJ and me as if we're gum stuck on the bottom of her Louis Vuittons. "Especially the gay Ronald McDonald one."

"*Oh no she did int!*" TJ narrows his eyes. He loathes being called Ronald McDonald because of his reddish strawberry-blond hair. "You look like something I drew with my left hand."

"Because that's the only action your left hand gets," she sneers.

"At least I can keep my man satisfied in the shower," TJ whispers loudly. He's referring to the incident of Brooke's husband Graham cheating on her with the French nanny.

Brooke growls and lunges for TJ, grabbing on to his fanny pack. TJ quickly unclips his pack making Brooke stumble forward. Kiki grabs on to her to keep her from falling on her face as TJ holds up a hand and waves it in Brooke's face. "I'm in my own lane, you ain't in my category."

"Oh my god, Mom, can you please stop her?" Kiki turns to her mom vibrating with anger. "I can't take any more of this! And TJ for the last time, stop talking like you're Nicki Minaj! You're a preppy white thirty-year-old gay man."

Mrs. Forbes quickly steps in between them and wraps an arm around Brooke to guide her away from Kiki.

"Brooke, honey, let's settle down. I'm sure you'll have plenty of opportunities to chat with Nicole. Dad and I would be honored to sit next to you and Graham. And TJ dear, let's use proper English."

Brooke regains control as she walks back over to us smoothing down her hair as she glares at TJ. She picks up her dreaded clipboard off the table. "We'll come back to the seating arrangement issue in the morning. Okay, next thing on my list…"

I lean against a chair as I tune out Brooke's incessant droning. Her voice is like nails down a chalkboard. I just want to shove her up against the wall and say to her… *'Listen, bitch, and listen good. This isn't your wedding. This is all about Kiki and her day. If I hear one more snide comment come out of your mouth, then I'm going to rip your hair extensions out WWF-style. So, if you want to mingle with Nicole and Keith, then you are just going to sit pretty and zip your obnoxious trap. Are we clear?'* And then TJ would give me a high-five and a butt-bump and say, *'Dayum, Gina!'*

That's what I want to say, but in reality I can't, because to be honest, Brooke scares the shit out of me.

"Hellooo! Is anyone home? Tell the aliens to bring Sare Bear back to earth!" TJ snaps his fingers in my face. I look up and see Kiki, her mom, and Brooke staring at me with odd expressions.

Brooke rolls her eyes. "Seriously, Kiki? Your maid of

honor just spaced out for like my whole speech on the proper way to toe-step step down the aisle. Ugh, she's going to get it all wrong now and ruin everything!"

"I wish I could have toe-step stepped on that obnoxious trap of hers," TJ mutters. "This bitch be cray-cray. You okay, hon? You were mumbling about Keith Urban and hair extensions…" TJ feels my forehead. I look over to Kiki. She gives me a watery smile as she points her index finger to her head like a gun as her mom and sister argue over the merits of ice sculptures.

"I was just daydreaming about shoving Brooke up against a wall and telling her to shut the hell up," I whisper back.

TJ hops in place and claps his hands giddily. "Yes, Sare Bear! Do it! Do it! Oh, what I wouldn't give to see that. I'll even hold the bitch down for you."

I giggle as I playfully elbow him. "I like my hair attached to my head, thanks."

Brooke claps her hands making me jump. I cringe as I zero in on her *"Leave the Judgin' to Jesus"* sweatshirt she has on. She's such a walking contradiction.

"Okay, one last thing before we get ready for dinner. I think we should change what you guys will be wearing tomorrow. It clashes with my outfit and will look *terrible* in pictures." Brooke digs some color swatches out of her bag.

"Wait, what? No!" Kiki cries. "We've had their outfit colors picked out for months, and the three of us designed them! No!" Kiki stamps her foot like a three-year-old having a tantrum. "Mom, no!"

Brooke huffs in annoyance. "Kiki, stop focusing on yourself and think of the bigger picture at hand, shall we? I'm wearing wine red, and it's Dior. As if I'd change *my* dress. It will clash with…what did you call it? Pantone 2562?"

Kiki growls. "It's Wisteria purple, and I'm *not* changing it, so wear something else. I'm sorry if you're pissed because I didn't ask you to be a bridesmaid, but for the hundredth time, Tatum only wanted Lex and his brother. Stop trying to change up my wedding!"

Brooke studies her freshly painted nails. "Well…I guess I could wear my white Stella McCartney dress."

TJ wheezes next to me. "Oh, hell no!" He rummages in his man-bag and retrieves a brown paper bag. He starts blowing the bag in and out as he hyperventilates next to me.

"No! You are not wearing white! This isn't your wedding, so stop trying to act like it's yours. Either wear your wine-red Dior or don't bother coming!"

Brooke gasps and drops her color samples. "Kiki! That is very hurtful. I seriously think you need some Jesus time and ask for his forgiveness. You're being really selfish right now, and frankly you're acting like an asshole."

"Agh!" Kiki launches herself toward her sister. TJ drops the bag and quickly grabs Kiki around the waist.

"Now girls, girls, let's not fight over this. Maybe we can compromise…" Kiki's mom belatedly swoops in and guides a shellshocked-looking Brooke over to the elevators as she shouts over her shoulder, "Kiki, we'll see you at dinner, sweetheart!" They quickly get on a waiting elevator and the doors close just as we hear Brooke sob that Kiki is acting like an animal.

"Ugh! I can't believe the nerve of her!" Kiki picks up Brooke's color samples and throws them toward the elevators. Tears track down her cheeks.

"For real…who wears wine red to a June wedding?" TJ asks solemnly.

Kiki, TJ, and I look at each other and burst out laughing.

"She's seriously mental." Kiki wipes the tears from her eyes. "She even asked Tatum's mom at breakfast this morning if she was going to color her hair for the wedding. His mom just had her hair done yesterday! I was so embarrassed. And then Graham was escorted out by Tatum's security guard Brad. I have no idea why, and I don't want to know."

I squeeze Kiki's hand. "Kiki, don't worry about her. Your wedding is going to be perfect in every way. You're marrying the man of your dreams, I will be wearing Wisteria to match the flowers, Keith and Nicole will have a delightful time at their table with TJ, *not* Brooke." TJ and I high-five. "Everything will be perfect, because at the end of the day, it's just about you and Tatum."

"And I solemnly swear that if she shows up wearing a white dress, I will douse her in red wine." TJ hold his hand up, as he takes his oath. Kiki and I both give him a high-five.

"Why in the hell did I decide on a big wedding?" Kiki asks miserably as she sniffles. "TJ, I'm sorry I snapped at you earlier. Brooke brings out the worst in me…this wedding has brought out the worst in me." She leans into him and hugs him.

"No need to apologize, Kinky. I know you're stressed. Let's forget about Martha Stewart's top-ten worst wedding nightmare guests and focus on bigger things."

TJ produces a bottle of champagne and three flutes from

his man-bag. Kiki laughs. "Oh thank God! Have you been carrying those around all day?"

"No, I got it from the bar when your sister was trying to teach us the art of flower arrangement…because apparently your award-winning florist doesn't know what she's doing." TJ pops the cork of Moet with flair and fills our three flutes to the brim with delicious bubbly.

"Oh my gosh, you guys, what would I do without you?"

TJ lifts his glass. "Cheers to a beautiful bride, a beautiful day tomorrow, and the most handsomely dressed Mister of Honor to ever walk down the aisle! And cheers to his beautiful partner in crime that will be draped in gorgeous Wisteria."

"Cheers!" We clink glasses and take a sip while laughing.

"And cheers to always believing in love and never giving up!" I say, my eyes misting over for my friend and the long journey that brought her here.

"Cheers!" we all shout in unison.

Kiki raises her glass. "And cheers to the two very best friends a girl could ask for. You guys are my true family and I couldn't have gotten here without either one of you. I love you both!"

"Cheers!" we all scream causing other patrons in the ritzy hotel lobby to look over at us.

We burst into giggles.

Kiki sighs. "And TJ, thanks for fighting for that seating chart like it was Justin Bieber's dick about to be tattooed with Selena's name on it."

"*Gurl*, Selena wouldn't have wanted that." TJ winks.

"I love you guys, I truly do." Kiki wipes a tear.

"We love you too, Kiki." I hug her and plant a kiss on her cheek.

"I wonder if Brooke is upstairs folding Graham's underwear into perfect little squares right now." TJ smirks.

I laugh at that. "What on earth are you talking about?"

Kiki gasps. "I never told you the story about the big black binder of suck?"

"Here, let me fill up our drinks, this is a good one." TJ smiles as Kiki goes on to tell me the story of when Brooke wanted to hire her as her nanny.

Chapter 4

Lex

EVEN THOUGH I'M not the sentimental type, Tatum and Kiki's wedding is truly a beautiful event. But I'm itching to find a quiet place and have a drink. It seems that everywhere I turn there's someone from the industry milling about that wants to stop and chat with me.

"There's my man!" Tatum suddenly grabs me in a head-lock as a photographer emerges from thin air and snaps a picture of us. "Are you having fun, man?"

"Of course, best day in band history!"

"Damn right it is! Best day of my life!"

"Tater Tot! There you are! We have to cut the cake soon." Kiki and Sarah emerge from the crowd. "Sarah had to help me with this marshmallow of a dress while I peed. She's the best! Oh, hey Lex!"

Sarah looks like a goddess, her golden skin flushed as she flashes me a brilliant smile. "Hey guys."

"Okay babe, just one minute. Can I get—"

"Oh my god, I love this song! Let's dance! Here Lex,

dance with Sarah!" Kiki pushes Sarah toward me and I awkwardly catch her in my arms as she trips over Kiki's dress. Kiki yanks Tatum onto the dancefloor laughing as she shimmies into his arms.

Sarah quickly releases her grip on my arm and straightens her satin dress, her cheeks staining a pretty pink. She looks like an old Hollywood film star, her long blonde hair is down and wavy, but one side pinned up with light purple orchid flowers. She looks fucking amazing—her hair, the dress showing off her hourglass figure, her beautiful dazzling smile. I hold out my hand.

"After you, Love."

"Oh!" She giggles nervously. "It's okay, Lex, we don't have to dance."

I raise my eyebrow at her and place my hand over my heart. "Are you turning me down, Sunshine?"

"I...um, no, I just..."

I quickly grab her hand before she can scurry off like a scared little mouse and pull her onto the dancefloor. A slow song starts to play and I look down at her as I take her into my arms. She smells incredible, like strawberries and cream.

"You look very pretty."

She visibly swallows and looks away. "Thanks, so do you. I mean not pretty. You look handsome, nice, shit!"

I chuckle as I stare at her. She's so beautiful when she's flustered. I dip my chin to meet her eyes. "I look like shit?"

Her eyes widen as she stares up at me in horror, her mouth opening and closing like a fish out of water. "I...no, I meant, you look really nice." She quickly shuts her mouth and scans the dancefloor, avoiding my eyes.

"Sunshine…"

She looks up and I get lost in her honey-colored pools. "Yes, Lex?"

"Relax, Love."

She smiles, but it looks strained. "Sorry, I just need a glass of champagne, I think. I'm not a great dancer."

"You're doing great. Want me to get you a glass of bubbly?"

"I'd love—"

"Hi, do you mind if I cut in?" A young pretty brunette dancing with an older man stops next to us, turning to Sarah.

"Oh, um, of course!" Sarah smiles politely as she steps away from me. I want to immediately reach back for her, but that would cause a scene, so I stuff my hands into my pockets. I smile cordially at the brunette, but I don't want to be dancing with her. I want Sarah in my arms. Sarah looks back at me and gives me a small smile as she graciously steps up to the white-haired gentleman and they dance away from us getting lost in the crowd. I stiffly hold the brunette in my arms as we start to dance.

"You don't remember me, do you?"

"Of course I do, Love, are you having fun?" I look over her head trying to figure out which direction Sarah went on the crowded dancefloor.

She giggles as she traces her finger along my collar. "You don't, but that's okay, we can get reacquainted if you want. We can go into the bathroom after this dance," she whispers huskily in my ear while she grabs my ass.

I scoot her away from me, as I look out into the crowd

desperate to find someone to shove this grabby-patty off onto. "Sorry Love, not tonight. Listen, I've got to find a friend. Thanks for the dance."

The lady pouts as I leave her on the dancefloor. "I'll be your friend!"

I don't give her a backwards glance as I head to the bar. I see Matt and Will and a guy named Jason, a producer I know from the record label, with their dates over at one of the table tops and I head toward them.

"Dudes and dudettes. What do I gotta do to get a fucking drink around here?"

"Lex, my man." Matt fist-bumps me. "I haven't seen a waitress in a while. I could use another too. Anyone else?"

I look around the table, and land on Jason's date Katie, who is seductively trying to eye-fuck me. She's hard to miss in her caked-on makeup and tight hot-pink dress.

"I can go get them for you." Katie winks at me. "What are you having, Lex?"

"I'll take a whiskey neat, thanks."

"Matt, another vodka tonic? Jason you want a beer?"

"Yeah that would be great, thanks babe."

Katie gets up and saunters away swaying her hips. She looks over her shoulder to see if I'm watching, and of course I am. Katie spells trouble. Normally my favorite kind, but not tonight. I scan the crowd looking for Sarah. I spot Tatum and Kiki by the dancefloor happily chatting to guests. They both look so fucking happy and in love. I smile as I watch her goofy friend TJ lead Carrie Underwood and Keith Urban in a round of the Macarena.

Matt leans forward as if reading my thoughts. "I'm really

happy for Tater Tot and Coffee Girl."

"Yeah mate, me too."

"I hope I get to find a girl as cool as Kiki."

"I hear ya." Jason grimaces as his eyes narrow on me.

"What about Katie?" Will pipes up.

"Well, when she's eye-fucking my friend right in front of me, that's kind of a red flag in my book."

I groan, "Sorry mate."

Jason shrugs. "I'm not. Just shows me her true colors. Besides, there was never serious interest. She's a good fuck, but that's about it."

Will covers his date's ears. "Jesus, Jason, have a little respect. You're starting to sound like Romeo right here." Will jerks his head in my direction.

Katie returns with the drinks and sets them on the table. She stands between Matt and I, and discreetly slides her hand over my ass. This girl has some balls, I'll give her that. This is the second time I've had my ass felt up in the last twenty minutes and I'm getting tired of it.

I move away from Katie's wandering hand just as I spot Sarah sneaking off by herself, away from the crowd. I grab my drink and excuse myself from the table. I pick up a champagne flute from a passing waiter and follow the path Sarah took.

My parents own their own landscaping business in Ireland, and when I bought this place, they came over for six months and built beautiful pathways around fountains and gardens. *Southern Style* and *Home and Garden* have begged me several times to let them do a spread on my home, but I've always declined. It's mine, and somehow sharing it with everyone else takes a little piece of me away. It's hard enough having all these strangers at my house for the reception; I can't imagine millions of people getting a sneak peek of my sanctuary.

I make a turn around a green hedge and stop short. Sarah is sitting on a large flat boulder at the edge of my upstairs patio overlooking the pastures, the setting sun bathing her in golden light. Her eyes are closed as she soaks up the fading rays, a light breeze ruffling her hair. She's a magnificent creature—pure and innocent and too good for the likes of me. I take a step back to turn and leave her alone when she opens one eye.

"Shit, Lex. You scared me!" she says breathlessly.

"Sorry Love, I didn't know you'd be here." *Lying fucking bastard.*

She blushes. "Oh sorry to wander your property, I just kind of had to take a breather. Know what I mean?"

I drink her in. Her blonde hair flowing down her back in beautiful soft waves, her satiny pale-purple dress fluttering in the breeze, her knees pulled up to her chest. I find her bare feet with the matching lilac toenail polish sexy as hell. I thrust the champagne toward her.

"Found you some champagne," I croak out. *What the fuck is wrong with me?* I usually don't get flustered around a woman.

"Ah thanks. I was wishing I had grabbed some before I left the party." She takes the flute and her fingers brush mine, making me shiver. She takes a deep breath. "Want to join me?"

I look around, desperate for an escape. A minute ago, I

did want to join her, but now I'm torn. Seeing her all glammed up is messing with my head. She's usually dressed in a tank and skinny jeans, and she's just *Sarah*. But tonight, she looks like a goddess. She's delicate and elegant, like the orchids pinned up in her hair.

"Skootch over," I say gruffly and sit down next to her on the boulder before I change my mind. I can feel the heat emanating off her skin and again that subtle scent of strawberries and cream. I inhale deeply before I take a sip of my whiskey. "How was the rest of your dance?"

She side-eyes me. "Miserable."

I laugh as I look at her acerbic expression. "Why? He looked like someone's sweet grandpa."

"Ha! More like a horny lecher. The dirty old man kept trying to put his hands on my ass. I finally told him I had to use the restroom and ran as soon as he loosened his grip."

Part of me wants to laugh and part of me wants to go hunt that bastard down and rip his hands off his body.

"Point him out to me later and I'll make him wish he didn't have feeling in his crotchety old arse."

Sarah giggles and it's the sweetest sound.

"Your horses are beautiful. Do you ride?"

"Eh, I used to. I try to ride if I'm home, but you know how that goes. Free time is hard to come by these days." I shrug. "Anyway, most of them you can't ride."

She chuckles quietly. "You have a lot of horses for not having time to ride."

I lightly bump her shoulder with mine. "Most of these horses are rescues. They've been abused or neglected."

"Awe, that makes me so sad. So, you're like their safe

haven?"

I shrug as we both stare out over the pastures. "They need a safe place to heal, to become whole again. I have the space."

"Hmm, I think you play a bigger role than that. Have they? Become whole again?" she asks in a hushed whisper. Our eyes meet, and hers are sad. This feeling of sudden protectiveness wraps around my heart. I don't ever want this girl to be sad.

"Some have…some can't quite move forward and forget the past." I sigh, really wishing I had a cigarette even though I quit years ago. I take a sip of my whiskey as I feel her stare at my profile.

"Are you having fun?" she asks nonchalantly, dragging me out of the edgy feeling creeping into my veins.

I look off into the distance. "Eh, weddings and me don't really mesh, but I'm really happy for Tate and Kiki."

"What do you mean?" She glides her fingers along a crease in her satin dress.

She looks up at me as I contemplate. I want to open up to her, but it's hard for me. I look out over the pasture and hear the chatter and music from the party down below. She's comfortable to be around. We haven't had much time alone together the two years we've been on tour. What's most comforting is that she doesn't make me feel like all she wants me for is sex.

"Have you ever wanted something so bad but it's just out of reach?" I quietly ask, tucking a lock of her silky hair behind her flowers. She visibly swallows; her golden-brown eyes burn into mine. They are like two pools of warm honey with a touch of liquid gold. She quickly averts her gaze and looks out over the pasture breaking the spell she has me under.

"I have," she says softly.

"And did you ever throw caution to the wind and just go for it?"

"Go for it?"

"Yeah. Did you ever take on the impossible and go after what you wanted?"

I can't help but touch her bare shoulder, sliding the silvery-purple satin bow from her halter strap back over her shoulder. My impulse is to untie the bow and plant soft kisses along her smooth golden skin, but I hold back. She's making me crazy and she doesn't even realize it.

"I uh...I don't...I mean...sure?" she says breathlessly as she stares down at my fingers as they linger on the satin. The wind picks up and stirs her hair causing the strawberries-and-cream fragrance to assault my senses. I breathe her in and all my muscles relax. I suddenly find myself wanting to tell Sarah every thought and secret my heart has been holding.

"I had a bad deal at a wedding once. I..." I rub my hands over my face, tired of the memories that linger.

She nods, looking off into the distance. "Lex, it's okay, you don't have to explain if you don't want to."

I chuckle. "Shite. I—"

"There you are! I've been looking everywhere for you!" We whip our heads around in surprise.

Katie, Jason's date, puts her hand on my shoulder and looks down at us. *What the fuck? Did she follow me?*

"I waited a couple minutes, but I didn't realize you went

on a nature walk." She giggles, her laugh sounding like an annoying chattering monkey.

"Oh, um, I need to get back to the party anyway. Kiki will probably be cutting the cake soon and I don't want to miss it." Sarah scrambles to her feet and grabs her discarded heels. She chugs the champagne in one gulp which I find pretty impressive.

She shoves the flute toward me as I stand up. "Thanks for the drink, Lex." A rosy blush spreads across her delicate cheekbones. Before I can utter a single word, she's run off back down to the party.

"Sorry, did I interrupt something?" Katie asks innocently, but I know she isn't sorry. I know her type all too well because she's the type of girl I normally seek out. She's what I deserve. Girls like Sarah are too good for me, too pure. Girls like Sarah deserve good guys that will love them back. Katie palms my dick and rubs up and down, instantly making me hard, but I'm not thinking about Katie, because all my senses are attuned to Sarah.

Fuck it, I feel bad for breaking my promise to Tatum, but the tension I'm feeling from this party has to be relieved and if Jason is stupid enough to let his horny date out of his sight, then the fault is on him.

I pick Katie up as she wraps her legs around my waist, rubbing herself against me like a cat in heat. I shove her up against the stone wall of the patio in the shadows, close my eyes and fuck her hard. I fuck out all my frustrations, my tension, but most of all I fuck the image of Sarah out of my head.

Chapter 5

Sarah

LEX RYAN…WHAT IS there to say? I have the crush of all crushes on him, even though he's a total playboy. In bathrooms all over the country you will find, *"For a good time, call Lex Ryan"* written in Sharpie with his actual cell number on it. And I'd bet my savings if you call, he'd probably answer.

But dang it, despite his playboy status, I still want him. There's something moody and mysterious about him that draws me in. I know he's a total commitment-phobe and yet I want to be the one he's willing to give up his womanizing ways for. But I also know Lex is the kind of guy that won't change for anything or anyone. It's that stubborn Irish in him. I'm aware of all of his issues, yet I'm still drawn to him like a moth to a flame.

Maybe Kiki is right, I just need to find a nice boy who will give me the time of day. I yawn just thinking about it. All I've dated in the past are nice guys, and they don't make my heart long for something more like Lex does. It doesn't matter though, because he doesn't see me that way.

He doesn't see me at all.

He's so incredibly handsome tonight, his Tom Ford gray suit fitting him like a glove. I've secretly been keeping tabs on him all throughout the party like a complete loser stalker. Even during the ceremony while my best friends were getting married, all I could think about was Lex and what it would be like if this were our wedding.

I'm a terrible friend.

I brush away the tear that slides down my cheek and slow down to catch my breath. My heart is galloping like a thousand wild horses racing to the finish. I stop on the path leading back to the party and slump against the wall.

I wanted to kill Kiki earlier when she shoved me toward him on the dancefloor. Slow dancing in his incredibly strong and sexy arms made me so nervous and frazzled. I can't even begin to tell you what song was playing or what we talked about. It took all my concentration not to step on his feet as I worried about moving my uncoordinated legs across the floor. But like always, we were interrupted by some floozy wanting a chance with Lex.

And then when he sat down next to me on the rock, my stomach tightened into a ball of knots. He smelled like fresh-cut grass, spice and man. The pheromones he was putting off were scrambling my brain. I wanted to crawl into his lap and rub my cheek along his day-old scruff. I wanted to run my fingers through his silky dark hair and skim my lips along his. If he wanted me, I was his.

But he doesn't want me. He wants all the one-night-stand skanks that just want to ride on the Lex Dick Express.

I swipe away another tear, frowning as I think back about our conversation on the rock. I'm pretty sure we were having a moment. I actually think he was about to open up to me about why this wedding is making him so tense. It's the first intimate conversation he and I have ever had…but then kittyslut Katie showed up ruining the moment, and like I always do in uncomfortable situations, I put on a bright smile and ran.

I can't believe I did it again! I pound my fist against the wall behind me. I feel like such an idiot. I let myself believe that Lex Ryan was interested in *me*, that he wanted to spend time with *me*! He must have been waiting for Katie that whole time. He was probably trying to drum up some excuse to get me out of there before she arrived. *So humiliating.*

What is my obsession with him anyway? Why can't I get past it? Clearly, he doesn't see me in a romantic way. Maybe I need to throw myself at him like all the other women do. Thrust my C cups in his face and wear a miniskirt for a dress.

I laugh humorlessly, because that's *so* not me. Skinny jeans and Converse are more my speed. I just need to forget about him. He's put me into the friend box and the lid is closed. I push off from the wall and wipe my cheeks dry, grabbing another champagne flute from a passing waiter as I reenter the party and I quickly down it.

TJ waves me over like he's landing a Boeing jet. "Sarah! SAR-AH! Your cousin is amazeballs! Heather! Heather! Do the worm again! Oh my god Trish, get it girlfriend! Sare Bear! Trisha Yearwood is doing the running man! Agh!! I heart her!"

I giggle as my cousin Heather does the running man with Trisha on the dancefloor and TJ does the robot with Garth Brooks. Never in my wildest dreams would I have imagined this moment happening. I'm quickly swept up into TJ's enthusiasm, doubled over laughing as he tries to teach Maren Morris the sprinkler when I look up in time to see Katie Skankbags return to the party straightening her dress and hair. No sign of Lex. Bile rises in my throat.

Kiki is right. This obsession with Lex has to end now. I can't let myself live like this anymore. I have to find a nice guy who won't continue to hurt me and make my heart slowly bleed. I have to move on.

Chapter 6

Sarah

One Month Later

I TRY AND heft my suitcase up into Tatum's Escalade right before his security guy Brad walks around to the trunk.

"I've got this. You just go get buckled up," he says gruffly.

"Okay, thank you, but don't smash that one. It has all my makeup in it." He nods as I head to the passenger side and open the door to a lip-locked Kiki and Tate.

"Ugh, gross. Is this how it's going to be on the nine-hour plane ride over?" I frown.

Kiki blushes and pulls away from Tatum. "Whoops, sorry, can't keep my hands off him."

"I know. It's called the honeymoon phase," I grumble as I throw my carry-on bag in.

"What's with the scowl? What happened to Little Miss Sunshine? She's been gone for a month now and I want her back."

"She's on vacation," I deadpan.

"Clearly."

Kiki pokes me and pretends to pout. But she's right, I haven't been myself since their wedding. Since I vowed to forget about Lex. I haven't seen him since that night. Every time my brain starts to go back to him I immediately busy myself with learning new hairstyling trends or watching some new YouTube video on makeup and then trying it out on Kiki for our business, *Nashville Style Studio*. Kiki, TJ, and I have been growing our styling boutique steadily over the last year. We style everyone from A-list celebrities to local brides for their events. I'm also still the stylist for the band which is why I'm going on this European tour, leaving my cousin Heather and TJ behind to run the shop in our absence.

I'm miserable. And my misery is about to increase tenfold because we are heading out on a ten-day tour to kickstart the summer. I'm so thankful Kiki is coming along to be with Tatum and be my sidekick, because I know it's going to be difficult for me. I've had a crush on Lex for over two years now and it isn't easy to turn that off, especially when I'll be seeing him every day.

I feel like I'm *Fatal Attraction* stalker level, but Kiki assures me I'm not. She said if I was, I'd have broken into his house, camped out in his closet for a week, smelling his dirty laundry and wearing diapers so I could pee on myself and not bring attention to the fact that I was there. I seriously don't know where she gets this shit from.

No, I haven't broken into his house or smelled any of his sweaty laundry after a concert. I go on dates with other guys if I'm not on the road, but they never work out because my head and heart circle back to Lex. No one can compete with him and it drives me crazy that I can't get him out of my head. If he ever does get a serious girlfriend, I might have to commit myself into some kind of Lex rehab, because there's no doubt in my mind I'd completely fall apart.

I put on a breezy smile. "You know what? You're right. I'm tired of wallowing. Time to get back to being me."

"That's my girl! We're going to have a blast on this trip." Kiki pulls me into a side-hug.

Tate reaches into his pocket and answers his buzzing phone as I check to make sure I have my wallet and passport. "Hey Lee." He shifts in his seat. "Well where the fuck is he?" Tatum sighs and runs his hand through his hair. "K, I'll call him."

"What's going on?" Kiki looks worriedly over at Tatum.

"Lee can't find Lex. And he's not answering his phone. Matt said he talked to him last night and he seemed fine. Fuck!" Tatum leans forward. "Brad, can you swing by Lex's place before we head to the airport?"

"Sorry boss, we're on a tight schedule. We don't have time to go across town."

"We can't miss our flight, Tatum. He'll be there," Kiki reassures him.

"Why on earth would he go missing the morning our flight leaves?" Tatum fumes.

"I hope he's okay. I'm with Kiki, he'll be there. I mean we're taking a private plane, right?"

"Yeah," Tate grunts. "But we're still on a schedule. We're not going to hold the whole crew up because Lex is sulking like a fucking baby." Tatum absently looks over at me. "Sorry Sunshine, I don't mean to sound like an asshole. I'm just frustrated with him. He's been so negative lately about doing this tour."

I shrug and look out the window while Kiki rubs Tatum's shoulder.

We get to the hanger and Brad loads our stuff onto the plane. Lee is already there waiting for us, pulling Tatum to the side as Kiki and I walk up the airplane steps. As we walk on board Matt and Will are lounging on plush leather couches playing a video game. This jet is incredible. It's decorated in pale creams with comfy buttery-soft leather seats and couches. Everyone gets their own cashmere blanket and pillow.

"Welcome back on tour, ladies." Matt smiles at us.

Kiki and I both smile and give them hugs after we set our stuff down. Kiki takes two reclining chairs and I take a loveseat. A pretty stewardess comes out from the cockpit to take our drink orders and to ask if we need anything to eat. I order a latte and Kiki gets a Diet Coke and some gummy bears. Tatum climbs on board and settles in next to Kiki after giving Will and Ryan a fist-bump. Jess—the band's stylist, Lee—the band's manager, and Jimmie—Tatum's personal assistant follow suit.

"Are we waiting for Lex?" Matt asks as he careens his car into Will's truck on the video game.

"No," Tatum says tersely.

I look over at Kiki and she gives me wide eyes. I open a bag of dark chocolate squares and munch on one as I flip through an *InStyle* magazine. What on earth is Lex doing? He can't just abandon the band right as they're about to leave for the European tour!

Suddenly, there's commotion coming from the stairs and a disheveled Lex climbs onto the plane.

"I'm here. Stop fuckin' blowin' up my phone."

"About fucking time, Dick Face!" Tatum shouts as he gets up heading toward the cockpit. "Where the fuck have you been, man? We've been looking for you for hours."

"I was on the lash…Doesn' matter," Lex slurs as he falls into a matching loveseat across from me. The amount of alcohol seeping from his pores is enough to get me plastered.

"Shooey buddy, you smell like you took a bath in whiskey. You didn't drive here did you?" Will tosses over his shoulder at Lex.

Lex ignores everyone and laser focuses in on me. "Hey." *Hiccup.* "Sunshine."

I've been hiding behind my magazine up until this point hoping he doesn't notice me. I slowly lower it.

"Hi, Lex."

"Howyouvebeen?" *Hiccup.*

"Ah…great. And you?"

"Fuck." *Hiccup.* "Fucking peach-ee." *Hiccup.*

I look over at Kiki, my eyes wide as she tries to contain her laughter.

"Um, if you're going to throw up, will you give me some warning? I'm not good with vomit." I scrunch up my nose just at the thought.

"Love." *Hiccup.* "I'm naw gonna puke. I'm gonna pass out." *Hiccup.*

"Awesome." *Dear Lord, please let this flight go by quickly.* I immediately return to my magazine and sip my coffee.

"Hey Sar—" *Hiccup.* "—ah".

I look up reluctantly. "Yes?"

"Knock, knock." *Hiccup.*

Kiki rolls her eyes, smiling. "These are so bad. Don't answer him."

"Coffee Girl!" Lex yells. "You shush." *Hiccup.* "I wuzn askin' you."

Oh geez, I'll just go along to appease him. Hopefully it won't be nine hours of this. "Who's there?"

Lex grins broadly, his one dimple popping out, and I want to pass out he's so freaking good-looking.

"A little ole lady." *Hiccup.*

Kiki snorts and shakes her head. "So bad."

I smirk at her and return my gaze to Lex. "A little ole lady who?"

"I didn't know you could…" *Hiccup.* "Yodel."

I replay what he said in my head and roll my eyes at him. He winks at me. Shit, even drunk Lex is a total babe.

"Knock knock."

Kiki groans. "I told you not to answer him."

"Coffee G," he growls.

I smile back at Lex. "Who's there?"

Hiccup. "Ice cream soda."

"Ice cream soda who?"

Within seconds loud snoring erupts across from me. "Lex! Ice cream soda who?"

He is completely passed out. Kiki throws a gummy bear at his forehead, but it just bounces off onto the carpet. She throws a few more. He doesn't even twitch. God, he's even freakishly good-looking passed out on the couch with his arms flung wide and his mouth slightly agape. I reach my leg out and toe him with my shoe hoping it will stop the snoring. If anything, it gets louder.

"Are you kidding me? How am I going to sleep with that?" I whine to Kiki.

She bursts out laughing. "Here, you can use Tate's noise-canceling headphones."

She tosses me his headphones, but what I really want is a pillow to smother Lex with. Kiki gets up with her bag of gummy bears and kneels in front of Lex's face.

"What are you doing?" I giggle as she extracts a red gummy bear from the bag and gently shoves it up Lex's nose.

She snickers, "I did this to TJ once when he fell asleep at his desk. My coworker Darren and I took bets on which colored gummy could shoot out the farthest when he snored."

"Oh my god, Kiki, this is so mean…" The one gummy bear causes Lex's nose to start whistling. "Do the other nostril!" We both start giggling hysterically.

She takes out a green gummy. "Okay do you want red or gree—"

"Kiki! What are you doing?" Tatum's booming voice interrupts our game as he comes down the aisle toward us with a stern frown on his face. "Are you sticking gummy bears up his nose?"

"Me? Uh … no? Maybe? Sarah told me to do it."

I huff out a laugh. "I did not, you little liar."

"Kiki, seriously? What are you, eight? Take it out. I don't need Lex snorting a gummy bear up into his sinuses."

Kiki looks at me desperately and then back at Tate. "But it's far up there. I don't want to stick my finger up his nose!"

Tate settles into his seat and gives her a pointed look. "Well that sucks for you, doesn't it?"

Just at that moment Jess walks on to the airplane swinging her wide hips down the aisle.

"Jess! We have an emergency. Lex was eating gummy bears while he was drunk and accidentally got one up his nose, and now he's passed out. Do you have any tweezers in your bag?"

Kiki rolls her eyes. Jess's back is turned to her as she points to her eyebrows and then at Jess. She shakes her head and mouths, '*You're kidding me, right?*'

I shrug. I must admit, I'm not the best at lying, especially on the spot. I look up at Jess's scraggly brows. Yikes. She definitely doesn't own a pair of tweezers. Jess turns around, getting down on one knee as she peers up into Lex's whistling nostril and then looks over at Kiki holding the bag. She shakes her head and crouches down in front of Lex. Sticking her fingers up his nose she extracts the red gummy causing him to snort in his sleep. She tosses it into Kiki's open bag.

"Easy-peasy. Next time don't shove it so far up, Mackenzie." She grunts as she gets up and saunters down the aisle.

"Eew, I can't believe she just did that! And then threw it in my bag!" Kiki looks down at her gummy bear bag with pure disgust. Tatum and I laugh as the stewardess makes the announcement to buckle up.

I settle in my seat, putting my headphones on as I catch one last glimpse of Lex. He looks so vulnerable. I quickly get up and cover him with one of the blankets. Maybe I can finally find my peace with him on this trip. Ireland, I've been waiting for you.

Chapter 7

Lex

I GROAN AS someone not so gently shoves my shoulder.

"Wake up dude, we're here." Matt tosses my bag in my lap as we exit the van to our hotel in Dublin.

"Home sweet home. I feel like shit beaten up in a bucket," I mutter as I carefully exit the car. I slept off most of the whiskey on the flight over and now I'm sullen and hungover. I almost skipped out on this tour, but I couldn't do it to Tatum and the guys. They don't know why I hate being back here so much. It's not their fault I can't man up and face my past and the invisible baggage that's tethered around my neck.

I stumble from the van grateful for the overcast day and my wayfarer sunglasses. Our fans are lined up behind blockades and they start cheering and waving posters when they spot us. I love our fans, but I can't stop and chat with them right now. I just want to pass out again. I wave as I duck through the hotel door as Tatum, Will, and Matt stop to sign some autographs.

Thankfully we're here in July, so the temperature is mild. I peel off my leather jacket as I walk into the hotel lobby and wait for the guys. I don't want to talk to anyone right now, I just want to sleep off this massive hangover. Tate announces to the group that we'll meet back in the lobby at eight tonight for dinner. We check in at the Westbury and I immediately go to my room, drop my bag on the floor, and pass out on my bed fully clothed.

A SHARP KNOCK on the door wakes me up from a dreamless sleep. I stumble to the door and open it a smidge to see Tatum standing there looking like a fucking spring daffodil.

"What the fuck are you wearing?" I open the door wider.

Tatum looks down at his bright green t-shirt with red lip kisses printed all over it. *Kiss me, I'm Irish* written in white script across his chest.

I bust up laughing. "Nah mate, you can't wear that out."

"What? Kiki bought it for me. I'm in Ireland. When in Rome and all that shit."

"That screams *I'm American and I'm a fucking eejit.*"

Tatum pushes past me into my room and falls into one of my leather lounge chairs. "Forget about the shirt. Tell me what the fuck is going on with you. I don't want to spend this whole tour worrying about you, wondering if you're going to show or if you're going to be piss-drunk every night. I'm not going to do it, man."

I sigh as I sit down and lower my aching head into my

hands. I feel something in my hair and extract a squished gummy bear. What the hell? When did I eat gummy bears? Tatum clears his throat and looks down at his phone.

"Give me a second, mate. I'm completely wrecked." I get up, go into the bathroom and grab two ibuprofens from my kit and come and sit down across from him. "This stays between us."

"Of course man, you know that."

"I mean, I don't even want Kiki to know."

Tatum rubs his jaw and then nods curtly. "Understood."

I scrub my hands down my face. "Well, before I moved to the States, you know my brother and I ran the pub in Kinsale. One day the most beautiful girl I had ever laid eyes on walked into the bar. She had strawberry-blonde hair, baby-blue eyes that completely undid me, curves in all the right places, legs for days... I was a complete stook for her. She was beautiful."

I wring my hands and look up to see if Tate is still following, and he is.

"See, I wasn't the womanizer back then that I am now." I huff out a humorless laugh. "I wasn't a virgin, but I definitely wasn't experienced. I was single and so was she. Her name was Alana. We hired her to work at our bar as a waitress even though she didn't have a lick of experience. One thing led to another and she and I started dating. We had that corny kind of love that was all sunshine and Leprechauns shootin' rainbows out of their fucking arses."

Tatum chuckles as he settles back into his chair. "Nice analogy."

I smile and scratch my jaw. "Anyway, after going together for about six months I asked her to marry me. She said yes and I was the happiest fucking sot I had ever been in my twenty-two years on this earth. My mum was beyond excited. She wanted ten grandbabies. My brother thought I was a donkey's arse, but that's neither here nor there. He didn't trust Alana for reasons I didn't understand or care to. Alana didn't have a lot of family and my parents took her under their wing. My mum wanted to throw us a big wedding, but I just wanted it simple. I didn't care about the ceremony…I just wanted the forever with her."

I take a deep breath as I run my fingers through my hair, agitated by this conversation. "I was so in love with her, mate, it was pathetic. I would have done anything this lass asked of me. She wanted the big wedding, the expensive dress, the flowers…I agreed to it all. We were to get married at a countryside resort near Cork. My whole family was coming—aunts, uncles, cousins, cousins twice removed. My parents were paying for everything because she and I didn't have two dimes to rub together, and she only had her mum on her side coming. You get the picture."

I get up and start pacing. Tatum watches me, his eyes following my jerky movements. "I was fucking clueless, dude. I had my head so far up her ass that I never saw it coming. We had our rehearsal dinner at a posh restaurant on the estate and then I played a song I had written for her. She had tears in her eyes, the whole place did. It was a beautiful fucking song. Afterwards I couldn't sleep, I was so excited to make Alana my wife. I snuck over to her room even though it was bad luck for the groom to see the bride the night before."

I huff out a breath as the suppressed memories tumble back into my brain. "I slid my keycard into the door, because it was our honeymoon suite and I wanted to surprise her. I walked in on her fucking the waiter from our rehearsal dinner on the couch. *The fucking waiter.* And the worst part? I know she saw me. She swears she didn't, but she fucking saw me and smirked and kept on riding that motherfucker until she came, like it turned her on that I was watching. I almost killed the fucking guy. Security guards had to pull me off of him after Alana called for help."

"Jesus, man," Tatum whispers, shaking his head.

"Yeah, just fucking imagine what you feel for Kiki and having her betray you like that. I wish..." My teeth grind together as I pause collecting my thoughts. "I don't know mate...It killed something in me."

"I can't imagine. I mean Savannah cheated on me, but I never caught her in the act."

"Not the same. You weren't in love with her."

"True, and it still hurt. Christ, so what happened?" Tatum rubs his jaw as he looks at me.

"I told her to pack her shit and get out immediately."

"Did she?"

"She cried and told me it was nothing, that she was just trying to relieve some pre-wedding jitter stress, but I just couldn't believe anything she said. Come to find out after the wedding was canceled that the waiter wasn't the only guy she was sleeping with behind my back."

"Jesus."

"I told her I was done. She was dead to me and to not ever show her face around Kinsale again. She stalked me at the bar for a couple weeks after, but my whole family made it quite clear she was no longer a Ryan and no longer welcome. I couldn't take seeing her around town, so I packed a bag and moved to the States. That was about ten years ago and well, you know the rest."

I take a sip of water and sit back down. "Even though she's a part of my past, I'm worried coming back here will dredge up old memories that I can't handle."

Tate is silent as he soaks in all the information I just gave him. "Thanks for telling me, brother. I think I understand you a lot better now, why it's hard for you to trust women and why it's so hard for you to come back home. I promise we won't let you slip through the cracks."

I nod in contemplation. "I wish I could be a better man. I wish I could find someone to love, but she killed that part of me." I shrug. "What's that saying? Wild hearts can't be broken? I don't mind writing and singing love songs, but I never want to live through that shit again."

"Not even for the right girl?"

"Not even for the right girl."

"Okay." Tatum nods and gets up out of his chair. "I guess you better go wash the dick off of your face. We have dinner reservations in an hour."

"What the fuck are you talking about?"

Tatum smirks. "Matt drew a dick on your face when you were passed-out snoring on the plane."

"Remind me to kill that cocksucker." I heave myself out of the chair. "Hey mate, thanks for listening."

"Anytime. Thanks for sharing. I know it wasn't easy." We fist-bump as he turns to leave.

"Dude?"

"Yeah?"

"Burn that fucking shirt."

"Is it really that bad? Kiki thought it was cute," he mumbles to himself as I shut the door on him.

Chapter 8

Sarah

"WHAT ARE YOU going to wear?" I ask Kiki over my shoulder as I finish putting light waves in my hair with a wand.

"Uh, probably just jeans and a long-sleeved top. The weather app says it gets down into the fifties at night."

"Hmm, okay, I'll wear my loose-knit sweater and moto skinnies."

"Ooh wow! Your hair looks great! You liar, you said your hair is stick straight, but it holds curl!" Kiki smacks my butt as she walks by me.

"Ha, this will hold for about ten minutes. The only reason it stayed at your wedding is because Heather put about a gallon of hairspray in my hair."

"Well, it looks good no matter what you do to it." She picks her sweater up off my bed and grabs her key card. "Thanks for doing my makeup. I'm headed back to my room to get dressed. I'll meet you downstairs?"

I sigh as I sit down in front of the floor-length mirror to do my makeup. "Sounds good."

"What's wrong?" Kiki arches an eyebrow at my deflated tone.

"Nothing. I'm just nervous about being on tour again."

"With Lex."

"Yes, with Lex. I'm scared I won't be able to mask my feelings for him, and I'm tired of not being able to act on them."

Kiki sits down on my bed. "So, why don't you act on them and see what happens?"

I lower my shadow brush and look at her with my mouth hanging open. "The girl that tells me to stay away from him, that I could do so much better, has changed her tune?"

Kiki shrugs and looks guilty. "I was just trying to protect your heart, but if he's truly what you want, then why not give it a shot?"

"Because what if he turns me down?" I chew on my lip. I never did tell her what happened at her wedding. I don't think she'd be pushing me toward him if she knew he did something with Katie. I don't want to feel that kind of dismissal again. I shake my head vehemently. "No, no way, I couldn't handle that kind of rejection. I'd rather just pine for him from afar."

"Suit yourself." Kiki stands up rubbing her hands down her thighs. "But you'll always have the 'what if' question in your mind for the rest of your life."

"What if he turns me down?" I snark back at her.

"What if he doesn't?"

"What if I meet the man of my dreams tonight?" I throw back.

"What if the man of your dreams has been standing right

in front of you all along?"

Shit, she has me there. Because even though I don't know intimate details about Lex, my attraction to him is off-the-charts impossible to ignore.

"What if I do take the leap and find out I don't like the man behind the gorgeous face and melt-your-panties accent?"

She grins. "Well, then you know he wasn't the right one for you and you can finally move on."

"Ugh, Kiki, why can't it be easy like you and Tate?"

"Easy?" she sputters. "It wasn't easy! It was scary as hell. Don't you remember all my insecurities? Shit, I still have them. Not to mention a famous country music star trying to sabotage my relationship. Easy? No. Worth the leap? Most definitely."

Poor Kiki and Tate went through an emotional wringer last year on tour when his ex, country/pop superstar Savannah Edwards, tried to write a scathing article about Tatum that could have ended his singing career. She tried to blackmail him by saying she wouldn't release the article if she could rekindle her relationship with him. It was an emotional rollercoaster for Kiki and Tatum, that's for sure.

"Yeah, you're right. You're *so* right! I just need to take the plunge!" My stomach rolls just thinking about it.

"Yes! Do it! Tonight!" Kiki fist-pumps in the air.

"Whoa, slow your roll there, pony. Tonight? No, no way. Not unless you get me super drunk."

"Okay." She smiles cheekily at me.

"Okay what?" I eye her suspiciously.

"Okay I'll get you super drunk. See you downstairs in

ten!" She starts to sing as she opens my hotel-room door. "I'm getting Sarah drunk and she's gonna kiss Lex and tell him she looooves him."

"What? Kiki! No, I was kidding!" The door closes and I'm left alone with my thoughts. Could I really ask Lex out? My palms perspire just thinking about it.

I look in the mirror and give myself a pep talk. *It's now or never, Sarah. Just do it! If he says no, yeah, your heart will break a little, but you'll recover…and we can put this little silly crush to bed once and for all! You've got this, girl!*

If I've got this why do I feel like I'm about to leap off the ledge without a safety net?

Chapter 9

Sarah

Our group of seven chooses to head into an old tavern after dinner. Jess decides to go back to the hotel because she was nodding off at dinner. The rest of us are determined to stay up so we can get used to the time change.

O'Shaughnessy's tavern looks straight out of something from Harry Potter with its lead glass windows and dark cherry wood bar. It's cozy with its huge stone fireplace burning at one end, leather couches and club chairs surrounding little cocktail tables. Table tops are filled with patrons along the windows and there's a pool table off to the left of the entrance.

Will and Matt immediately veer toward the pool table and wait their turn. Tatum and Lee order beers for all of us as Lex stops to talk to some of the locals. Kiki and I head to the surprisingly empty leather couch and chairs near the fire. The tavern is crowded but not claustrophobic. Mostly people are hanging out at the bar keeping the bartender busy. I'm stuffed from dinner and the heat emanating from the fire is making me drowsy.

"Uh Kiki, I don't know if I can hang much longer. I think the time difference is catching up to me too."

"No Sare, you have to stay up. You'll adjust to the time change so much faster if you do."

Lee, Tatum, and Lex bring our beers over and sit down with us. Lex sits down across from me and eyes me over his beer mug.

He looks so damn sexy in just a black button-down with the sleeves rolled up, dark jeans and boots. He has black leather bands around his wrist, the tattoos on his arms peeking out from beneath his rolled cuffs giving him his signature rocker look. His dark hair is shorter than at the wedding and he's styled it into a kind of faux Mohawk look. He's more rock than country, and it always surprises me for some reason. His ocean-blue eyes are piercing as they hypnotize me. I try to look away, but I'm drowning in his gaze.

Fingers snap in front of my face and I feel my cheeks heat. "Sarah, did you fall asleep on me?" Kiki elbows me.

"No, just kind of got lost for a moment," I murmur as I catch Lex smirking as he responds to something Lee is saying.

"Maybe we should dance!" Kiki starts bouncing on the couch.

I laugh. "Where are we going to dance? There's no dancefloor."

"I don't know." She looks around. "Right here I guess!"

I take a couple sips of my beer for liquid encouragement because there's no stopping Kiki. She's already dancing in place to some Irish rock band I've never heard of. I join her as The Corrs' "Breathless" comes on. We're jumping all around as the guys watch on with amusement. Kiki and I laugh like fools as we bump and grind each other. She has a pretend microphone she's singing into as she twerks me. Patrons from the bar stare at us, but we don't care.

We fall back down on the couch in a sweaty mess, laughing our asses off as the song ends. Tatum grabs Kiki and pulls her practically onto his lap as they kiss. Not wanting to be a third wheel on the couch, I head to the restroom to make sure my makeup isn't melting down my face. When I return, Kiki and Tate are talking with their heads together, Lee is gone, and Lex is at the bar ordering more drinks while a blonde flirts with him. Jealousy and annoyance for the blonde flare up in my veins as I flop back down in Lee's chair, giving Tatum and Kiki some privacy. I hate feeling this way because he's not even mine to be jealous over, but we can't go anywhere without some woman trying to get her hands all over him. It gets old pretty quickly.

I'm surprised when he looks up and excuses himself from her, his eyes on me as he makes his way back from the bar. U2's "One" starts to play. Tatum grabs Kiki and pulls her up off the couch, slow dancing with her. They really are so cute together. I sigh as I watch them, wishing I had a guy like Tatum Reed in my life.

Lex places a fresh beer down in front of me. I'm about to thank him, when he suddenly reaches out and pulls me out of the chair. I'm unexpectedly wrapped in his strong arms, my head hitting right to his chin. He takes a deep breath in, and I'm in such shock wondering what the hell is going on that I'm frozen in his arms.

"Sarah."

I look up into his aquamarine eyes as I have a major déjà vu moment. "Yes, Lex?"

"Breathe, beautiful."

I nod my head once and move my hands up to his shoulders. *Is this really happening? I can't believe this is happening!* Would it be weird if I did a little cheer jump and then resumed my dance position with Lex? Probably best just to do kicks in my head.

I smile as I stare at his chest mentally unbuttoning his shirt. What I wouldn't give to run my fingers over his hard-chiseled pecs. I know what he looks like under there from seeing him shirtless more times than I can count when he goes onstage or when I have to wipe sweat off of him at a concert. I know I won't be disappointed; he's built like an Adonis.

We slowly move to the song and his fingertips slide down my back making my whole body break out in goosebumps as he presses me closer to him. When I danced with him at the wedding, we definitely were not this close because I was so worried about tripping over my feet, but here I'm just holding on to him, along for the ride while he controls how we move. My fingers glide up into his rich silky hair. *Oh my god, I can't believe I'm touching Lex Ryan right now. I am freaking touching Lex Ryan!* I have waited over two long torturous years for this moment.

I'm lightheaded and burning up. I'm not sure if it's the beer, lack of sleep and the warm fire, or if it's the effect Lex has on me. The song floats around us like a dream. I must still be on the couch having one of those weird daydreams again because this can't be real.

"Lex?"

"Yeah?" He leans in closer to hear me and this must be one good fucking dream because he smells delicious.

"Am I dreaming?"

He chuckles. "I don't think so, beautiful." His breath is light on my ear giving me goosebumps as his nose dips and nuzzles my neck. He softly kisses me there and I want to die. I let out an embarrassing strangled groan. Hopefully the music is loud enough to cover it up. His masculine scent of leather, forests, and spice pulls me under. I am limp in his arms as he moves his kisses back up to my ear. "God, you're so beautiful, Princess," he whispers into my ear. "I can't take my eyes off of you."

I exhale the breath I've been holding, "Ah, uh…" This is it. This is my chance. *Now or never, Sarah.*

I take a deep breath. "Lex, um, would you consider…" *Crap! I can't do this.* His teeth graze my neck and the blood rushes out of my head. I can't think. I don't even know what I want to ask him. Sleep with me? Can we go on a date? Can we be more than friends?

Lame, lame, lame. How do you go from friends to something more? I've been so complacent in this relationship for so long, too stupid not to ask for what I really wanted from the very beginning.

He tilts my chin up so that I'm staring into his bottomless Caribbean eyes. He arches an eyebrow. "Would I…"

I swallow, trying to gather my courage. Bono croons on and on about being one. *Come on Sarah, one life, one chance, man up and just do it!*

He leans in and brushes his lips against mine. The whole tavern becomes muted as I'm enveloped in his arms, his scent, his taste. It's just the two of us swaying to the music that I can't even hear anymore over the loud beating of my heart.

It's just a simple, soft kiss, but it packs a walloping punch to my core. His eyes are hooded as he stares down at my lips like he's about to lean back in and devour them.

I place my hand on his chest. *This is it girl, you've got this. Just ask him out and then you can have as many kisses as you want.* "Would you consider…" I clear my throat. "Would you consider…getting a whiskey?" I squeak out.

Chicken, chicken. Total chicken.

The song ends and Lex takes a step back from me and smirks. "You want a whiskey? Right now?"

I shrug as I stare at his throat, unable to meet his eyes. I'm pissed at myself for breaking the moment between us and not being able to tell him what I really want. *No, I don't want a goddamned whiskey, I want you!* Why can't I just say that?

I glance around and notice that we're alone. Tatum and Kiki must have snuck off after their dance. "Why not? We're in Ireland, right? I've never tried it before." I paste on a fake smile and avoid his penetrating stare.

He smiles, showing off his gorgeous straight white teeth and dimple. "Aye Love, yer about to taste the finest whiskey in yer life. Stay right here and I'll get us some."

I plop down on the leather sofa and fling my head back against the cushion looking up at the exposed wood beams of the ceiling, relieved for a little respite to gather my wits.

Did Lex and I just really make out? Okay, maybe *making out* isn't the right term. It was the Sesame Street version of making out, but still…I'm in shock. The kiss was soft and tentative, and perfect as far as first kisses go, and not what I was expecting from him. I brush my fingertips over my lips as I sit up. I definitely want more.

He's taking his time with me, savoring me, and I think that shocks me more than anything. Usually he has his hands up some girl's shirt within two minutes after name introductions. Ugh, I don't want to think about him with other girls right now. I need to relax and just follow his lead. I'm not going to push him any further than he wants to go. *Just play it cool, Sarah.*

He returns with two tumblers of whiskey, one finger for me, two for him. He sits down and turns toward me handing me my glass. "Sip it slow. It will burn at first going down yer throat."

I laugh. "Sounds awful."

He smiles and looks down into his tumbler. "Some things are meant to be savored. It may go down in flames, but the end result is worth the punch to the gut."

"God, I'm kind of scared, Lex." I cringe as I smell the whiskey.

He chuckles. "Don't be scared. Just don't treat it as a shot. Sip it slow. It's Auchentoshan, so it's an excellent smooth whiskey."

I bring the glass to my lips as he watches me. I take a small sip of the amber liquid and it burns, but I like the taste. I take a bigger sip and it goes smoothly down my throat burning in the pit of my stomach before the fingers of liquid fire spread out through my belly causing a warm tickle. "Mmm, I think I like whiskey." I turn toward him and tuck one leg under me as I lean my shoulder into the soft buttery couch.

Lex snorts. "Aye, not many lasses do. This could be trouble." He grins as he takes a large sip of his. He watches me over the brim of his glass. "Your eyes are the same color as this whiskey. Amber lit by the fire."

I smile shyly at him. "Just plain old brown."

"Nothing plain about you, Sarah." He shifts and mirrors my position. "Do you like Ireland so far?"

I shrug. "I'm not sure? I haven't seen much except for the hotel. I can't wait to go explore and take some pictures tomorrow after the interview."

"Shite. I forgot about the interview." He rubs his hand over his forehead. "What kind of pictures do you like to take?"

"Well, I take pictures of Kiki for the blog we run, so we'll do a couple of those, but I've found I really like taking landscape photography."

He reaches out and takes a piece of my hair that has purple running through it. "Are you ever in the blog pictures?"

I laugh. "Sometimes, but not often. Kiki is a horrible photographer. Bless her heart she's tried, but in every photo either my head is chopped off or it's blurry. So, it's better if I take the pics."

"I like the purple." He rubs my hair between his fingers.

My skin pebbles with goosebumps, I want him to touch

me so badly. I swallow. "Thanks, I was going to do green for Ireland, but I was worried it would look like algae."

He bursts out laughing. "I think any color of the rainbow would look beautiful on you. I like how it's just this piece under your ear. Like a secret color only some people get to see if they look close enough."

I smile as I take another small sip of whiskey. "Hmm."

"Sarah?"

"Yeah?"

"Can I kiss you again?"

Before I can answer he takes my whiskey and places it on the table and leans forward. His fingers thread through my hair and he pulls me to him. His lips brush against mine, but they are hungrier this time, bruising mine as he takes. My lips part on their own accord, inviting him to go deeper. His tongue meets mine, as my body melts against him. He deepens the kiss and holy hell, it's the sexiest kiss I have ever received. The warmth of the fire behind us kindles with his scent and my senses go into overdrive. I'm sleepy, but wide awake at the same time, unable to stop this runaway train I'm on. And I don't want it to stop.

Kissing Lex is the most exhilarating thing I have ever done, because his kisses aren't G-rated. Oh boy, no Siree. They are X-rated, whole body, blow-your-top, toe-curling, brain-consuming, sex kisses. If this is how he kisses, I can't begin to imagine what he's like in bed. My sex clenches at the thought and blood heats my veins. I slide my fingers up into his silky black hair and he groans as he sucks on my bottom lip.

This has got to be the hottest make-out session I have

ever experienced. He pulls me closer as we continue to kiss. I hum with need because I need him to touch me, I feel like I'm about to explode. He breaks the kiss as he puts his hands on my wrists.

"Slow down, Love."

Not exactly the words I want to hear. His hooded eyes are glazed with desire as we both pant. He licks his lips and my eyes flicker to his mouth. Pure lust makes me dizzy with need. I know he wants me as much as I want him. I can feel it in my bones.

"I don't want to slow down. I want more," I say truthfully. I gather up some courage, fueled by the whiskey. "Come back to the hotel with me?"

He smiles ruefully and gently moves me away from him. "Sarah…look…" He sighs and runs his fingers through his hair as he looks down at the ground.

Oh shit. Here it comes. I can feel the rejection on his lips. I mentally slap my palm against my forehead. I can't believe I asked him back to the hotel, what was I thinking? How did I read this situation so wrong? Damn whiskey making me do stupid things. I don't want to hear what he has to say. I don't think I could stomach being humiliated for the hundredth time by this beautiful man.

I hold my hand up and sigh. "No, Lex. I get it. Just…don't." I hurriedly grab my clutch and stand up, wobbling a bit in my heels, the alcohol finally settling in my veins making me woozy.

"Whoa, Love. Let me help you."

He grabs my elbow helping to steady me. Tears threaten to spill over. *Don't let him see you cry, pull yourself together.*

I shrug off his hand. "I've got it." I rudely push away from him and start walking toward the front door of the bar.

"Sunshine, let me at least walk you home."

"No, I'm good," I snap back at him over my shoulder. I can hear him mutter a curse behind me.

I slam through the front door. The cool air snaps against my heated skin, and the tears start to flow. *What a fucking fool I am!* I look up to the starless sky as wet lines track down my cheeks. I quickly wipe them away. *Are you ever going to fucking learn? He is not the guy for you!*

But why isn't he? Why can't he be? What's so wrong with me that he chooses those skanky hoes over me? He made me feel so pathetic a minute ago, like he was doing *me* a favor by kissing me.

But it was such a hot kiss.

No, Sarah! Just…no. Move on, he's not good enough for you.

I hug myself as I walk the couple blocks back to the hotel internally battling with myself. I look back over my shoulder and see Lex walking about a block behind me. The fucking Irish asshole is following me back here. Ugh, I love him for that and hate him all over again in one shuddering breath. I scowl at him as I push myself through the revolving door and head straight back up to my room to hate on Lex Ryan…and to think about that incredible kiss that can never happen again.

Chapter 10

Sarah

"Oh my god, Kiki, it was so humiliating."

"But I saw you guys, I was so excited for you! Tate and I made our escape so that maybe you two love birds could have some alone time."

"Oh, we had our alone time, all right. Right after he completely dissed me."

Kiki gives me a side-hug as we walk behind Tatum and Lee on the sidewalk. We're on our way to the local Dublin TV station so the guys can do an interview on their morning show to get fans hyped for their tour.

"Quickly give me a low down on what happened."

"Hmm, well in a nutshell, I had the hottest make-out session of my life. I told him I wanted more. He said no. I walked back to the hotel. Alone. That's it."

"No! He said *no* to you? What the hell? He doesn't say no to any girl."

I cut my eyes at her. "Thanks, I'm aware."

"Oh sorry, that came out wrong." Kiki chews on her

thumbnail, lost in thought.

"He didn't even say no, he didn't say *anything*, he just gave me this pathetic smile like I was some charity case and gently pushed me away. I guess he prefers the floozies and hoe-bags." I shrug as I sip my latte. "Doesn't matter, you were right all along, Kiki. I need to look for a nice guy. Lex is just a tease."

Kiki links her arm in mine. "I'm sorry, Sunshine. I hate it that he can't see what an awesome, beautiful girl he has right in front of his face. It hurts my heart."

"Yeah, it hurts mine too. I need a nice guy like Tatum. Someone who knows what he wants and takes the bull by the horns."

Kiki giggles. "He does do that. Maybe Lex wants you, he just doesn't realize it."

"Oh, he knows exactly what he's doing. He played me like a fiddle last night. I hate him."

"Whoa, I don't think I've ever heard you say that word before…hate is… healthy-ish."

I laugh. "It's definitely not in my vocabulary, but today I hate Lex Ryan!" I say forcefully.

We get to the studio doors and Tatum holds the door open for Kiki and me. He looks behind us. "Lex, my man, where's Will and Matt?"

"They should be right behind me," Lex says gruffly. "I'll wait for them in the lobby."

I look over at Kiki like a deer caught in headlights. *Oh my god, was he behind us for our whole conversation?* Kiki looks constipated. I duck my head, grab her arm, and pivot quickly toward the elevator.

"Sarah, can I talk to you for a minute?" Lex asks quietly.

No! Shit no! I'll just pretend like I didn't hear him. Kiki pinches my arm and tilts her head in Lex's direction.

"No!" I whisper to her harshly.

"Yes!" Kiki hisses back and pushes me in his direction as she gets on the elevator with Tatum and Lee. She reaches out and quickly jabs the button to close the doors before I can utter a word. The elevator closes leaving me alone with him.

Thanks a lot, best friend.

Chapter 11

Lex

SARAH HUFFS OUT a breath as she turns toward me. She's not happy to see me and I can understand why. Like the total gobshite that I am, I turned her down last night. I know it took a lot of courage for her to ask me back to her room, but I couldn't take it any further than that kiss. Shit, it took all the self-control I had to stop myself from devouring her. The simple fact is she deserves better than me.

She looks like a ray of sunshine on this gloomy morning, her hair up in a high ponytail with little silver star stud earrings that twinkle in her earlobes. Memories of sucking on them last night and the cute little moans she made suddenly invade my thoughts. I instantly get hard. Jesus, since when have a girl's earlobes ever made me hard? What the fuck is wrong with me? This no-sex sabbatical I've put myself on since Tatum's wedding is starting to make my eyes cross and my wires go haywire. I've never gone this long before.

Her pouty pink lips frown at me as she stands with her arms crossed over her perky little tits. The same tits that were pressed up against my chest as we danced last night. She had me so hard and aching when we were on the couch I couldn't see straight. I wanted to strip her clothes off with my teeth, in front of everyone. I wanted to bend her over the couch in front of that fire and hear her scream my name.

Jesus, why am I torturing myself with images of last night? Tossing and turning thinking about her all night was torment enough. I rub my hands down my face. I have to stay away from her, for my own sanity.

"What do you want, Lex?" she grits out.

I scratch my jaw, my scruff getting a little longer since I haven't shaved in a couple days.

"About last night…"

Sarah scoffs, "Seriously? You're doing this all over again? I don't need a play by play of what happened last night, I was there. I get it. I'm not what you want. You made that loud and clear." She takes a step back and holds up her hand. "So, no problem, you won't have to worry if pathetic Sarah will be mooning over you like a lovesick puppy dog, because this girl won't be looking in your direction *ever* again."

She whirls around and something inside me snaps. The thought of Sarah never smiling at me again kills me. I catch up to her and grab her elbow and guide her to the bank of elevators.

"Get off me, Lex." She tries to shake me off as people turn to stare but I hold firm.

One of the elevators going up dings and I immediately shuffle her onto it. Just at that moment Will and Matt arrive.

"Hey guys! Top of the mornin' to ya!" Will says cheerfully, clueless that we're having a moment.

I turn around. "Get off the fucking elevator."

Matt's eyes go big. "Whoa dude, what's wrong?"

"Take another fucking elevator, pissants!" I growl.

I don't have to tell them again. They slowly step off the elevator, hands up in surrender and the doors slide shut. I press the emergency button.

Sarah quietly chuckles. "Are you fucking kidding me?"

I turn around and face her, but she looks anything but happy. I crowd her into the corner of the elevator. My arms cage her in and both our chests are rising up and down as I stare down at her. "I'm not fucking done talkin' and yer gonna hear what I have to say."

Her eyes go wide and she subtly nods.

"Last night I wanted you. I wanted you so badly it hurt. But I'm a Mr. Right Now, not a Mr. Forever kind of guy. I can't give you what you want. You need the hearts and flowers and forever." I run my hand through my hair. "Shit, you *deserve* that…I shouldn't have kissed you."

She clucks her tongue and looks away from me, blush coloring her cheeks. I turn her chin back toward me. "Sarah…I—"

"I hate you, Lex Ryan."

"Don't hate me, Love."

"I do." A single tear escapes her eye and it breaks my heart. I gently glide my thumb over the tear, stopping its descent down her cheek.

She tries to push me away but I gather her in my arms and lift her up, pressing her to the elevator wall. Her legs automatically wrap around my waist and my hard-on pushes into her sweet spot. She gasps and that sweet little noise makes my control snap.

I swoop down, ravishing her perfect petal-pink lips. Our tongues clash, fighting in a battle of who-wants-this-kiss-more. I take all of her, coaxing her tongue in a rhythm with mine. Her fingers tug harshly at my hair making me groan with need. It's not a sweet kiss, it's an angry all-consuming kiss. I can't get enough of this woman and I want to take her right here and now against the elevator wall.

"Lex…" Sarah pants as she breaks for air. "Oh my god, Lex, please…"

"*Ba mhaith liom grá a dhéanamh leat.*"[1]

I murmur in Irish as I kiss down her neck, pushing her V-neck t-shirt down to expose her lacy bra. I want to take my time with her, but time isn't on our side. I run my tongue over the fabric and she arches into me. I lower the lace cup and suck her sweet little bud into my mouth. It's like milk and honey, the sweetest taste.

"Oh god, oh god," she pants as she grinds against me. "Please don't stop."

I release her nipple and stare down at her beautiful flushed face. Suddenly I snap out of my lust-filled haze. I can't do this to Sarah. Not in a dirty elevator. Not like this. She deserves a good guy that will make love to her properly on satin sheets with rose petals and candles. Not jammed up in the corner of a dingy public elevator. Our chests heave as I stare down into her whiskey-amber eyes.

She's shaking in my arms as I put her back down on the ground. I carefully pull the cup of her bra up and straighten

---

[1] Irish translation: I want to make love to you.

her shirt. Her cheeks bloom bright pink as I look down at her.

I feel so ashamed that I lost control again.

Shit, I can't believe I let it get this far like I did last night. I lose all my senses when she's in my arms. I'm serious when I tell her I'm not the right guy for her. I'm a mess. In my fantasies Sarah would be mine, and mine alone. In reality it just isn't possible.

"Sarah…" I say, my voice tinged with regret.

Her eyes widen in disbelief. "Lex Ryan, are you fucking kidding me? Don't you dare!"

She shoves me roughly away from her. Lunging forward she hits the emergency button causing the elevator to lurch up. She's strong for being such a little thing. "I swear to God, if you say that was a mistake, I'm going to knee you right in the balls. I mean I can't *believe* I let that happen again. I'm such a fucking idiot! Agh!"

I huff out a humorless laugh. "You're not an idiot, Sarah."

"Just shut up! I'm not even talking to you; I'm talking to myself!" She angrily crosses her arms over her chest.

I sigh as I lean against the wall. The resentment emanating off of her washes over me in waves of regret. "I meant what I said—I'm not the right guy for you."

She twists her lips into a bitter scowl as she picks up her bag. "For not being the right guy, you sure like to keep on trying."

The elevator doors open and she storms off. I catch up to her and grab her hand. "Sarah, wait. I don't want to hurt you."

"Too late for that, *Asshat*." She tries to wrench her hand from my grip as we turn the corner. "Let go of my hand!"

Everyone is standing in a group talking to a woman dressed in a navy suit as we approach. Kiki's eyes widen as she drinks us in. The woman interviewing us turns around.

"Why Lex Ryan, what a little surprise!"

"Alana," I choke out as I drop Sarah's hand.

Chapter 12

Lex

WHAT THE FUCK? Is this a nightmare? I rub my eyes with the heels of my palms hoping this is just a really bad dream. My fucking past is standing right in front of me with a wide smile on her face.

"What the fuck are you doing here?"

"Is that any way to talk to your fiancée?" She giggles as she leans in for a hug and a kiss on the cheek. I'm stiff as a board. I hear Sarah quietly gasp beside me as she takes a step back.

"*Ex*-fiancée," I bark out. "You have some fucking nerve."

"Lexy…I'm so happy to see you too," she purrs as she runs a fingernail down my arm. My jaw ticks in annoyance as I grind my teeth. My head is about to explode with anger and confusion. My hands clench and unclench as I try to remain calm.

"Whoa, whoa." Lee steps up next to me and puts his hand on my shoulder. "Okay then, now that we've all said hello, let's go get some coffee, Lex, before the interview starts. Ms. McKenna, if you'll excuse us." Lee quickly steers me away from the group to the greenroom set up for us down the hall. I glance back over my shoulder; every single face in the group is slack-jawed except for Alana who is smiling confidently. She looks like a cat that just caught the canary and swallowed it whole.

"Uh, want to tell me what's going on?" Lee hands me a bottle of water as I lower myself onto the couch.

"Not particularly," I grumble. I'm shaking as I gulp some water. I think I'm in shock. "What the hell is Alana Walsh doing here?"

"Alana McKenna. She's the journalist covering the tour. How do you know her?"

"She's someone from my past. McKenna? Is she married?"

"Uh, not sure bud." Lee chuckles. "Did I hear her right? Fiancée?"

"No. Yes. Not anymore."

Lee nods. "Are you going to be okay with this? Do I need to fly Kimberly over here?"

Kimberly handles the band's PR. She took over when Tatum needed help rebuilding his image after his ex-girlfriend Savannah Edwards tried to drag him through the mud and ruin his career.

I grimace. "No, I can handle her. This won't turn into a PR circus." I rub my hands down my face.

Lee nods. "Sorry, Lex. If we had known we could have requested someone different."

I huff out a laugh. "Oh she knew exactly what she was doing. Name change and all. She wanted it to be a surprise."

Tatum comes barging into the greenroom. "Shit, Lex. You okay man?"

I'm really glad I told Tate about my past last night. "Not really, but I can get through it. It's just one interview." Tatum and Lee exchange a look. "What? What the fuck was that look for? What do you two know that I don't?"

Tatum sighs. "Uh, Alana McKenna will be going on tour with us to write an exposé for *Ireland Shout* magazine."

The blood drains from my face. "Fuck that. No fucking way."

Lee leans back against the counter. "Like I said, if we had known, we could've gotten someone different. As it stands, we can't change it."

"So, it's my fucking fault that I didn't tell you about my past? This is stupid," I seethe.

"No man," Tate tries to soothe, "it's just that the ball has already started rolling and we can't stop it. But I promise we'll have Lee draw up a contract that says she'll remain strictly professional with the band, especially with you. Right, Lee?" Tatum glares at Lee.

"Right, absolutely. I'll call the lawyers and have them draft something for her to sign after the interview. Just stay away from her, Lex, and we won't have any problems."

"Right." I frown at them. "You obviously don't know Alana like I do."

Ten Years Earlier

"YO IRISH, GREAT show tonight, I think we killed it, well, everyone except for Deuce."

"Eh it was some craic." I nod my head at our band's drummer Scotty as I follow him to the side of the stage of the seedy Los Angeles club we played at tonight called The Velvet Tread.

"Deuce is being such a crackhead tonight. He could barely hit his notes. I think we should get rid of him."

I nod as I help him move the amp. "He's got the devil in 'im that's fer sure."

"I heard there were some label reps in the crowd tonight."

"In this cesspit?" I ask dubiously.

"Yeah man…that's the word on the street."

"Huh, we'll see." I look out into the dark club, a sea of bodies dancing to some beat on the sound system.

I'm drowning out here in LA. This isn't my scene, and the band I've hooked up with is total shit, despite Scotty's enthusiasm. I'm slowly dying and I don't even care. My brother is visiting because he knows I'm sinking, but even he can't help me. No one can. I'm a ghost of who I used to be, but the pain is too raw and real to do anything about it.

I see a familiar-looking girl sitting at the bar, causing me to do a double-take. I swear it looks just like…no, it can't be. She's in a different country. I shake my head and head backstage. These drugs are starting to mess with my own head, making me paranoid. I need to bury this shit down further until I'm so numb I can't even imagine I'm seeing her.

"Yo Scotty, have any more blow?"

Scotty grins. "Always for you, Irish. Wanna go take a hit right now?"

I nod as we head back to our crappy little dressing room. I down a couple shots of shitty whiskey as Scotty begins to cut lines on a mirror.

"Ready man." Scotty snorts a line and then hands the mirror to me.

I quickly snort up a line, watching my eyes in the mirror glass over as the euphoria hits my system instantaneously.

"It's laced with some shit, so be careful." Scotty laughs.

I get up and punch him in the arm. "What the fuck dude? Ye need to tell me this shit."

"I just did!" Scotty laughs hysterically.

"I'm gonna bust yer dial ye gobshite when I come down off this high."

Our bass player Martin saunters into the room. "Anyone seen Deuce?"

"Ah, he's probably fucking one of the waitresses in the bathroom or shootin' up." Scotty stretches out on the couch as hc lights up some weed.

"Irish, there's someone looking for you, she's outside." Martin kicks my boot.

"By all means, send her in."

"I'm not your fucking pimp, get off your ass and get her yourself." Martin grabs the reefer from Scotty and takes a long toke.

I groan as I get up and open our door. "What the fuck are ye doin' here?" I spit out at the sight of Alana slinking against the opposite wall. So, it really was her, not my imagination. Relief washes over me that I wasn't totally losing my shit. The relief is short-lived though because anger punches through my system at lightning speed as soon as she opens her mouth.

"Lex, I needed to see you, don't be mad, baby. I followed yer brother here from yer apartment."

"What the fuck for? Ye know where I live?" I'm going to kill Connor for not paying attention to his surroundings. "How long have ye been fuckin' stalkin' me here? How did ye even get here?"

I'd already lived through this fresh hell back in Ireland. I had to leave the country just to remain sane because she was relentless, showing up wherever I turned a corner. I see now it's impossible to escape her.

"A few weeks. Your cousin told me Connor was visiting ye. I needed to see you, Lex. Please take me back… I messed up, I see that now. I need you, we were so good together." She launches herself off the wall and lands against my chest with a thud. I take a step back against her sudden impact.

"Only ye could steal the blessing from the holy water. There is nothin' in the world that ye could ever give me that I would want. Take yer ratty-ass wagon back to Ireland." I push her away from me. "I swear to God, I'll get a restrainin' order against ye. I will put yer ass in jail if ye get within a yard of me."

"Jesus Lex, don't ye think yer being a wee bit dramatic?" She folds her arms over her chest. I grind my teeth in irritation and my left eye starts to twitch. Just the sight of her makes me want to puke up all the alcohol I drank tonight.

"Get the fuck outta here, ye lyin' rat. I'll knack your melt in wee doll if ye don't back off of him," Connor says darkly from the end of the hallway.

Thank Jesus for Connor, she was seriously starting to kill my high.

"Connor, take her to the airport and personally make sure she gets on an airplane. I'll meet you back at the apartment."

Connor nods as he grabs Alana's arm. "You won't get rid of me that easy, Lex! I love you! We were meant to be together!"

"Jesus woman, just shut the fuck up! Why can't ye take no for an answer already? No one wants ye here, just go back to the hole ye crawled outta." Connor drags her down the hall and out of my sight.

I walk back into my dressing room and grab Scotty's stash. I quickly snort the remaining three lines. Fuck whatever's mixed in with it. I want...no, I need to forget everything.

Chapter 13

Sarah

Present Day

MY EYES MEET Kiki's and she mouths, *'What happened?'* Her eyes quickly cut to the person suddenly standing behind me.

"We haven't met! Hi, I'm Alana McKenna!"

I plaster on my best smile and whirl around. "Hi, Alana! I'm Sarah."

I just jumped your fiancé in the elevator, hope you don't mind. I think I'm going to be sick.

"And what do you do, Sarah? Are you a team member, part of the band, or one of the guys' girlfriends?"

"I actually do hair and makeup for the band. Kiki and I also run our own styling company called Nashville Style Studio."

"Oh, that's so awesome, you're a makeup artist! Who knew a bunch of grungy country guys needed their hair and makeup done?" She giggles.

I muster a laugh. "Oh, you'd be surprised. Sometimes I have to remind them to take showers and trim their nails."

Alana chortles. "Like babysitting a bunch of preschoolers, eh?"

"You have no idea."

Goddammit I want to hate her, but she's really sweet and pretty. Her butterscotch-colored hair falls in soft waves to her shoulder. She's tall and leggy like a baby giraffe; but elegant, not gangly. She reminds me of a young Julia Roberts.

"So, you and Lex…are engaged?" I squeak out, ashamed I have to go there, but too desperate and curious not to.

She waves a hand and leans into me, her voice going an octave lower as she talks quietly. "Well, we were. We broke up, but now that he's back and I'll be on the tour I'm hoping we can pick up where we left off. He's the one that got away. I can't *believe* he's still single," she confides in me as she winks.

Kiki chokes on her water as I nod like a bobblehead doll.

"Are you okay?" Alana thumps Kiki on the back as she doubles over. Kiki gives her a watery smile and a thumbs-up.

So, Alana the journalist, aka Alana fiancée, aka Alana freakin' gorgeous is going on tour with us. Even though I'm still super hurt and pissed at him, any iota of hope I had with Lex just went up in flames.

My smile widens as reality slams into me. Now that Alana is back in the picture, I'll be back in the friend zone permanently. My heart starts thumping a crazy irregular beat as I desperately look around wanting to escape. This is pure torture talking to Lex's future girlfriend, wife, or whatever the hell she is and I'm about to burst into tears.

"Oh, well that's super exciting, Alana! Welcome to the

tour!"

"Are you a fan of country music?" Kiki loops her arm in mine.

Alana nods enthusiastically. "I am! Of course, I've always followed Lex's career."

I laugh a little too high-pitched. "Of course!"

Kiki squeezes my arm. My crazed eyes feel like they're about to pop out of my head. I start to giggle out of pure hysteria.

"Oh goodness, look at the time!" Kiki looks at her Apple watch. "Alana you've got to get the interview started. Sarah, we need to go and make sure Tatum is okay, touch up the guys' hair, maybe an outfit change, brush our teeth... And then we've got to head out to take pictures and grab lunch, and pick up the guys, and change clothes again, oh my gosh, tons to do—"

"Right!" I cut off Kiki's ramblings. "Alana, so nice to meet you! Can't wait to see you on tour!"

Alana looks between Kiki and me like we've suddenly grown two heads. The smile frozen on my face starts to hurt. Kiki tugs on my arm and we practically run to the greenroom.

WE SLAM INTO the greenroom causing the guys to look up from their phones as they lounge on the couches eating the catered food. Kiki looks around at each guy, nodding her head.

"Yup, yup, everyone looks good, okeedoke off to the interview!" She claps loudly.

Tatum gives her an amused look. "Did Ms. McKenna say she was ready?"

"Yes!" we shout in unison.

"You guys are acting weird," Matt mumbles as he gets up off the couch.

My eyes seek out Lex as I wait for him to look up and notice me…some kind of acknowledgment, but he has earbuds in and is completely engrossed in his phone. Even though he's surrounded by the guys, he looks alone and closed off. It leaves me feeling confused and conflicted. I want to go give him a hug and knee him in the balls at the same time.

Ugh, he's a frustrating man. I don't understand why he didn't tell me about Alana and why he would kiss me in the elevator when we were on our way up to see her.

"All right guys, you heard the ladies, let's do this." Lee stands up and the guys shuffle past us.

Will shakes Lex letting him know they're on the move. Tatum reaches down and kisses Kiki, whispering something in her ear. She blushes as she pushes him along. Lex follows behind him. He glances at me, but his eyes are a dull flat blue, devoid of emotion. I offer him a small smile because I have no clue what's going on in that gorgeous head of his, but he doesn't return it. I want to be angry with him for earlier but the desolate look on his face has my ire dissolving because he looks completely broken. My emotions are all over the place, scattered like papers in the wind. He shuts the door behind him and I blow out a breath.

"Shit." I look at Kiki.

"No shit." Kiki nods.

"I don't even know where to begin…"

"What happened to you guys in the lobby? You were gone forever and then you come around the corner holding his hand, looking mad as hell, but also like you were just sexed up."

I twirl around and throw myself down on the couch in exasperation. "Pretty much sums it up."

"You had sex in the lobby?" she whispers loudly, her eyes going wide.

I huff out a laugh. "No, you crazy. He got me alone in an elevator and pressed the emergency button. He told me even though he was attracted to me, it wouldn't work between us because he wasn't the right guy for me. I might have cried a little." I wince remembering my pathetic state. "Then suddenly we were kissing again, and then he stopped and said it was a mistake." I shrug, feeling numb and tired.

Kiki plops down beside me and grabs a carrot stick. "So he kisses you, rejects you, kisses you again and then says just kidding, you're everything I want, but I'm not the right guy for you…and then you turn the corner and there's freakin' Alana Legs, his ex-fiancée standing there ready to devour him."

I nod. "Good summation."

"Thanks." She pauses as she crunches her carrot. "Geez, this sucks, Sunshine. What are you going to do?"

I shrug. "Nothing. I mean we've made out twice and after each time he rejects me. My heart can't handle more. Besides, now he's got Alana on tour with us. He'll be hittin' that in no time." I scrub my hands over my face as I stare at the ceiling. "What I don't understand is why he never mentioned her. I mean why make out with me on our way up to meeting your ex-fiancée?"

Kiki chews on her carrot in contemplation. "I don't think he knew she was going to be there. Did you see the look on his face? And I'm pretty sure he isn't as in to getting back together with her as she is to him. There's a reason she's his ex, right?"

"I dunno," I say miserably.

"I think we need to call in the big guns." She whips out her phone and hits the speaker phone. It rings once before it's picked up.

"Seriously, I already told you the cats and Mabel are doing fine! Do we really need to do hourly check-ins?" TJ sighs loudly into the phone. "OMG, I forgot to tell you, Heather is the bomb. She handled this really big B that came in to request an appointment with Sarah like a pro. She was like—"

"TJ, shut up for one second! Jesus, don't you ever take a breath? We have an emergency on our hands."

"Ooh did Tatum's pants rip again?"

"No, bigger than that. Sarah and Lex hooked up!"

I cover my eyes. Great now TMZ will be posting this on their front page.

"Woo hoo! Finally! Sare Bear, that's great news!" he squeals. "I'd sure like to mash his Irish potatoes. Give me the deets!"

"Tug and Jerk, I will disown you if you say deets again!" Kiki yells.

"My end is getting crackly. Connection must be bad..." We can hear crinkling paper through the phone.

Kiki rolls her eyes. "Weren't you just bragging that your new iPhone is so state of the art you could hear a grain of sand drop in Egypt?"

The paper crinkling stops and TJ sighs. "Okay I'm getting exhausted by this convo. What's the emergency?"

Kiki fills him in on the last hour.

"I think I need to come to London," TJ says excitedly.

"What? Why? What's in London?"

"Duh, you two are, obvi. Geesh, did the time change damage your few remaining brain cells?"

"Seriously, I don't know why I bother telling you anything. We're in Ireland, you goob. London is at the end of the tour."

"Oh snaps! Green suits me better anyways."

"No. You can't leave Heather stranded alone with the business or my animals. We need you back home to hold down the fort."

"But I want in on the drama!" TJ whines.

"I promise we'll update you daily. Now listen, we need to know what Sarah should do."

I smile and whisper, "He's probably going to suggest measuring Lex's penis before we make any kind of plan."

"I heard that. Not a bad idea actually."

Kiki laughs. "Wow that connection suddenly got crystal clear!"

"Ooh Kinks, speaking of measuring, I forgot to tell you, I thought your bedroom was looking a little drab so I had a sex swing installed next to the window. You're welcome."

"A what?! I don't want a sex swing! Ugh, gross, TJ."

"Geese, someone's a little grumpy. A simple thank-you would have been acceptable…"

"Ugh, you're impossible. Focus! Just tell us what to do!"

"Okay, okay, okay…take a chill pill. If I were Sare Bear, I would keep my eyes on the prize. Don't give up on Sexy Lexy. He wants you, he just doesn't realize it yet."

"I really wish I could unhear that nickname for him," I mumble.

Kiki giggles. "Sexy Lexy, I love it!"

"And I think I would kill Alana with kindness. Keep your enemies close and the bitches closer."

"Hear that, Sunshine?" Kiki looks up at me and winks. "Eyes on that Irish prize."

"You guys make me sound like some kind of man-eater."

"Yes girl! Man-eat that Irish sex god!"

"Oh my god." I rub my hand down my face. "I don't even know if he's what I want anymore."

"Oh puhlease, you've been pining after that sexy beast for two years, don't pretend you're suddenly over him," TJ admonishes.

I laugh, because dammit if he isn't right. No matter how mad Lex makes me, I still circle back to wanting him.

"And don't forget to get those dick measurements. No one wants peas and a baby carrot, they want the bangers and mash. I feel confident he has the latter."

"Seriously, what is wrong with you?" Kiki mutters as she hangs up on him laughing.

Chapter 14

Lex

SWEAT DRIPS DOWN my back as I finish lifting my last set. I was hoping an hour in the hotel gym would help calm my nerves, but no such luck. I woke up sweating, tangled in my sheets after having the same fucking nightmare. It irks me so much because I can't figure out who the woman is in the dream and I wake up every time in a complete panic.

I slam the dumbbells back on to the rack and pick up my water bottle, guzzling the iced liquid down. I shake my head. I'm still in disbelief that Alana Walsh…McKenna, whatever the fuck her last name is, is back in my life. She hasn't changed much. Her hair is a little shorter, and she's a little curvier in all the right places. The years have definitely been kind to her.

I'm still curious how she became a journalist. When we were together she wanted to be a nurse. I have to admit, she looked polished in her suit and she still has those amazing long legs. I tried to avoid her eyes during the interview, but my attention kept returning to those baby blues. I hate that she still has that effect on me.

And then there's Sarah. Sweet, innocent, incredibly beautiful Sarah. What the hell was I thinking doing what I did to her in the elevator? It's killing me that I have to keep telling her no, to stay away, when in fact I'm the one who keeps bringing her back in. Whenever she looks at me with those big doe eyes, I'm a complete sucker at her mercy.

This is the *exact* reason I don't want to be tied down to a girl. I hate the feelings I have for Sarah, and I hate that I want to fuck that smile right off of Alana's face, showing her once and for all what she gave up.

I head up to my room to take a quick shower and grab my guitar. I get a group text from Tatum. *Rehearsal at 2 PM today.* Just enough time to head out and collect my thoughts before getting ready for the concert tonight.

After my shower I catch the Dart to Howth and get off on the east pier. I zip up my leather jacket against the blustery wind coming off the sea. Even though it's sunny, the wind has a bite to it. I hike along the bluffs toting my guitar on my back, looking for the perfect spot. The views are incredible up here and my heart aches that I've stayed away from my homeland for so long. I stop and stare out at the rough waters as they crash against the craggy bluffs. The sapphire-blue ocean pulls me into its depths, lulling me into a false sense of security. I breathe in the crisp salty air. My soul has missed this land and the siren song it sings.

I turn inland and the terrain changes from heather and swooping seagulls to lush greens, fuchsia and Buddleia plants blossoming along the path. The wind isn't as bad up here so I find an outcropping of rocks and settle down on one. I pull my guitar out of its case and strum a few chords, playing an old Irish lullaby my mum used to sing to me.

It's strange being back in Ireland after all this time. It's no longer where I reside, but in my heart it will always be home. I berate myself for staying away for so long, all because of a broken heart and bad memories.

All because of a woman.

My fingers still on my guitar. Maybe the dream that has been haunting me isn't about a woman. Maybe it's my homeland whispering to me. The woman asking me to come back is Ireland. I'm happy in Nashville, but maybe my subconscious is telling me to come back here. But even with this new revelation, the puzzle pieces don't seem to click into place; it doesn't feel right.

I sigh in frustration as my fingers automatically pluck out another tune playing it from muscle memory. I push the dream out of my thoughts and think about my family. I'm looking forward to seeing them tomorrow. I know I've hurt them by staying away, but they understand…at least I hope they do.

I look up just in time to see a long blonde ponytail blowing in the breeze, the most gorgeous creature I have ever laid eyes on, crouched down taking a picture of a butterfly flittering amongst the flowers. She's wearing black Nikes, black running tights and a hoodie, and she's…perfect. I laugh to myself, because of all the places I could have gone to today, we end up here together overlooking the same bluffs on a cloudless day. She hasn't seen me yet and I'm tempted to just quietly go back down the path because I have no business messing with her emotions again.

My fingers automatically start to strum The Rolling Stone's "Wild Horses". I watch her as I sing the tune quietly. She's completely unaware of her surroundings except for the subject she's photographing. She suddenly stands up and looks into her viewfinder. Her lips curl up into a little playful grin. God, she's so adorable. The song lyrics ring true for me, wild horses couldn't drag me away. I swallow as that painful unexpected truth lodges itself in my heart.

She heads up the gravel path toward me, looking off in the direction of the ocean. There are other people on the path, we're not alone, so she hasn't spotted me yet, but I know the moment she does because her eyes widen and she stops suddenly, causing a tourist behind her to nearly run into her. Apparently, I'm not the only one who wants to play the avoidance game today.

She knows I've seen her and she gives me a small smile and a wave as she continues toward me. She plops down on the rock beside me.

"Hey, Lex," she says quietly.

"Sunshine," I grunt.

She sighs and runs her hand through her long ponytail. "Fancy meeting you here. Did you follow me?"

I chuckle. "No, *mo chroí*[2]. I came here thinking I'd be alone."

Strawberry-pink blush colors her cheeks. "Oh, well then I'll let you have your peace and quiet." She begins to stand up but I grab her hand and gently tug her back down.

"Sunshine, please stay."

---

[2] Irish for my heart.

She sits back down and we sit in awkward silence for a moment.

"What were you…"

"Can I see your…"

I chuckle. "You first."

She smiles. "I was going to ask you what you were doing up here."

"Just trying to clear my head." She nods in understanding. "Can I see what you were taking pictures of?"

She pauses a beat then hands her camera over to me. "They aren't great, but this landscape is just too beautiful to not try and capture it."

"Aye, that it is." I open up her Nikon viewfinder and scroll through her pictures. There are close-ups of the butterfly I saw her taking, flower petals, couples strolling along the path, craggy bluffs and the ocean. They look like postcard pictures. "These are beautiful, Love," I murmur as I return to the beginning.

"Eh, thanks. It's just a hobby. Kind of like you said, it clears my head."

I nod and hand the camera back to her. "Well don't stop. You're very talented."

I can tell I've flustered her by the way she busily starts messing with random buttons and then she sighs and her hands still. "What were you playing? One of your songs?"

"Ah, a little of this and that."

"You know what I've always been curious about?"

I shrug and give her a small smile. "What's that?"

"Why is it that when you sing, I don't hear your accent?"

I chuckle and sigh as I look up at the clouds skittering

across the sky.

"What? Dumb question? Don't answer that. Move along to the next. When did you start playing guitar?"

I smile wryly at her. "Are you interviewing me, Sunshine?"

"What? No! I...I'm just trying to...to make conversation?"

I bark out a laugh. She's so damn cute when she's flustered. I bump my shoulder to hers to let her know I'm okay with her questions. "I don't know why I don't sing with my accent, it's not like I try and disguise it, it just doesn't come through." I pluck a few strings on the guitar and play an old Irish tune. "I picked up my first guitar when I was three. As I got older I had the innate ability to hear a tune and immediately start playing it. It drives my twin brother Connor nuts because he can't. He does all right on the guitar though. He's better at the piano than I am."

"Play something for me?" She smiles.

I look at her and a hundred different love songs come to mind. I slowly strum the guitar strings, not really sure what to choose.

"Is this your first time to Ireland?"

"Yes, and I love it. It's so lush and green. And the people are so friendly."

"Aye, they are."

"But a little hard to understand. Your accent doesn't seem as thick...except I've noticed it comes out a little stronger when you've been drinking or you're mad." She blushes and looks away.

I study her profile as she watches some hikers nearby. "I

tried to get rid of it ten years ago when I moved away from here."

Her head whips around, her attention laser focused on me. "Why? It's beautiful and unique…and so innately you."

I shrug. "I tried to erase a lot back then. Doesn't really matter." I strum a few chords. "Where are you from?"

"Nashville, born and raised. Pretty unexciting." She pulls her knees up and rests her chin on them. "Sometimes I wish I came from an exotic, exciting place like this, and had a kickass accent."

I chuckle. "Hmm…"

I start to sing Old Dominion's "One Man Band". Sarah watches me intently, her head still resting on her knees, as I play and sing just to her. I should feel self-conscious of her unwavering attention on me, but I don't. If anything I'm comfortable and at peace.

She looks up at me and gives me a lopsided grin once the song ends. "I love that song."

"I know."

"How did you…" She shakes her head. "Never mind."

"You practically tackled the band when we played with them at Route 66 last year. When this song came on you went all crazy fan-girl."

She laughs and blushes. "Oh god, I did? So embarrass-ing."

"Yeah, it made me a little jealous."

"It did?"

"Yeah, I missed having that attention on me." I lean into her and wink.

"Oh geez…that obvious, huh?" She adorably hides her

head in her hands.

"Mmm."

She shifts nervously on the rock. "So…um, what made you kiss me in the bar the other night? I mean why now?"

I rub my jaw wondering how the hell to answer her question. I can't be a total spanner and tell her I've loved her from the moment I laid eyes on her in that coffee shop.

"I dunno. You kept staring at me with your big brown eyes, and I couldn't take mine off you. I looked up and saw you watching Tate and Kiki dance, and you had this beautiful smile on your face…I wanted to dance with you. Once I had you in my arms, I couldn't let you go. I couldn't help myself." I smile sheepishly at her. "Why did you let me kiss you?"

"Truth?" She looks at me nervously as she bites her lip.

"Truth."

"I've wanted you to kiss me from the first moment I laid eyes on you."

I nod, my head and heart sparring with conflicting emotions as I watch her cheeks bloom rosy pink.

"And the elevator?" she quietly asks me.

I strum my guitar and sigh, my head winning out over my heart. "The elevator, the kisses…it was all a mistake, Sarah. I meant what I said…I can't give you what you want."

She balls her hands into fists. "How do you know what I want? You've never even asked me."

I shake my head. "Let me ask you a question. Why do you think I have a different girl every night? Why I don't settle down with one?"

Her face pales. "Because you're afraid of commitment."

"Wrong. I can go the distance in a relationship; I can be a one-woman kind of guy. I just don't want to get emotionally involved. I don't want to care. Not anymore."

She sucks in a breath. "Ouch."

"Yeah. So when I say I'm not the right guy for you, I mean it." I slam my guitar back in its case, driving the point home. I get up and leave her sitting on the rock completely stunned, feeling like I just kicked a puppy.

Chapter 15

Sarah

THE FIRST CONCERT of the tour goes off without a hitch. The guys are pumped as we head down the coast to the quaint little oceanside town of Kinsale where Lex grew up. It's been a pretty confusing turn of events since we arrived in Ireland. I haven't talked to him since he abruptly got up from our conversation two days ago, leaving me completely stunned. To be honest I've been trying to avoid him. My feelings for him are convoluted at best. These mood swings he's causing me to have are driving me crazy. One minute my heart is in my throat and I'm dizzy just wanting him to kiss me again, and the next I hate his guts and want to push him off one of these cliffs. This seesaw we're on is exhausting.

I look over at Alana who's riding with us in the luxury van and wonder what the hell happened between the two of them. Knowing Lex, it's probably his moody ass that ended the relationship. She seems so nice and normal, not like the typical girls Lex screws around with. She's chatting amicably with Kiki and I about our blog and has been nothing but pleasant and outgoing. Lex, Matt, and Will are riding in another van much to my relief. I honestly don't want to have another 'I'm not the right guy for you' talk, and I definitely don't want to see Alana getting cozy with him reminiscing about what could have been.

We pull up to a beautiful modern wood and glass one-story house overlooking the ocean. Lush gardens sprawl away from the house, beautiful topiaries are meticulously groomed. Grass so green and manicured it doesn't look real. I step out of the van and breathe in the fresh salty sea air. The wind whips my hair around as I wait for Kiki, Tatum, and Alana to get out. The front door bursts open and a large busty redheaded woman comes charging out the door.

"*Oye*! *Dia dhuit*! Hello! I'm so happy yer here!" she cries out and giggles as she reaches us and pulls me into her bosom before I can retreat. She smells of detergent and roses. "I'm Lex's mum, Mrs. Ryan, but ye can call me Maggie!"

"Nyshe to meech you…" I try to breathe but she's smothering me with her bosom. She squeezes one last time and abruptly lets me go and pulls Kiki into the same hug followed by Tatum.

"Oh Tatum, Love, it's been too long! Just as handsome as ever! Is this yer bride?" Since I'm standing next to her she grabs me into another hug making me giggle.

"No ma'am. This is my wife, Kiki." He pulls Kiki into a side-hug and Mrs. Ryan sighs as she claps her hands together.

"Such a beautiful couple." She looks over their shoulders where Alana is hovering by the van. Her face falls into a grimace. "Well look ye here what the cat dragged in." She straightens her shoulders and her voice has a chill to it. "Well, Alana, come here and give me a hug. It's been a long time."

Alana slinks over to Mrs. Ryan and gives her a stiff hug with a quick awkward pat to her back. "It's nice to see you, Maggie."

"You can call me Mrs. Ryan, dear." She quickly turns from Alana, dismissing her. "Where's Lex? Oh his da will be so excited to see him!" she gushes to us.

"He should be right behind us," Tatum responds checking his phone.

"Well, let's not dawdle out here. Come on in! And what's your name, dear? You are such a pretty lass! Are ye married? Do ye know my son Lex?" She links her arm in mine as we head toward the front door and I try not to giggle over her barrage of questions.

"My name is Sarah, I'm the band's makeup artist."

"How excitin'! I'm in desperate need of some new makeup, maybe ye could help guide me?"

I look at Maggie's rosy cheeks. She's not wearing a lick of makeup and her skin is smooth and creamy. I love her instantly. "I don't think you need any, but I'll help you however I can. Thank you so much for letting us stay with y'all."

She waves her hand. "Oh I just love yer American accents! When Lex said ye were goin' to stay at the local bed and breakfast I wouldn't hear of it! No friends of me son's stays at someone else's home. Not while I'm still alive."

We walk into the foyer and I'm instantly blown away by

the house's beauty. White-washed wood floors with walnut-stained wood-beamed ceilings. Glass doors stretch out across the back of the house so that the great room has a magnificent floor-to-ceiling view of the cliffs and ocean. The furniture looks soft and cozy done in white with shades of blue and coral accents.

"This is amazing," I breathe.

"Aye, Finn and I have been very lucky in life. We built this house about five years ago." Maggie claps her hands. "Well, ye all must be tired. Let me show ye to yer rooms so ye can get settled before supper." She looks over at us and smiles. "Let's put you in the ocean room, Sarah. Tatum, you and Kiki can have the rose room. Um…Alana…I wasn't quite expectin' you…" Mrs. Ryan looks around worriedly as she wrings her hands.

"Oh I'm staying in town, Mrs. Ryan," Alana says quickly as she gawks at the sunken living room.

"Oh well, good then. That's good."

Just then the front door swings open and Lex steps in with Will and Matt trailing behind, their eyes wide and mouths hanging open. My breath catches as he looks up and our eyes connect.

"There's ma boy!" Maggie shouts as she runs toward Lex. She wraps Lex into a big bear hug and I stifle a laugh as he groans in protest. It's funny to see bad-boy rocker Lex being smothered by his mama.

"Ma, put me down!"

"Oh! I've just missed ye so!" she cries. "You need a haircut, and did you get more tattoos? What am I gonna do with ye boys? Oh Will, Matt, where are me manners? Come in lads, come on in!"

She claps her hands together after hugging Will and Matt. "Let me show ye to yer rooms and then we'll have dinner. A big feast I've have prepared fer ye."

"Ma, ye didn't have to do all that."

"Ssh lad, ye know I love havin' ye home. It's been too long." She hugs Lex again and quickly wipes a tear from her eye. "I've missed ye, my little starkeeper."

"Where's Da?"

"He's out in the gardens pluckin' me some vegs. Anyone want a cuppa? No? Okay off to yer rooms ye lot and get washed up for supper!" She sends us off in a scurry before we can utter a word.

My room is spacious with a queen-sized bed covered in the fluffiest white duvet I've ever seen. Aqua throw pillows and a chenille blanket lay across the bed making me want to snuggle under it in a cocoon of safety. This room is so cozy and comforting. I set my bag down on a seashell-printed fabric chair with a matching ottoman as I look out the glass doors leading out to a small balcony overlooking the ocean.

Wow, this guest room is exquisite, like something out of *Southern Living*. I finger the delicate coral fan sculpture on the dresser. If I had a home on the ocean this is exactly how I would decorate it. It feels so fresh and clean. I open the doors and breathe in the salty air. Hushed voices carry over from the room next to mine. I start to close the doors, but pause when I hear Lex's voice.

"No, Ma! I didn't invite her along."

"Well, she's here, and she couldn't keep her eyes off of ye. Don' think I couldn't see. I know exactly what's gonna happen. Alana is a destructive force."

I hate to stand here and eavesdrop, but I can't stop myself. I'm so curious to know why Maggie dislikes Alana so much.

"Nothing's goin' to happen, so just drop it."

"I jus' don' want ye goin' down that road again. She's trouble."

"Ma! I've got it under control. She means nothing to me."

"That's what you said last time too, and yet here she is back in your life again…What about that sweet blonde girl? Sarah? She seems like a nice lass."

I hold my breath as I wait for his response. I know I should go back into my room, but I'm frozen in place. I need to know what he says.

"I just got here, can we not talk about this right now? I love you, but you know yer meddling drives me insane. Nothing is going to happen on this trip except that I'm going to play the guitar and enjoy my time with my friends and family."

"Sarah seems very lovely."

Lex growls in frustration. "Ma! Sarah is just a friend, I don't have feelings for her in that way."

"But Lex—"

"That will never happen so get it out of yer head now."

I quietly close the doors not wanting to hear any more of the conversation. I sink down onto my bed and a tear slips out. I've never felt more homesick and alone than I do right now.

AT DINNER I squeeze in next to Will and Matt at the opposite end of the table from Lex and Alana.

"You okay?" Will elbows me gently.

"Yeah, why?" I ask, sipping my water.

"You're usually always smiling. You seem down tonight."

"Ah, just tired I guess."

"Yeah, we've been non-stop haven't we?"

"Steak, my dear?" Mr. Ryan holds a platter out to me. He's the exact opposite of Mrs. Ryan. The yin to her yang. He's tall with black hair and striking blue eyes. He's reserved and quiet, but very nice.

"Thank you, Mr. Ryan." I take the platter from him, adding some steak to my plate and pass it down the table.

"Steak, Alana? You don't have any on your plate dear." Mrs. Ryan grabs the platter from Matt as he's about to take some meat off and shoves it toward Alana who scrunches up her nose.

"I'm a vegetarian, Mrs. Ryan. I'm good with just the vegetables."

Maggie sniffs. "An Irish vegetarian, I've never heard of such! You could use some meat on yer bones, couldn't ya."

"Ma! Quit it," Lex admonishes quietly. Alana looks up at him gratefully.

"I'm just saying, it's not natural for humans not to have protein."

"Oh I get plenty of protein from spinach, broccoli, and nuts." Alana laughs forcefully.

"Sounds like a squirrel diet to me," Mr. Ryan says quietly down at our end of the table.

"*Enough*," Lex says through his teeth.

"So, Maggie," Tatum pipes up. "Kiki and I took a walk through your gardens earlier. What was that huge purple plant? It smelled—"

"I mean really, Alana, if you're going to be a *guest* in someone's home you should eat what they are serving, am I right Finn?" Maggie doesn't wait for her husband to answer as she continues her tirade. "We worked hard over this dinner. Finn tenderized the meat for two days. *Two days!* It's so tender you don't need a knife. Am I right, dear?"

Mr. Ryan nods. Alana keeps her eyes on her plate and remains silent.

I catch Kiki's eye across the table, raising my eyebrow. This is getting kind of weird. Why is Mrs. Ryan insisting on making Alana eat meat? She seemed so friendly earlier, but now this dinner has turned into an interrogation of sorts…over meat.

"It's excellent meat, sir." Will smiles. "I'll eat her portion, Mrs. Ryan, don't worry, nothing will go to waste." He reaches for the platter.

"Oy, there's plenty for ye Will, not to worry!" She smiles genuinely at Will as she keeps the meat platter out of his reach. Her gaze narrows as she eyes Alana across the table. She forks a filet onto Alana's plate, challenging her with her eyes. "So what have ye been up to all these years, lass?"

"Oh. Well, I went back to school and got my degree in journalism. I started working for the *Dublin Times* and now I freelance." She smiles, but it doesn't reach her eyes. She nervously looks down at the steak on her plate.

"So yer in Dublin these days and now ye have found yerself on my boy's tour…his first tour in Ireland, how…convenient." Maggie starts stabbing her fork into a pepper.

"Ah…yes, quite fortuitous actually." Alana nervously looks around the table at us.

"Hmph…to be sure." Maggie reaches over and starts viciously cutting the steak on Alana's plate. "And do ye think yer goin' to worm yer way back into his life again and drag him under—"

"Ma, enough!" Lex stands up. He grabs Alana and pulls her up. "Come with me." They quickly leave the kitchen and walk out a side door into the gardens. Awkward silence descends over the table as we all stare at one another.

"Hmph. So, Matt, are you dating anyone?" Maggie asks sweetly like nothing just happened.

What the hell is going on? There's definitely more to this story than we are privy to, that's for sure. Kiki smiles at me and I know she's thinking that I'm back in the game. I shake my head subtly at her causing her to scrunch her face in confusion. If only she'd heard what Lex said on the balcony earlier.

Mr. Ryan turns to me and asks me about my life back in the States. I focus my attention on the conversation at hand, but I can't help wondering where Lex and Alana escaped to and what they could be doing. Maggie may not like Alana, but Lex defending her at dinner shows that he still feels some kind of loyalty to her.

Chapter 16

Lex

I STEER ALANA out the side door into the evening rays of the setting sun. There's a breeze coming off the ocean, and her hair sticks to her cheeks where tears track down her face. Shit.

I take my thumbs and wipe the tears, my fingers lingering on her face as I look into her baby-blue eyes.

"She didn't mean it. She's just mad," I say as old emotions start getting the best of me.

I'm angry with my mum for making everyone at the table uncomfortable. I knew it was going to be a bad idea for Alana to come back here with us, but she insisted she could handle my parents. Clearly, that isn't the case. My mum will never forgive Alana.

"Your mum has never liked me. I'm not the same girl I was back then, Lex. I've grown up. I'm more mature." She wraps her hands around my wrists, her eyes shimmering with tears.

"Why did you change your last name?"

Her eyes nervously dart around. "I was blacklisted here. I was a pariah. Everyone loved you and your family. I couldn't get a job within three townships. Especially after what happened in Los Angeles...so I moved to Dublin and used my mum's maiden name."

I swallow as I feel the old familiar feelings of longing I used to have for her, back in the beginning of our relationship. She's like a drug slowly pulling me under. Maybe she has changed...I know I have.

"I made a mistake. Haven't you ever made a mistake that you know you'll regret for the rest of your life? I'm different now, Lex." She tenderly strokes my cheek. Her lips curl up into a seductive smile. "We could still be good together, you know. I've missed you."

Her eyes land on my lips as she sways toward me. My hands go to her hips to steady her. Recollections of Alana and I from the past flash-flood my brain as muscle-memory reflexes replace any ounce of brain control.

I need to push her off of me. I breathe in her familiar scent. I try to gain a grip on the situation, but my hand fists the back of her dress as she stumbles into my body. She trails her fingertips over my chest.

"I want you." She licks her lips and my eyes flicker down to them as she closes the gap and presses her lips to mine. It surprises me, but I don't push her away. I don't return the kiss either. She moans as she moves against me, trying to arouse a reaction from me.

What the fuck am I doing? It's suddenly crystal clear in my head that I don't want her. I don't feel anything from this kiss...it's nothing compared to the intense desire I feel when I touch Sarah. I know I don't deserve sweet girls like Sarah, but what the fuck possessed me to think I wanted Alana? How did I so easily forget the torment she caused me in my past?

I gently take her by the shoulders and push her back, breaking the kiss. I look down into her surprised eyes. "You may be different, Alana, but so am I. The old Lex is gone. You've ruined me."

A throat clears behind me. "Lex, we're heading out to your brother's pub."

I look over my shoulder to see Sarah abruptly turn on her heel and march back into the house.

Shit.

"Sarah! Wait!"

Alana narrows her eyes. "Sarah, huh?"

"It's none of your business," I bite out as I leave her to head back into the house.

"But Lex, we're not finished!"

"You may not be, but I am."

Chapter 17

Sarah

OH GOD, OH Jesus, I think I'm hyperventilating. I reenter the kitchen and find Maggie washing the dishes.

"Did you find Le…? Goodness heavens lass, are ye all right?"

I nod yes and then no, unable to take a breath.

"Sit down, Love, sit down. Hold on a sec." She finds a paper bag and hands it to me. I shake my head no.

"Just breathe into it, lass. It will help, I promise." Her Irish lilt calms my nerves. "What happened? Did ye get stung by a bee? Oh me gots to tell Finn no more beehives. They are wonderful for the garden, but wallop such a sting."

I breathe in and out into the paper bag slowly coming back into my body. Once I get my breathing under control, I set the bag aside. "Thank you, Mrs. Ryan, it wasn't a bee sting. It was nothing." I'm so embarrassed I actually hyperventilated over seeing Lex kissing Alana.

"Hyperventilating can't be nothin', and call me Maggie, Love."

"I'm okay, I promise, Maggie. I need to get ready. I think we're leaving soon." The kitchen door handle rattles as it's being pulled open. "Thank you." I give Maggie a quick hug as I bolt from the kitchen to the safety of my room.

Lex's voice carries. "Have you seen Sarah?"

"She went to her room, me little starkeeper. I think ye should give her some space," Maggie says gently. "Lex…"

"Not a word, Ma. I can't do this right now with you."

I QUICKLY WASH my face and run a brush through my hair. My cheeks have red splotches, so I redo my makeup in the hopes of covering up evidence of my tears. I can't believe I just hyperventilated in front of Lex's mom. But worse than that, I can't believe I caught Lex and Alana kissing!

It broke something fragile inside of me, something resembling my hope. Hope that Lex could have changed his mind and decided I was worth the fall. Hope that Lex could have changed his ways for me. Hope that Lex felt the same way as I did.

So stupid, Sarah. How many times has he told you he doesn't want you and that he isn't going to change? Ugh! What's that book? *He's Just Not That into You?* All the neon arrows are pointing right at me. The biggest one being Lex and Alana kissing. I take a deep breath and open my door just as Kiki lifts her fist to knock. We both let out a little scream.

"Shit you scared me!" Kiki laughs. "Why are you

splotchy? You okay?"

I shrug. "I'll be all right."

Kiki eyes me over and shoves me back into my room.

"Hey!"

"Spill it, sister. You look like someone just ripped your heart out and stomped on it."

"Ha," I say weakly looking down at the floor as I sit on the edge of my bed. Kiki taps her foot impatiently as she folds her arms over her chest. "When Tatum asked me to go find Lex to let him know we were getting ready to leave, I did. I found him with Alana wrapped around him, lip-locked."

"What? No!" Kiki plops down on the bed next to me wrapping her arms around me.

"Yup."

"What did you do?"

"I interrupted them and said we were ready to go. Then I went inside and had an epic meltdown in front of Mrs. Ryan...there were paper bags and mascara tracks...and I'm so embarrassed!"

"Paper bags?"

"Yeah, I kind of...might have...hyperventilated."

"Awe sweetie, did you say anything to Lex?"

"What's there to say? I mean, he's told me multiple times he's not the guy for me. I overheard him tell his mom before dinner that we were just friends and that's all I'll ever be." I shrug. "Maybe it's time I listened."

"Oh Sarah, shit. I'm so sorry."

"Yeah, so it's time to move on." I shudder as I take a deep breath.

Kiki rubs my back. "Wanna get drunk tonight?"

"You have no idea."

Kiki claps her hands and stands up. "Yeehaw! Let's do this! I promise to get you so drunk you won't even remember *what's his name.*"

I giggle as she grabs my hand and drags me out of my room, out to the waiting car. I thank God again for Kiki being here with me.

Chapter 18

Sarah

WE ARRIVE AT Lex's twin brother's pub a short car ride later. It's on a cute cobblestone street overlooking the waterfront. Lex and Alana have not arrived yet. They're probably having hot sex in the car. *Ugh, get that image out of your head, now!*

We walk in and Connor, Lex's brother, grabs Tatum, Will, and Matt into a barrel hug.

"Se craic! Look at ye fuckin' ugly mugs!" He laughs.

He looks exactly like Lex minus the broody moody personality. They even have the same sleeve tattoos. Connor is all smiles and laughter. He exudes goofiness. His hair is a bit longer than Lex's but they share the same mischievous glint in their gorgeous blue eyes.

He turns to Kiki and me. "Ah Sarah, my love, I've missed ye!" He grabs me into a hug. I met Connor when he was visiting Lex when I first started touring with the band. "When are ye gonna run away with me, lass?"

"Get yer muggy paws off of her, ye tosser." I stiffen in Connor's arms as Lex steps up right behind me. "Thanks for leaving me at the house by the way." He punches Tatum in the arm before turning to his brother.

"Brother! Ye look like a bucket of snots." Connor releases me as he pulls Lex into a hard back-thumping hug.

"Feck aff, ye donkey. Yer ugly mug looks just like me."

"I'm definitely the better-looking one. And who is this?" He turns toward Kiki.

She looks like a deer in headlights as he picks her up into a bear hug.

"The Ryans sure do love to give hugs," Kiki squeaks.

"Put her down, ye gobshite. That's Tatum's wife, Kiki."

Connor winks at Kiki. "I know who she is, ye feckin' lemon. It's nice to meet ye, Kiki."

The door opens and Alana slinks in and hovers behind Lex. Connor gives her a once-over. "I smell a rat in my bar." He arches an eyebrow at Lex. "May ye be afflicted with itching without the benefit of scratching." He quickly does the sign of the cross over his chest and then turns away from her. He leads us into the main part of the bar. "Drinks on the house! Me brother is back!" Connor yells to the crowded cheering bar.

"Sarah, can I talk to you for a minute?" Lex whispers in my ear as his hand guides my lower back away from the group.

"There's nothing to say."

He walks me over to the hall leading to the bathrooms where we have some privacy. "I'm sorry about earlier. What you saw…it's complicated."

I look down at my pointed heels. "I'm sure it is."

He tilts my chin up so I'm drowning in his ocean-blue

eyes. "I know what's going on in your pretty head, and it's not what you think."

I shake my head slightly. "It's something." I push away from him as I head back to the table.

"Sarah."

"Let me just enjoy my night, Lex," I toss back over my shoulder as I head to our table.

Alana is watching us with hawk-like eyes, her mouth turned down in an angry scowl. I walk away from Lex as he gets swallowed up into the crowd of well-wishers and old friends. She immediately fixes her face into a pageant smile as I approach the table.

"So ladies, what are ye drinking?" she asks brightly as I grab a chair next to Kiki.

I plaster on a fake smile. "I think I'm in the mood for a cranberry-whiskey sour."

Kiki smiles and winks at me. "Sounds good to me too. What do you want, Alana? I'll go tell Tate."

"I'll have a Black and Tan please."

Kiki gets up and I want to strangle her for leaving me alone with Alana. The silence starts to get awkward as I look around the bar. It's a pretty Irish pub. Stone walls, shiny wood floors with a beautiful polished mahogany bar. There's a stage at one end where a house band is tuning their instruments.

"Listen Sarah, about earlier...I had no idea you and Lex were an item."

I look back over at her, surprised she's bringing this up. "Oh, um, we're not."

"Are ye sure? It doesn't look that way to me."

My smile widens and I just shrug as I strum my fingers on the table. I don't want to have this conversation with Lex's…whatever the hell she is. *Where the fuck is Kiki?*

Kiki rushes back with the drinks, mouthing *'I'm sorry'* to me behind Alana's back.

"Ah, I haven't been back in this bar in the longest time. Nothing has changed. I remember this one time Lexy and I had to break up a bar fight. Oh my goodness, it was so hilarious…" she muses as she takes a sip of her drink.

Kiki and I exchange glances wondering if she's going to continue the story. Not that I really want to hear it, but it's weird she just left us hanging.

Kiki mouths *'Sexy Lexy'* at me with a smirk and I kick her under the table. "Owe! So…why was it so funny?" Kiki prompts Alana.

Alana waves her hand in front of her face. "Oh, it was just funny because the local hurling team was in here and two guys started fighting over me and Lex came to my rescue telling the guys I was *his* woman. He is, I mean *was*, my knight in shining armor."

Oh barf.

The three of us sit in silence drinking our cocktails. Then Kiki starts, "I wonder what—"

Alana giggles, cutting Kiki off. "Then there was this time I got knocked into while holding a tray of beers, the tray tipped, soaking my t-shirt and you could see *everything*. I wasn't wearing a bra that night. All the guys started chanting 'wet t-shirt contest.' And well, it was a bit nippy in the bar if you know what I mean." She winks at us.

Eew, where the heck is this story going?

"So Lexy stripped off his shirt for me. Of course, he couldn't keep the girls off of him after that. I was so mad at him. But the make-up sex was ahhmazing. From that point on, I insisted the bar keep t-shirts in stock. It was my idea to have the staff wear Ryan's Pub t-shirts. They sold like hot cakes after that." She smugly smiles.

"Oh my gosh, that's so crazy." I flash a quick smile as I look around for the guys, wishing I could be anywhere else but here right now.

"I'll be right back, I'm going to the jacks." Alana scoots back from the table and saunters to the bathrooms.

"Seriously?!" Kiki screeches as she leans in across the table from me. "Did she really just talk about their amazing sex? Eew!"

"Yeah, it's really awesome to have to sit here and listen to it."

"Maybe you should start telling her your Lex stories from being on the road with him. That will make her jealous."

I arch my eyebrow at her. "Hmm, which ones? There are *so* many. The one where I styled his hair? Or…wait…the one where I styled his hair. Or maybe the one where I watched him leave with a different skank after each show?"

Kiki chews on her lip. "Ugh, yeah, never mind. You did get to wipe down his body though!"

"Hmm. 'Oh hey Alana, you want to hear about the time I wiped sweat off of Lex? Oh! You had sex with him? Ha, yeah no, I never had that pleasure'." I grimace at Kiki.

"I see your point. Okay, plan B. Let's just get drunk and then we won't give two shits what she says."

"I like this plan." I clink my glass to hers.

"Okay, here's our game. Every time she says *Lexy* we have to do a shot."

"Omg, we'll be shitfaced in no time."

"Isn't that the point?"

I smile. "I'm in."

Kiki heads to the bar to get us a round of shots. The house band starts to play and they aren't bad if you're into Irish folk music. I feel the sudden desire to get up on the small stage in this quaint venue and sing. I love to sing and have a pretty decent voice; I just never wanted to do it professionally.

Alana comes back to the table just as Kiki arrives with a tray full of shots. My eyebrows shoot up to my hairline. *Jesus, how many did she get?*

"Ooh shots! I remember this one time I laid myself down on the bar and Lexy lined up tequila shots. He licked the salt out of my belly button and then proceeded to pour a shot of tequila on me. He licked it up my body until he reached my mouth where I was holding the lime." She smiles sweetly at me. "Have you ever had a guy do that to you, Sarah?"

Kiki raises her eyebrow at me and we both grab a shot and down it.

"Oh! Wait for me!" Alana quickly snatches a lemon drop and slams it. "Woo! Tart!"

"So, Alana, how did you and Lex meet?" Kiki asks.

"Oh, it was love at first sight. I walked into this pub looking for a job. I was just out of high school and on my own. He was so handsome and rugged. I remember it like it was yesterday. I sat down on one of the barstools and talked to him for about five minutes and then I walked around the bar, threw my arms around his neck, and kissed the hell out of him.”

“Wow! Guess you got the job then, huh?” Kiki sips her cocktail.

Alana laughs lightly. “Yeah, I sure did. Lexy wouldn’t let me out of his sight after that.”

Kiki and I clink shot glasses together and slam another lemon drop. The alcohol starts to dull my senses in a much-needed good way.

“So, if things were so amazing between you two, why did you break up?” Kiki asks innocently as she kicks my foot under the table.

“Kind of nosy, aren’t ye? Guess Americans are like that though,” she titters.

Tatum, Lex, Matt, and Will drop down into seats at the table before Alana can answer. A waitress comes behind them depositing a tray of beer and waters at our table.

“I saw the shots and thought you could use some water.” Tatum leans down and kisses Kiki’s neck.

“Lex, sit here!” Alana pulls out the chair on the other side of her and practically drags him down into it.

“Geez, Alana, okay. Easy.” He looks over at me and I compose my face into a mask of indifference.

“Oh my gosh, Lexy, remember that one time when that group of tourists came in here lost? That was sooo funny!” Alana giggles annoyingly. Lex smiles uncomfortably. Kiki and I pick up another shot and down it.

“Whoa you two, you better slow down.” Tatum slides a water in front of us.

Alana scoffs. “They’ve had like ten shots.”

"Hardly," Kiki snaps back. "I ordered us some food, Sarah, don't worry."

"Well that was dumb, now you'll just vomit," Alana snickers.

Ugh, what happened to the nice girl from earlier today? This version of Alana is quickly grating on my nerves.

"Well then I'm sure Connor can give us bar t-shirts since you implemented the extra t-shirt plan." Kiki winks at me.

Connor walks over to the table. "Hey guys, the band is taking a break. Do you want to play something?"

Lex looks over at Tatum. "Eh, I'm not feeling it tonight, bro. Can we just play a small set tomorrow night?"

"Yeah, yeah, absolutely."

"I'll sing something," I pipe up, fueled by the alcohol and wanting to escape from the table. Everyone looks at me in astonishment.

"Yeah, Sarah!" Kiki claps excitedly. "She rocks it at karaoke."

"You do, do ye? That's grand." Connor smiles at me. "I can play guitar or piano if you want."

"Sure!" I smile broadly at him.

Lex starts to get up. "I got it, Connor."

Feeling snarky after all the Alana stories, I hold up my hand. "No thanks, Lex. Like you said, you aren't feeling it tonight." I flash him a bright smile, but then feel bad when I see the hurt in his eyes. I quickly swallow some water and walk toward the stage before I change my mind.

Chapter 19

Lex

SARAH WALKS AWAY from me, and I'm completely helpless. I want to be the one she wants up there with her, but I'm not. Perhaps it's better she chose my brother. At least that's what my head is telling me—my heart is a fiery ball of jealousy eating me up inside.

I slowly sit back down as Connor and Sarah talk on stage. She laughs, and I realize with a pang that I've missed that beautiful sound. I haven't heard it much lately and I know it's my fault. Shame and longing punch me hard in the gut.

"So Lexy, remember when we used to sit on stage together when you played?" Alana coos in my ear. I see Kiki doing a shot by herself out of the corner of my eye.

"Whoa there pony. Let's saddle back on those." Tatum quickly removes the tray of shots and passes them to the table behind us. Kiki quietly starts to hiccup.

"But they're sooo good," she slurs. Tatum hands her a glass of water.

"And remember that time when we were being naughty behind the bar?" Alana whispers in my ear as she trails her fingers up my arm.

I'm not sure what her end game is, but it's not going to be me. Her other hand runs over my crotch. After the kiss in the garden I don't want her to think she can touch me as she pleases. Especially after seeing the look on Sarah's face after, it nearly killed me. I don't want this girl anywhere near me. I grab her fingers and squeeze them hard.

"Ow! What was that for?"

"Keep your fingers to yourself, Alana," I grit out. Kiki snorts on the other side of Tatum.

"So can Sarah really sing?" Tatum asks Kiki.

"Oh yeah, she's *so* good. I keep telling her she should try out for you guys, but she doesn't want to sing. She loves doing makeup."

Alana huffs. "Who would choose doing makeup over singing for the number-one country band in the States?"

Kiki leans forward. "Uh, a super talented one, that's who. She's a makeup artist to the stars and makes mega bucks doing it. It's an art form to her. She's fucking fantastic and brilliant!"

Alana ignores her and takes a sip of her drink. "Whatever."

I smile as Tatum pushes Kiki back telling her to take it easy. Listening to Kiki makes me so proud of Sarah. She's come a long way since I first met her in that coffee shop.

Connor steps up to the mic. "Hey everyone, thanks for making it out tonight!" The crowd whistles and claps. "I want you to give a big round of applause to my girl Sarah.

She hails from the States...Nashville, Tennessee to be exact, and she's fuckin' amazin'!"

Sarah blushes as she steps up to the mic. The whole bar continues to whistle and clap, the loudest coming from our table. Alana sits silently next to me, pouting. I return my gaze to Sarah. She's so goddamn beautiful standing up there under the spotlight, her golden hair glowing giving her an ethereal appearance.

Connor sits down behind her at the piano and one of the bartenders lowers the lights in the bar. Connor's fingers expertly play over the keys as she takes a deep breath, her eyes closed. She starts to sing "Ocean" by Lady Antebellum, and she hits the notes perfectly, flawless really, sounding just like Hillary Scott. I'm hanging on every word and it's not lost on me that she's singing this song to me. I want to crawl into her arms and rest my lonely heart there. And I'm not the only one—the whole bar is completely enraptured.

"Holy shit, our girl can really sing," Tatum whispers over Alana to me as Sarah starts to sing the refrain.

Not wanting to miss a second of her intoxicating voice, I nod in response, powerless to tear my eyes from her. I'm drunk on her. It's just another facet of Sarah I didn't know about. As she continues the song, Connor joins her to harmonize. Their voices blend perfectly.

Sarah looks back at my brother, smiling as she gives him a wink. I'm so fucking jealous that I'm not the one singing with her I can hardly stand it.

She turns back around and her eyes find mine as she sings. I can't look away. I'm completely hypnotized by the siren singing her song to me. Her eyes are sad as she sings about begging her love to let her in, to take a chance on her. *For me to let her in.* The lyrics hit me in the chest like a ton of bricks. Her eyes close and my heart breaks open, clarity spreading through my veins. She is what I want. I want to let her in, to let her love me and try to heal this tormented heart.

The song ends and the whole bar remains silent for a moment before erupting in cheers and whistling. Everyone is completely blown away. Sarah blushes and waves.

"Thank you, everyone, for indulging me tonight."

"Sarah darling, you can come sing in my bar anytime your little heart desires. That was amazing!" Connor grabs her in a hug.

I scoot back my chair surprising everyone at the table and stride toward the stage. Hoots and whistles echo around the bar.

"Ye change yer mind?" Connor asks.

I tersely nod as I reach for the guitar the band left on stage. Sarah starts to walk off the stage but I grab her hand. I look down into her whiskey eyes.

"Stay, *mo rogha*[3], please. Sing one with *me.*" My voice is gruff, leaving no room for argument. She doesn't answer me but nods slightly, our eyes staying connected. Connor brings both of us a glass of water and she drinks it thirstily.

"I'd like to do one more if ye don't mind," I speak into the mic.

The crowd claps and shouts their approval. I have no idea what I'm going to play until I look over at Sarah. Her

---

[3] Irish for my chosen one.

eyes are sad, but she gives me a quick smile and shrugs her shoulders. We sit down on the chairs facing each other onstage, the noise and people from the bar dimming as we lock into our own little bubble of just Sarah and Lex.

I strum a few chords of the song and her smile widens as she recognizes it. I nod at her and she returns it.

"You with the sad eyes don't be discouraged…" I sing the first few verses of "True Colors" and nod at Sarah to come in whenever she's ready.

When she starts to sing with me it's the sweetest blending of sound I have ever heard. It's a soothing balm for my soul. And I mean every word I sing to her—to not be afraid to show the world who she really is, because she's beautiful. We sing to each other, her eyes blazing into mine as our heartbeats synchronize with the beat of the song. *Don't give up on me, mo chroí, my heart,* the little voice in my heart shouts out.

I don't want this moment to end. But eventually it does as I strum the last chord. You could hear a pin drop before everyone goes nuts. I wink at her and give her a smirk. She smiles back at me shyly and ducks her head as she quickly stands. Before I can reach for her hand she hops off the stage and heads back to the table.

Will and Matt reach her first, giving her a big hug. "Who knew our little ray of sunshine could sing like that? Holy shit girl, you're singing on stage with us next time!"

"Ha, no, no. I just like to do it for fun."

Kiki barrels into her next, jumping on Sarah and squealing. Sarah laughs as she untangles herself. "Did you do more shots without me?"

"Yes, someone kept saying the code word until Tater Tot took them away." Kiki frowns and then quickly smiles. "Holy shit, the chemistry up there between you and Lex was on fire!"

Sarah smiles weakly and shrugs, looking at me over her shoulder.

She makes it back to her chair in one piece. Tatum gives her a high-five across the table. "We need to talk, Sarah." He grins widely.

"Stop with the dimples, I'm not singing with you guys." She laughs. "Besides, Lex and Connor can make anyone sound good."

Tatum grins. "I don't think so."

I come around the other side of the table from her, keeping my hands to myself because what I really want to do is drag her across it and kiss the hell out of her. Alana's chair is vacant as I sit back down. Hopefully she left and I won't have to deal with her wandering fingers or annoying stories.

"You guys sounded like Justin and Anna in *Trolls*. It was awesome!" Kiki gushes.

"That's because that's this dope's favorite movie." Connor laughs as he pulls a chair out next to Sarah.

"Shut yer mouth or I'll slap ye a kick, ye cabbage."

"Wait a minute." Kiki holds her hand up. "Wait. One. Minute. You're telling us *Trolls* is Lex Ryan's favorite movie? Oh god, this is too good!" Kiki bursts out laughing, clapping her hands gleefully. Connor nods as he ducks away from me trying to land a fist on his arm.

I shrug as I sit back in my chair, folding my arms over my chest. "I like Branch, what can I say?"

"Oh my god, that's awesome." Kiki wipes tears from her cheeks. Sarah smiles at me across the table.

"Another round!" Connor shouts. A waitress comes by and drops a tray full of beers on our table. "Sarah, seriously Love, when are you going to run away with me?"

"Piss off, mate." I shove my boot against his leg under the table.

"What? She's free to date the better-looking brother!"

Alana snorts as she pulls her chair out and sits back down, much to my dismay.

"Awe, piss off, Alana. I'll knack your melt in, wee doll."

"Shut the feck up, Connor. I'm on a job assignment, ye tosser."

"Feck away aff ye lying rat. Wouldn't take ye to the spuds."

Shit, this is escalating fast and could get ugly. I put up my hand in front of Connor. "Relax, Brother."

My brother *hates* Alana with a fire of a thousand suns. He has good reason to. He blames her for hurting me, driving me away, and tearing our family apart.

Everyone else at the table is watching their interaction like a tennis match when suddenly Connor looks up and huffs out a laugh. "Get a load of this copper knob."

We all turn to look as a tall Leprechaun wearing a green button-down, green skinny jeans, and a green sequined vest strolls into the bar.

Chapter 20

Lex

"TOP OF THE mornin' to ye!"

"Oh my god! TJ? It's nighttime, but whatevs…What the hell are you doing here?" Kiki cries as she launches herself at him.

I chuckle because what in the hell *is* he wearing? He's dressed head-to-toe in bright emerald green. He's even sporting a green bowtie and suspenders under his god-awful sequined vest. I don't even want to know where he finagled one of those. His suede bucks are emerald green, dyed to match his skinny jeans. Everyone at the bar watches him saunter in cool as a cucumber, because he actually looks like one.

"I was needed, so here I am!"

Sarah gets up and grabs onto the both of them. "TJ, you're the best."

Kiki releases him and stands back with her hands on her hips. "Whoa, wait. What about Heather? She can't run the business by herself! What about my babies?!" she screeches.

"Turn that shit down, Ace of Base. Heather gave me her blessing. She knows Sare Bear needs me more than she does. Your brother is staying at the Animal House." He snaps his fingers. "It's all taken care of. Now let me see what we're dealing with here." He strides over to the table and everyone fist-bumps TJ.

"Hey Lex. Hey Matt, Will, Tatum. Hi again, Lex." He does a double-take and we all laugh. "There are *two* Lex Ryans? Holy mother of hay-zeus I'm going to faint." He dramatically sits down in a chair on the other side of Sarah. "This is just so unfair," he mutters as he turns his attention to Alana. "And *you* must be Elaine."

"It's Alana." She smiles politely.

He waves her off. "It *is* hotter than a sauna in here! Totes agree!"

"No, I said—"

"So, who do you have to screw to get a beer around here?" He winks at Alana and whispers, "I've always wanted to say that!"

Connor puts a beer down in front of TJ. "Oh! *Well* then, thank you, hot IT brother!"

"He's not an IT techie, dumbass. He owns the bar." Kiki throws an olive at him.

TJ rolls his eyes as he sips his beer. "Identical twin? Get with the fucking program, Kinks."

"And *who* are you again?" Alana rudely asks TJ.

"You mean you don't know who I am?"

Alana looks around the table and we all smirk. "No? That's why I'm asking."

TJ holds his hand up. "Thank you, next," he says sassily,

dismissing her as he turns to chat with Sarah and Kiki.

Alana huffs out an annoyed breath as she leans into me. "Lexy, can you take me back to my hotel? I feel a headache coming on."

Sense of duty and being a courteous gentleman has me nodding my head, but the last thing I want to do is leave. I lean into Tate to let him know I'll be right back. I scoot my chair back and help Alana stand up. I try to catch Sarah's eye, but she's deep in conversation.

Alana and I walk out into the cool July evening. It's starting to get dark out as we walk down the sidewalk toward her hotel. There's a light breeze coming off the harbor as I look up at all the pastel buildings and shops, loving the quaint colorful town of Kinsale, and missing the place I used to call home.

She wraps her arm with mine and leans into me. I don't think she's drunk, but she's hanging onto me like she needs me to help her walk.

"Lexy, I've missed you."

I sigh as I look out at the boats in the harbor. I don't answer her, but she continues anyway.

"It could be just like old times. Don't you miss it? Don't you miss this?"

I grunt, because I'm not heading back down memory lane with her tonight. Not ever again.

"Stay with me tonight, Lex. Let me remind you how good we used to be."

"No."

She huffs, "Why? Because of *Sarah*? She doesn't even seem to like you."

I chuckle. "No, she doesn't, does she?"

"Then why are you wasting your time with her when you have me right in front of you telling you I want you back?"

I sigh. "Alana, it's none of your business."

"It is my business! I need to talk to you about something."

"Why are you fighting so hard for me? I haven't heard from you in what? Ten years? Why now, eh? Is it because I'm famous? Because I have more money than I know what to do with?"

Alana sputters, "Are you insinuating I'm a gold-digger?"

"I'm not insinuating anything. I'm just asking. I don't understand."

She stops and turns to me. "Because I've never stopped loving you! Seeing you again makes me believe we can start over. Clean slate. I know you feel it too, Lexy, and I'm going to make you see—we are meant to be together."

I shake my head and look down at the ground, avoiding her pleading eyes.

"Don't you see? This is fate that we are back together on your tour. The magazine could have picked any other journalist, but it was me! Me!"

"I don't want you, Alana. It's coincidence you're on this tour, that's it. Not some magical alignment of stars pushing us back together." I shake my head and shove my hands into my jean pockets as I turn to face her in front of the hotel. "I don't want anything from you. What we had is in the past. You hurt not only me, but my family too. I'm not willing to put them or myself through your drama and bullshit again. I understand that you need to be on our tour for work, and I'll be courteous to you, but that's all I'm willing to give you. I'm over you."

She stomps her foot in frustration. "When are you going to stop blaming me? It's been ten years! When are you going to get over what happened? I feel like you've made this into a way bigger issue than it really is!"

"Seriously? How can you say that? What you did to me killed a piece of my heart with your betrayal. Not only do I have trust issues, but I don't ever want to fall in love again. You made me crazy." I run my fingers through my hair as I pace in front of her. "So fuck you for saying I've made this into a bigger issue than what you think it is."

"Lex, baby, I'm sorry. I'm so sorry. You're right, I shouldn't trivialize your feelings." She steps in my path and puts her hands on my chest. "We were so good together." Her perfume assaults my nostrils making me feel sick. I take her hands and push them off of me, but it doesn't seem to faze her.

"That's just it, we *were* good. A long time ago, but it turned out it was all a lie. You were never in love with me. You just used me. I'm not going to make that same mistake again. That I *can* promise you."

"Think about it, baby. This isn't over for us." She opens the hotel door. "I'm not giving up that easily."

I look to the heavens as I sigh. "We can be friends, Alana. I'm willing to give you that much."

She walks into the hotel without a backwards glance. What a fuckin' mess. I ponder what to do as I walk back to my brother's pub.

I WALK THROUGH the doors and cover my ears. Horrible screeching is coming from the stage. Sarah, Kiki, and TJ are on stage singing (if you can call it singing). I make it to the table and sit down next to Tatum.

"What the hell happened in the forty minutes I was gone? They're completely fluthered."

"Lots of shots, man. Lots of shots."

The song ends and the three buffoons stumble off the stage and everyone cheers. I'm not sure if it's because they like their performance or if they're happy they won't be singing anymore. I'm thinking it's the latter as Kiki trips and lands flat on her face. A couple near the front help her up as she giggles and apologizes.

"Shit, this is going to be a disaster. We better get them home." Tate sighs.

I nod and signal to my brother that we'll be wrapping things up. "Where are Matt and Will?"

"Uh, they left with two girls right after you."

"Good for them, they need to get laid."

Tatum laughs. "One was leeched on to Matt's neck. I think she was a sure thing."

I smile absentmindedly as I watch Sarah stumble to the table, with TJ making a beeline toward the bar. Kiki bumps into Sarah from behind and they both start laughing uncontrollably.

"Shite."

"You're telling me. I tried to stop them, but they kept

saying sexy and sauna and taking shots after you left. It was three against one, and they kept calling me their mood-killer."

"Hmph. Well, you grab Kiki, I'll get Sarah. I'll have my brother call a cab for TJ if he wants to stay. I can drive, I've only had a beer."

Tatum nods as he quickly grabs a squealing Kiki and hauls her over his shoulder. "Oh god, Tater Tot, I think I'm going to be sick." She giggles as she slaps his ass. "Have I ever told you how much I love your ass? It's the perfect view from here. Don't mind me, I'm just going to squeeze it for the rest of the night."

Sarah crashes down into the chair opposite me and smiles lazily. "I'm reaaaally hammered Leeeex."

"I know ye are, gorgeous."

Her face twists into a frown. "Ugh, don't call me things you don't mean."

"I always say what I mean."

"I hate you, Lex."

My lips lift into a smile. "I know, Love."

Her head thunks down on the table as she passes out cold. I lift her over my shoulder and follow Tatum outside. We buckle them into the van and Tatum hops into the front with me.

We're five minutes into the drive when Sarah comes to life and says she's going to be sick. I quickly pull the van over and spring into action. I open her door as she stumbles into my arms.

"Move, Lex..." she mumbles right before she vomits on the road, some of it hitting me, causing me to curse. She starts to cry and it kills me. I hold her long hair back from her face as she throws up again.

"I ha…I hate puking," she cries.

I chuckle. "Awe, it's the pits, I know. Get it all out, baby girl."

She turns into me and starts to cry against my leather jacket. I get in back with her, gently pushing a passed-out Kiki over. "You're up, man."

Tatum climbs over to the driver's seat and starts to drive. "She okay?"

"Yeah, just too much of the lemon juice I think."

Sarah whimpers into my jacket as she clings to me. I stroke her head and whisper to her that she's going to be okay.

We make it to my parents' house in record time which is quite impressive since Tatum isn't used to driving on the opposite side of the road in the dark. The front door is unlocked and thankfully my parents aren't waiting up for us as Tatum carts Kiki to their room and I take Sarah to hers. She looks so miserable I just want to wrap her in my arms and hold her.

"I'm going to puke again," she mumbles as I set her down. I quickly guide her into the bathroom and wrap her hair in a pink ponytail holder I see on her sink. She hugs the toilet and vomits two more times. She starts crying again as she leans back against the clawfoot tub and I place a warm washcloth to her face. Her eyes are red-rimmed as tears track down her cheeks.

"I'm never drinking again."

I bite back a smile. "I hear ya, Love."

"Why are you here? Weren't you with skank-bags Alana?"

I chuckle. "I walked her to her hotel, but I came back for you."

"You did? Why?"

"I wanted to make sure you were okay."

She shifts her body and lays her head on the thick floormat next to the tub, closing her eyes. I think she's asleep again until she mumbles, "Lex, why do you hate me?"

"Why would you think I hate you, Love?"

"I dunno. You're moody sometimes."

"I know I can be a moody bollix, can't I?"

"Did you just call yourself a moody buttlicks?"

I chuckle as I wipe her again with the washcloth. "I don't hate ye, Sunshine. Don't ever think that."

"Lex, knock knock."

I smirk because apparently I do the same shit when I'm drunk beyond repair.

"Who's there?"

"Ice cream soda."

"Ice cream soda who?"

"Ice scream soda I don't friggin' know because you passed out before you told me the punchline."

"I did? When was that?" I sit down opposite her on the cold tile.

"On the airplane. It's been driving me crazy."

I grin. "*I scream so da* people can hear me."

She doesn't open her eyes, her mouth curling up into a smile. She lifts her hand and points her gun fingers at me and shoots. "That's bangin'." Her hand drops like a dead weight and she groans. "I hate puking. It makes me cry."

"I know, Love. Let me help you change into a clean t-shirt." She dutifully sits up and lifts her hands in the air like a toddler and it's adorable, making me laugh. "Let me find one first. Don't move."

"I not goin' anywhere." She lies back down on the tile floor and moans.

I don't want to dig through her suitcase so I quickly run to my room and grab one of mine for her and a change of clothes for me. I toe off my puked-on boots and set them out on the balcony. I come back to her room and find her slightly snoring on the bathroom floor as I crouch down beside her.

"Sarah, wake up."

Nothing.

I try to hold her up to take her clothes off but she's like a bag of potatoes. She falls to the side if I let go of her. I gently shake her. "Sarah, I need you to help me, Love."

Her eyes remain closed as she mumbles, "I heart you, Lex Ryan."

"I heart you too, Love."

One eye pops open. "You do? Awe, you just made my lifetime."

I smile. "I'm glad I made your lifetime. Can you sit up?"

"Lex? Have I ever told you I loooove your accent. It makes me so horny."

"Really?"

"Say something."

"I like that I make you horny."

"Oh yeah, so so good," she moans as she smushes her

face against the cold tile. "Hey, Lex?"

"Yes, Princess?"

"Do you like me?"

I chuckle as I stare at her in a fetal position with her face kissing the floor. She's a hot mess. "How could I not? You're my ray of sunshine."

She sits up. Her blonde ponytail flops to the side, silky strands falling out. "Don't laugh! I'm Siri...dammit, not Siri...I hate Siri, she's so goddamn annoying with her 'I'm better than you' voice. Like she's got one up on you 'cause she has all the answers and you need her to give you those answers. She never gives me the right answer and when I tell her to go away she asks if we can still be friends. I don't wanna be her friend. She sucks..." She takes a shuddering breath. "Wait...what were we talking about? That was exhausting."

I just grin as I stare at her in amazement. I help her to her feet.

"Sexy Lexy I smell like puke." She starts to cry.

"Did you just call me *Sexy Lexy?*" I smirk.

"Kiki and TJ call you that. I said no, no way. No, no, no, nope."

"I think I got it, it was a solid no."

She sways to the left, so I reach out and steady her. "But it stuck."

I wipe her tears with a washcloth. "Do you not think I'm sexy?"

"I think you're super..." She yawns.

"You think I'm super?"

"Uh huh... I'm really sleepy, Sexy Lexy." She starts to

sink back to the floor.

"Okay, hang on babe, can you help me out here and lift your arms up?"

She flops her arms up and down like a baby bird taking flight. "Ugh, they're so heavy." She starts to giggle. "Heavy sounds like sexy. I think you're *sex-eeee*."

I smirk. "Heavy does not rhyme with sexy, but it's better than super, so I'll take it. Can you hold one arm up, maybe?"

"You'll take heavy? What does that even *mean?*" She starts to giggle uncontrollably. "Oh my god, stop tickling me! I'll pee in my pants."

I grin because I'm not even touching her. Jesus, she's a disaster. "I'm not tickling you, Love. Please don't pee in your pants. Give me your arm."

She quickly lifts an arm socking me in the eye as I reach for the hem of her shirt. I see stars…bright white ones.

"Holy shit, Sunshine!"

"Oh no, did I hurt you?" she coos as she pats my stomach and leans in to kiss it.

"It's okay, I didn't need that eye anyway." I step out of her reach. "How about this, you just stand still and I'm going to wrangle this t-shirt off of you. But I need you not to tip over. Okay?"

She solemnly nods her head and salutes me. "Aye Aye, Captain. Such a stern face."

She giggles as she watches me out of red-rimmed eyes as I approach her like I'm about to wrestle a feral cat into a carrier. The quicker I can get it off, the better. I step forward as she sways toward the floor. I grab her hem and roughly pull the shirt over her head.

"Owe! Jesus, Lex, you just tried to take my head off!"

I quickly pull my much bigger t-shirt down over her as I try not to stare at her chest.

Whew, done! I mentally clap myself on the back. She sinks back down to the floor like a deflated balloon.

"Lex," she whines.

"Yeah?"

"What about my bra? And these jeans have puke on them. And my shoes. Oh my poor little cute shoes. I love my poor little pukey shoosey-wooseys." She starts to pet her heels.

Shit. I tug her back up to standing and quickly reach around her and unsnap her bra clasp.

"Whoa, I may be super drunk but that's the quickest I've ever had a guy undo my bra."

"Just a flick of the wrist, Love."

I grimace as I look at her jeans. I pick her up and she wraps her arms around my neck as she sighs into my chest.

"You smell like heaven."

My heart does something funny as it begins to beat faster. I place her gently on the bed and remove her heels and put them outside her door. I undo her button fly and yank her skinny jeans off roughly.

"Owe, Jesus! Easy tiger, they aren't glued on!" she gripes as she accidentally kicks me in the stomach making me grunt as she rolls to her side. "I can't imagine you're much of a ladies' man if you remove everyone's clothes like that, Buttlicks," she mumbles as she buries her head into the pillow.

I chuckle as I pull the comforter over her and get her a

glass of water and two aspirin and set them on her nightstand. I watch her shoulders rise up and down with her breathing, her beautiful silvery-blonde hair splayed across the white pillow. I should leave her and go back to my room, but I'm worried she might puke again.

I'll just watch her for a few minutes, no harm in that. I climb into bed next to her after taking off my shirt and pulling on some pajama pants. The bed dips and she rolls away from me.

"Shib rum det. Mum dee."

I smirk. "Did you say something, Sunshine?" I gently move the silky strands off her cheek. She sighs in her sleep.

"Shilo rum do, Lex."

"Shilo rum do, Princess." I allow myself one moment of weakness and softly kiss her temple. "Goodnight, beautiful."

Chapter 21

Sarah

I PEEL ONE eye open as the light comes through my balcony window. Even though the curtains are closed, there's a tiny sliver peeking through that is making my head pound. I squeeze my eyes shut, but my brain is now wide awake. Oh god, my throat feels like sandpaper and I'm so thirsty I could drink out of a toilet. Okay, just kidding, that's super gross. I'm not *that* thirsty, but I'm pretty damn parched.

Memories slowly ebb in like the tide as I remember bits and pieces from last night. One thing I do know for sure, I'm going to kill Kiki and TJ since they were the ones pushing the shots like a pimp pushing crack. I remember throwing up several times. Why do I feel like I puked on a dark country road with sheep bleating in the middle of the night? Maybe that was a dream. I remember hugging the toilet like it was my lifeline and then falling asleep on the ice-cold tile of the floor. So how on earth did I get back in bed? I must have crawled.

I open my eyes again and slowly turn my head. I'm cocooned in a cloud of comforter and pillows and it's so cozy I don't want to move my body, but I need to reach the nightstand where I see a glass of water and two aspirin. I covet them like a kid craves candy. I love Lex's mom, she is my savior. I gingerly sit up and down the aspirin and take some cautious sips of water. Even though I'm incredibly thirsty, the fear of puking all over again overrides guzzling the whole glass. I set the glass down and turn to see a muscular tanned back next to me. I quickly duck back under the poufy duvet.

Um…hello? Who the hell is this? I start to panic. Did I bring someone home from the bar with me? *To Lex's parents' house?* No, no way. Even though I was super pissed and hurt he had left the bar with Alana, there's no way I would bring a stranger back to his house, and sleep with him. *Oh Jesus, did I have sex with this guy?*

I lift the covers and see that I'm wearing only a black t-shirt and panties. And the humungous t-shirt is definitely not mine. I stare at the bathroom door in horror, barely breathing because I do not want to wake this guy up. I turn back to starc at his body as it movcs slowly up and down with his even breathing. He's still asleep, thank goodness.

I gingerly sit up to get a better look and feel a second of relief when I recognize Lex's Celtic cross on his bicep, and his black tousled hair against the white linens. Thank God, it's not some random dude.

Wait a minute, what the honky-tonk is Lex doing in *my* bed? Did he take me out of my clothes? Is he wearing clothes? Did we have sex? I clutch the sheet tightly in my fist. Did I finally have sex with Lex Ryan and not remember one iota of it? Nooooo! I want to cry…for being hungover, for missing out on possibly the most amazing sex of my life, for letting Kiki and TJ hammer me with shots, for this stupid headache…for so many reasons.

I pull the comforter up to my neck as I sink back against the pillows and my head begins to pound. I'm so confused about why he's here. The last thing I remember is him leaving the bar with Alana. I was so upset that I just started doing the shots TJ and Kiki were pushing on me to numb the pain.

I huff out a deep breath as I stare up at the ceiling. Lex rolls next to me and I suddenly feel his arm drape across me and pull me into him. *Shit.* I shift my eyes to him but I can't see his face. I'm like a frozen mummy cocooned by him and the comforter. His breathing is even and deep letting me know he's still asleep.

Normally, this would be heaven—all my fantasies coming true. But I always imagined waking up in Lex's arms in a hot passionate embrace, our bodies slick with sweat as we make love to the sunrise breaching over the water. Sadly, reality isn't quite the picture I painted in my head. All I want is my toothbrush to brush the fuzz off my teeth, the aspirin to kick in for my splitting headache, and the sheets off because I'm starting to sweat from this super fluffy comforter and Lex's body heat. His arm feels like a thousand-pound steel beam as I gently try to move it off. I manage to lift it off and then I kick my leg out from under the comforter. Dang, that took monumental effort.

"You know, you really should try out for the Nashville Soccer Club. You kick like a pro."

I yip in surprise as I roll to my side at the sound of his gruff raspy voice and come face to face with the most beautiful aqua-blue eyes framed by sooty black eyelashes. *Oh Jesus*, his chiseled chest is on full display. I just want to reach out and place my hands on him as if his pecs had the technology to scan my fingertips for granted access. *Damn it, now is not the time, Sarah!* I knew I shouldn't have watched all those Jason Bourne movies on the plane ride over.

"Hi." *Please don't let me have morning dragon breath. Please don't let me have morning dragon breath.*

"*Maidin mhaith*, Princess."

"Uh...I think I'm still drunk because all I can hear is gibberish coming out of your mouth."

Speaking of that mouth, good god he's perfection. His beautiful lips tilt up into a smile, one dimple popping out and I can't tear my eyes from them.

"It's Irish. I said good morning, Princess. How are you feelin'?"

"Like shit." *Jesus, quite the sexy talker you are, Sarah.*

"Did you take the aspirin I put on your nightstand?"

"I did...thank you." I clear my throat. "So, um...about last night...thank you? And maybe I'm sorry? To be honest, I can't remember much. I thought you went home with Alana?"

He tucks a piece of hair behind my ear and I want to melt. "Aye, I did walk her to her hotel, but I came back for you."

"You did?"

He traces his index finger down my cheek as we stare at each other. "Aye. Lot good it did me. You puked on me, punched me, kicked me, and told me you hated me."

I inwardly cringe. "I did? Wait, what do you mean I punched you?"

"I'm finding out there's a lot more to you, Princess. You sing, you take beautiful pictures, you have one hell of a right hook…"

"Uh." I laugh. "What do you mean right hook?" I nervously start to scrunch the sheets in my hands.

"You socked me in the eye last night as I was trying to change your t-shirt." He points to his left eye and smirks.

"Oh no, I did? I'm so sorry." I gingerly reach out and run my index finger under his left eye.

His eyes close for a brief moment. "S'okay." His beautiful blues slowly open as he stares at me before he suddenly gives me a quick kiss on the lips, throws the covers off, and hops out of bed. The sudden motion makes me want to hurl.

"Get up, Sunshine. We're taking the boat out today."

"Ugh, I don't think that's a good plan for me." *Did he just kiss me?*

"Take a hot shower. Mum will be making some good stuff for breakfast. You'll feel right as rain in an hour."

I roll to my side and silently plead with him, but he ignores me as he pulls a shirt over his glorious body. Jesus, why can't I remember if I even got to run my fingers over his silky skin last night? I'm ninety-nine percent sure nothing happened. I feel like I would be tender down there if Lex ever got a hold of me, but I have to be sure for my own sanity.

"Uh, Lex?"

"Yes, Princess?"

My cheeks warm. "Um…did I? Er…did I say or *do* anything I might regret this morning?"

He chuckles as he pulls the comforter off. I shriek as I pull his t-shirt down hiding my pink panties.

He smirks. "No Love, you were the perfect gentleman."

I blink. "Okay, but if I said or did anything embarrassing…you'd tell me, right?"

He grins devilishly. "Come on, get up, we've got a date with a sailboat."

"Ugh, okay…"

He turns his back as he heads to the door and starts to sing. "If I were sexy then my name would be Sexy Lexy. The girls would all scream for me…"

The door shuts and I'm left alone in sudden silence feeling totally mortified. Oh god, did I really call him Sexy Lexy last night? Please let that be it. I groan as I pull myself out of bed and stumble to the shower.

Chapter 22

Sarah

"Ahoy, mate-ies!" TJ sing-songs from the dock.

"Fuck off, TJ," Kiki grumbles as she throws her bag over her shoulder.

"Will you guys *please* stop yelling," I groan.

"We're not Ms. Lemondrop Shot USA."

"Ugh, please don't say that word. I'll spew. Why did we drink so much last night again?"

"Check yourself sister, *you two* drank that much, I was perfectly buzzed. And that's the reason why."

We turn to see Alana walking down the docks with a large sunhat, kimono billowing in the breeze, a sexy barely there two-piece, like she's modeling for some exotic getaway. I'm suddenly feeling very frumpy in my baseball hat and one-piece that Kiki convinced me was eat-your-heart-out sexy. Nothing can compete with barely there dental floss. Matt, Will, and two girls I vaguely remember from last night trail behind her carrying an assortment of bags.

Tatum, Connor, and Lex have been getting the boat

ready to sail all morning. And holy cow, this isn't some small fishing dingy. This boat is like a mini yacht with two bedrooms and a kitchen underneath. Polished teak wood decks, gleaming glossy bannisters. Lounging chairs with soft cushions positioned for intimate conversations.

"What are we looking at?" Tatum sets a cooler down next to us.

"The arrivals," I say flatly.

"What the feck is that manky slag doing here?" Connor mutters. "I'm going to kill my feckin' brother." He hands us some more towels. "Lex!" Connor retreats below deck.

"I wonder why Connor doesn't like Alana," Kiki whispers to me as we put our bags down on some toweled chairs.

"I don't know, seems like the whole family hates her."

"Hey beautiful, here's a water for you." Tatum leans down and kisses Kiki. "I'm going to fish up front with the guys. You want to come?"

"Nope, I'm good right here on my soft cushioned seat! Thanks, babe." Kiki stands up on her toes throwing her arms around him as they kiss. He squeezes her before murmuring something in her ear. "See you guys in a little while. Hey, Alana." Tatum smiles as he leaves our group.

Alana breezes up to us as she plunks her bag down.

"Well, you two sure boozed it up last night. Couple uh drunkards ye were."

"We weren't *that* drunk," Kiki retorts as she puts on her oversized sunglasses.

TJ snorts. "Yeah you were."

"Shut up, TJ," we both gripe in unison.

"Hey, drunky-ducks! How ya feelin'?" Will and Matt

grin as they head to their chairs down the way from us. "Kiki, TJ, Sarah, Alana, this is Melody and Rhiana. Hey, great performance of 'Baby Got Back' by the way! TJ, you nailed the intro."

We wave at the girls and TJ fist-bumps Matt and Will. "Thanks!"

"We sang 'Baby Got Back' last night?" I look over at Kiki and TJ with wide eyes.

"Yes, it was so awesome. We had the crowd eating out of our hands." Kiki smiles.

"Oh Lexy, there you are!" Alana says breathily. "Could you be a god and put some sun cream on my back?"

"The ol' sunscreen trick," Kiki mumbles beside me as she opens up a magazine. "That'll reel him in."

"Uh, yeah sure, just give me a minute." Lex scoots by Alana and stands in front of my chair. Before I can process what he's holding, he plunks a bright orange life preserver over my head. A big devilish grin spreads across his face as he places a bucket next to my chair.

"Princess, it's going to be a little rough out there today. Thought these could help."

"Hardy har-har," I deadpan. Not only am I feeling frumpy, but now I'm the only one on the boat wearing a DayGlo-orange life preserver.

"You look adorbs, Sare! In that safety cone kind of way..." TJ chirps from his seat. Kiki chuckles beside him until I slap her arm.

Lex laughs as he turns to Alana who has taken a chair across the way from us.

"Let me know if you need anything." He winks at me

and heads toward her. She looks like she's posing for a Victoria Secret ad as she lounges, waiting for her cabana boy. Lex saunters over to her and sits down on her chair as she giggles passing him the sunscreen.

"I can't read lips, but she's definitely flirting with him. Someone needs to push her overboard. TJ, I vote you." Kiki watches them behind her shades.

"Do you think her boobs are real?" I ask trying not to openly stare at her massive bouncy boobs that are spilling out all sides of her bikini top.

"Oh honey, she doesn't need a life preserver with those flotation devices." TJ licks his fingertip before he turns the page of his magazine.

"I hate that style of bikini. It's the same one Tyra had on the *Sports Illustrated* cover." Kiki passes the sunscreen to TJ. "It looks like one of those things doctors and nurses wear over their mouths."

"Uh, you mean a surgical mask?" I giggle.

"Why are the easiest names for things so damn hard to remember?" Kiki muses.

"It's called hangover memory loss."

Laughter erupts from Alana and a twinge of jealousy ignites in my belly.

"Oh Lexy, you're so funny! I just love your big muscular arms…they're so…big," Kiki says in a falsetto breathy voice as Alana rubs her fingers along Lex's arm. She throws her head back in exaggerated laughter.

"Oh Lexy, remember that time we went out on the sailboat and we made passionate love in front of your whole family? Wasn't that so funny?" I say in the same breathy voice and we start giggling.

A throat clears. "Over my dead body would that ever happen."

I have to do a double-take because Connor looks so much like Lex, but sure enough Lex is still sitting with Alana. My cheeks heat up at being caught in our little game of *"what is Alana saying"*. Connor sits at the foot of TJ's chair and places his hand on his leg for a second before removing it.

"We're going to fish at the front of the boat. Want to join us?"

"Um, not really my thing. I'm good gossiping with the girls." TJ smiles at Connor.

Is TJ blushing? I poke Kiki in the side, but instead of paying attention to what's going on in the chair next to her, she looks at me. "What?"

I roll my eyes and tilt my head toward TJ.

"Oh god, are you going to puke? We've got a puker!" She sits up and yells, shoving the bucket in my face. Everyone turns to stare at me.

"Oh my god, shut up!" I hiss, holding my hand up to reassure everyone. "I'm not going to puke!"

"Oh, sorry. You had a weird head-tilt thing going on and your eyes were rolling."

"You're hopeless," I mumble.

"All right then, well I'm going to gather up the guys. If you need anything…uh, let me know." Connor gets up before smiling and winking at TJ.

TJ watches him walk toward Matt and Will.

I sit up in my lounger and turn toward Kiki and TJ. "*Oh*

my god! What is going *on*?"

"What? What happened? Is Lex getting it on with Alana?" Kiki arches her neck to look over at them.

"Seriously, let's never go into detective work because you are clueless."

"Hey, that's not nice! You're mean when you're hungover."

"I'm sorry, you're right. That wasn't nice. I'm just stressed over the two kanoodling over there."

"Wait, I thought we were on team *I hate Lex*. We've been back and forth so much I can't keep up."

I sigh. "I know. Don't hate Lex. He took care of my drunk ass last night."

"Awe, he did?"

"I uh…he was in my bed when I woke up this morning."

"What?!" Kiki screeches as she sits up. "And you're just now telling me this?"

"Ssh, everyone is looking at us! Nothing happened. He just fell asleep making sure I was okay after I vomited all over him."

"No you did not!" Kiki giggles.

"Yes, and apparently I told him we call him Sexy Lexy."

"Did you make out with him?"

I cringe. "God, I hope not. That would be nasty after I just puked. To be honest, I don't remember much."

"Oh my god, do you think he slipped you a roofie?"

"What? No! *Who are you*?"

Kiki shrugs. "I was just making sure."

"He's your husband's best friend *and* your friend. He can also have any woman he wants with a crook of his finger…I think it's safe to say he doesn't need to slip a date-rape drug."

"Sorry, you're right. I've been watching a lot of weird shit on Netflix lately. It's made me paranoid of everyone. So, what now? Your man over there is flirting with the enemy."

"So…nothing. We're just friends." I shrug.

"Ooh! I have a plan." Kiki claps. "You need to start flirting with his brother. It will drive him crazy."

"Eh, I don't want to make him insanely jealous. I just want him to want me for me. Why can't it be simple like that?" I sit back in my chair. "Besides, I'm pretty positive his brother isn't interested." I stick my finger out and point toward TJ. Kiki gapes.

We both turn to TJ who is unusually quiet and humming to himself as he flips through a *Vogue* magazine.

"Hellooo, earth to TJ." Kiki flicks his ear.

"Don't mind me, I'm just ignoring you bitches."

"You're keeping secrets from us, Thomas Jean, and that's a big no-no."

"I will push you overboard, you slut, if you say my full name out loud again."

"Ooh, Sare, he's fired up. We got him right where we want him." Kiki pokes his rock-hard abs. "TJ, it's so unfair you're gay. You seriously have a rockin' body."

"I know I do. Don't try and butter me up, I'm not telling you anything."

"So…that little flirt-flirt sesh I just saw happening was totally made up in my head?" I arch my eyebrow.

"What flirt-flirt sesh?" Kiki sits up.

I roll my eyes. "When Connor came over here and was all chatty-patty with Tammy Jean here."

"Tammy Jean, I love it!" Kiki muses as TJ gives me the stink eye.

"So Sarah, let's get back to you and your man problems." TJ throws down his magazine.

"Oh no, Mister. Spill it or I'll tell Connor about the time you sharted in your pants at the company pool party."

"You wouldn't dare!"

Kiki solemnly nods her head.

"Ugh! You are the *worst* best friend ever, Mackenzie Leigh!"

"I know, now spill it."

TJ turns on his side to face us. He really is so adorable in a Prince Harry kind of way. And Kiki's right, he does have a rockin' body.

"So when I met him last night my gaydar went haywire."

"Seriously? I had no clue he was gay."

"Me neither." I shrug.

"Well, he's not out of the boudoir yet. His family knows, but that's it. It's very on the DL. Tatum doesn't even know." He looks at Kiki pointedly. "Connor just isn't ready yet. We got to talking and I don't know, we just hit it off."

"Wait, that's it? That's all you're going to say?" Kiki pokes him again.

"Stop trying to feel me up. You have your own man for that."

"Seriously? I spill everything about Tatum and I and you're not going to give me one tidbit of info?"

"A gentleman never shares the details, ladies."

"I'll remember that when I see one. Come on! We want to know!"

TJ smiles secretively, turns onto his back, and sighs dreamily. "All I'm going to say is that I seriously want to pillowtalk him."

"What the hell does that mean? Is that some gay-club term?"

TJ rolls his eyes. "Kinks, seriously…pillowtalk means I want to lay next to his hot sexy bod and just pillowtalk, you know, share our secrets and desires. Duh."

"Awe, that sounds sweet," I say dreamily and TJ winks at me.

"Have you done that already?" Kiki lowers her glasses.

"Not yet. I'll share soon. But this secret stays with us."

"What secret?" Alana pipes up, appearing out of thin air. We all freeze in uncomfortable silence.

"Ugh, I guess it's not a secret anymore. Sarah has a huge crush on Matt," Kiki says drolly as she picks up her magazine again.

"Wait…what? Kiki!" I growl.

Alana looks confused as she grabs a water from the ice chest next to us. "I thought you and Lex were an item."

"Lex Shmex. He's too moody. She's on to bigger and better things." She smiles cheekily up at Alana.

"Huh…well, good luck with that, Sarah. He looks pretty into his new girlfriend right about now."

We all look over to see Matt sensuously putting sunscreen on Melody's chest. Oh god, gross, I did not need to see that.

"Nasty," I automatically blurt out. Kiki pinches me.

"What Sarah means is he's so hot, I bet he likes it nasty. We're just deciding when she should make her move."

"Oh! I'll help you!" Alana says brightly.

"I'm sure you will," TJ mutters as he resumes flipping through his magazine.

"Nope, no, I'm good. I can handle Matt on my own."

God, can we please end this discussion? I need to shut this shit down before word gets back to him. The thought of hooking up with Matt makes my stomach flip, and not in a good way. He's like a brother to me—an annoying brother who teases and tortures. Don't get me wrong, I love Matt, but this conversation is making me want to heave again.

"Well, dibs on Lex!" she says cheerfully as she saunters away.

"*Dibs on Lex*," I mimic. "God, she sucks. *Kiki, what the fuck?*"

Kiki and TJ start to giggle. "I'm sorry! I had to say something. Besides, if word gets back to Lex he's not going to like this new turn of events."

"This is totes true. Good call, Kinks."

"Thanks." They high-five each other.

"I hate you both," I say miserably. "And why am I still wearing this dorky life preserver? Ugh!" I throw off the vest in frustration.

"You're right, hungover Sarah *is* really cranky," TJ whispers loudly.

I'VE JUST DOZED off when loud cheers erupt from the front of the boat.

"Let's see what's going on!" Kiki pushes my leg as she gets up.

The three of us head to the front of the sailboat toward the commotion. I stumble at the sight of four incredibly gorgeous shirtless men drinking beer as they cheer on Lex who's currently fighting to pull in a fish. His muscles are straining as he lets the line out a little and then aggressively winds it back in. My mouth waters as I see his tanned back muscles bunch, his abdomen taut as he twists to fight the fish. Then all of a sudden he pulls up this huge thrashing gray metallic fish. Connor and Tatum lean over to help bring it in with a net.

The three of them hold down the fish as they get the hook out of its mouth. Lex turns around holding the fish in his hands. He's seriously a beautiful specimen in his red board shorts and his black snapback turned backwards on his head. His olive skin is tanned and his abs ripple as he holds up the four-foot fish. His gorgeous baby blues crinkle as a devastating smile spreads across his face. It's contagious, automatically making me smile at seeing how happy he is.

Lex proudly stands between Tatum and his brother holding the fish up as Will takes a picture. His eyes land on me and he calls me over.

"Sunshine, look at this beauty! Can ye believe it?!"

"It's beautiful! Is it a shark?" I ask as I cautiously touch its smooth rubbery skin.

"Aye, it's a tope fish, a species of shark. They won't bite you though. Take a pic with me. It's a big deal to catch one."

Will takes a pic of Lex and I with the fish and then Kiki and TJ join me for more pictures. Lex kisses the shark and then tosses it back over the side.

"Wait, you're not going to keep it? I thought you guys were trying to catch fish for dinner tonight."

"Aye, we are, but these fish are protected, so back it goes. Will and Connor caught some cod."

His happiness is a heady thing and I feel like I'm deliriously spinning in it. He washes his arms off with a wet towel and then grabs a beer from Tatum and pops it open and taps his bottle with everyone, cheering, "*Sláinte*." I'm hyperaware of his arm as it wraps around me and pulls me to his side as he jokes with Tatum and Will.

He smells like ocean, mint, and man. His fingers lightly trail over the exposed skin from the side cutouts of my swimsuit. I shiver as his arm automatically tightens around me. I'm trying to act casual, like *hey no big deal, Lex has me tucked into his side where it feels so right*, but I'm frozen, unable to follow the thread of conversation around me. My heart is singing its own love song as it thumps fast in my chest.

Why can't this be real? Why can't we be more than friends? It's like we're a couple as we laugh and joke with all of my favorite people surrounding us. Kiki raises her eyebrows up and down at me and I smile sheepishly because nothing can beat this ecstatic mood that I'm suddenly in. Lex looks down at me and tips my hat up.

"You feeling better, Sunshine? You don't look as green as you did this morning."

I smile ruefully. "Yeah, a little bit."

"Good. I like this swimsuit…" His hooded eyes flicker from my lips to my eyes and back to my lips. His fingers trace and skim over the soft exposed skin alongside my boob. Forget what I said earlier about feeling frumpy. *Thank you Kiki for making me buy this suit.* He bends his head slightly down toward me and my eyes shutter closed. I hold my breath because I know he's going to kiss me, and I want it more than ever.

"Hey, Lexy! What's all the commotion about?" Alana yells as she walks up the steps to the front of the boat.

The moment is lost as Lex looks up. A gust of wind wraps Alana's long kimono around one of the ropes as she stumbles in her high-heeled sandals, her floppy hat falling forward obscuring her eyes. The boat bounces at that moment catching her off guard. She tips to the side and falls overboard. We watch it all unfold as if in slow motion.

"Oh shit! That water is freezing." Lex being the closest to her quickly hands me his beer and runs to the side and jumps in after her. All I can see is her stupid kimono hanging on the rope blowing in the breeze.

We all run to the port side and look over at them bobbing in the frigid sea. Alana is screaming for dear life in the choppy water.

"Oh my god, there are sharks in there." Kiki looks at me with wide eyes. TJ flings my life preserver over the side, hitting Alana in the head. She shrieks again as Lex reaches for her. He swims her over to the side and Will pulls her up to safety.

Rhiana hands her a towel and Alana snaps it from her. Her lips are quivering and she sends me an evil glare as if I pushed her myself. Lex climbs back up onto the deck and Connor hands him a towel. Alana turns to him and starts to cry.

"Lexy, I was so scared. It was freezing and I swear I felt sharks all around me. Thank you so much for jumping in after me and saving me!" She flings herself against his wet chest. "I've lost my sandals and my hat," she whines.

I turn away and look to the heavens for some patience. "It's like a six-foot drop and she's acting like she was chum sitting in the water. I didn't see one fin," I mumble.

Lex escorts her to a chair and sits her between his legs as he rubs a towel over her arms. "That water is cold, we've got to get you warm again…Ssh, don't cry, you're okay. I've got you," Lex coos to Alana.

TJ sidles up to me and flings an arm over my shoulder. "Well, you had him at vomit, but I think Alana just stole the show for drowning victim."

"Thanks for hitting her in the head with the life jacket."

"You're welcome."

Alana lets out another wail and Lex holds her closer.

"She's good, she's real good."

TJ hugs me. "But you're better. Don't throw the towel in just yet."

I rest my head on TJ's arm. I wish I could believe that.

Chapter 23

Lex

THE EVENING IS breezy as I sit out on the back deck outside my room thinking about the day. Everyone retired to their rooms after dinner, exhausted from the boat ride today. We played for a little bit at my brother's pub after we got off the boat, but no one was in the mood to stay and party. Sarah was practically turning green as she sipped water at the bar.

The boat ride was so much fun. I still can't believe I actually caught a tope. I enjoyed myself until Alana fell into the water. I felt bad for her, but she turned into a stage-five clinger and wouldn't leave my side the rest of the day. I asked her not to come back to my parents' place for dinner because my mum didn't want her there. She threw a minor temper tantrum and then huffed off to her hotel when I wouldn't budge.

It's our last night at my parents' before we head on to Glasgow. I strum my guitar as I think back to dinner. My dad grilled the fish we caught, and Mum made a vegetable ragout that was out of this world. Sarah was quiet. I'm not sure if she was tired or if it was all the Alana drama, but I didn't want to push her, so I left her alone.

I push all thoughts out of my head concentrating on a melody I'm working on. It's on the edge of my brain, but just out of my grasp and it's driving me crazy. I pluck a few chords and my thoughts roam again so I give up on the song. It's weird and confusing to be back here and to have Alana back in my life. She's familiar and reminds me of the old days, but the past is the past and that's where I want her to stay. There's just too much drama and bad history between us.

I start to play and sing "Stuck" by Imagine Dragons. As if on cue, Sarah's French doors open and she steps outside. She turns to me as she leans on the balcony railing, her long blonde hair blowing in the breeze. She's silent as I sing, drinking it in.

She is my future.

Holy shit, where did that thought come from? It's dangerous for me to think that way. I can't get attached to Sarah. The kind of relationship she wants isn't in my DNA. Not anymore. I know I'll just hurt her, and yet when I'm around her and getting to know her more, I can't keep away. It's confusing as hell. I finish the song.

"I love that song. Am I bothering you? I just needed some fresh air, but then I heard you playing. I can go back inside if you want to be alone."

"No, it's okay. Come join me." I scoot the chair next to me out a little, inviting her over. My fingers automatically strum the tune I'm struggling with.

"Um, okay, if you're sure. What are you playing?" She

sits down primly in the chair.

"Nothing…something…not sure." I grin. "I have a song I want to write, but it's being evasive. So I play other songs or listen to music until I get inspired. Do you play?"

"I…"

"Here, let me show you." I hand the guitar over and crouch down in front of her. I place her fingers on the strings, adjusting them. Her eyes widen as she watches my fingers over hers.

"Now, just strum."

She glides her thumb down.

"Yeah, that's it." Her strawberries-and-cream scent wafts over me, drowning me in her signature fragrance that drives me so crazy. Our eyes connect and all I want to do is kiss her. So badly.

"Um, Lex?"

"Yeah?" I croak out.

"I have a confession to make."

"What is it, Love?" Our lips are a breath apart.

She swallows. "I know how to play the guitar."

I sit back on my heels and laugh breaking the moment. Of course she does, and here I thought I was being a total stud teaching the girl of my dreams something special. The girl of my dreams…

That thought pierces my heart.

"But, you can still show me…I mean, you can teach me new stuff, I'm sure."

I sit back in my chair and take a sip of my beer. "Who taught you how to play?"

Sarah's quiet for a moment as she strums a few chords.

"My dad."

I give her a lopsided grin. "Well tell your dad, thanks a lot for ruining my mojo."

"I can't. He died when I was fourteen."

"Oh shit, I'm so sorry, Sare." I quickly sober up. "That must have been hard for you and your mom."

"Not exactly. My mom left my dad when I was a baby. Said she wasn't ready for kids and she needed to explore the world." She shrugs. "I guess she's still exploring because I haven't heard from her since."

"Oh Love, I'm so sorry." And I truly mean it. How awful for a girl to grow up without a mum and then to lose her dad. "What happened?"

"My dad's sister took me in. Heather's mom. She was divorced and barely hanging on, working two jobs. My dad had life insurance, but all the hospital bills and funeral stuff pretty much ate that up. He had cancer. Anyway, my Aunt Susan wasn't home much. Heather was a senior in high school, getting ready for cosmetology school, so I was pretty much on my own. But it was okay, I managed. At least I wasn't put into foster care."

"Jesus, I'm so sorry, Love." I want to wrap her in my arms and hold her, she looks so vulnerable. I'm lucky to have such a great support system like my parents. Sarah doesn't have that luxury. She strums the guitar and looks out over the ocean.

"I'm okay. I've come to peace with it all."

"Why haven't you ever told us you could sing? You're amazing."

"It's not a big deal." She shrugs. "I like my life the way it is."

"But Sarah, you have this amazing talent...don't you want to see where it takes you?"

She flashes me a quick smile. "No, I'm good."

"Love, you could—"

"Lex, please, just drop it."

"But Sunshine—"

"I don't want to sing because my mom was a singer!" she yells, then lowers her voice to almost a whisper, "I promised myself I'd never be like her."

I run my fingers through my hair. "Shit. Sorry, babe. I didn't know." Her knee is bouncing as I put my hand on it. "Hey, it's okay."

She shakes her head. "I love to sing, but my cards weren't dealt to me that way. When my dad died, I didn't have the luxury of going off on my own and starting a singing career. I had bills to pay, a part-time job at the coffee shop—I needed a steady career. I started taking online classes for business management at night and enrolled in cosmetology school during the day."

She holds up a hand as I'm about to protest. "It's okay. Singing has become more of a cathartic release for me. I don't want a career doing it. I've worked my ass off to be a makeup artist and I'm damn good at it. It wasn't something I was born with, it was something I created and built upon. It's mine, Lex, and no one can take that away from me. I now have a degree in business management and a lucrative career doing what I love. I'm pretty damn proud of myself."

She sighs as she strums the guitar. "Music brings me joy, but it doesn't complete me. It doesn't make me whole like it does you." She stares out at the crashing waves. "I'm good, Lex, I've come to peace with my parents, my career choice. I miss my dad every day, but I know he's in my heart."

I grab her hand, giving it a gentle squeeze. "Sarah, you amaze me. You've always been such a bright ray of sunshine even with all the shit you've been dealt. I'm sorry if I've ever made you feel less than happy."

She squeezes my hand back, then pulls away. "It's okay." She looks down at the strings on the guitar as she glides her fingers over them. "Enough about me." She smiles brightly.

I study her for a minute. "You hide behind that beautiful smile, don't you?"

"Sometimes it's easier to. Sunshine always follows the rain, doesn't it?" She shrugs and strums the guitar again. I want to reach over and tuck her into my heart. "So…*Trolls* huh? Badass Lex Ryan's favorite movie is a kid's cartoon. I was thinking more along the lines of *John Wick* or *Mission Impossible*."

I laugh, letting her change the subject. "I'm gonna kill that gombeen Connor." I shrug. "I guess I'm a sucker for Princess Poppy. She's upbeat and positive, she saves the troll kingdom, she loves to sing, and she has a secret thing for grumpy Branch."

"Ha! I think it's the other way around. Branch has a thing for her. She just wants all the hugs."

I chuckle. "She does love to hug. I know I'll never hear the end of it from Kiki."

Sarah giggles. "No, you won't. So where's Alana?"

"Back at her hotel. I asked her not to come tonight. My mum isn't too fond of her."

"Why is that? I mean every time your brother sees her he's spitting nails."

I take the guitar back from her, needing to do something with my hands. "Alana and I were engaged, as you know. We never got married. Turns out she was messing around with several other guys the whole time we were together."

Her eyes widen. "Shit. I'm so sorry, Lex."

"Yeah, I found her with another guy the night before our wedding."

"Oh my god," Sarah gasps.

"I went into a tailspin after that. Moved to Los Angeles to get away from here. Got involved with a rock band and started abusing drugs to numb the pain. It got pretty bad." I take a sip of my beer as I reflect on those dark days. "My brother was visiting and he found me one night after a gig face-down in my apartment. I had accidentally overdosed on a concoction of crap after a surprise visit from Alana. He apparently freaked out and rushed me to the hospital. I would have died if he hadn't found me."

I look over at Sarah and see tears running tracks down her cheeks.

"Don't cry, Love, I'm here." I wipe her cheek with my thumb. "So my family blames Alana for causing duress during that time. She wouldn't leave me alone and that's why I had to move to the States, to get away from her, then she followed me there and I spiraled out of control."

"What made you move to Nashville?"

"I had to get out of LA. It was too toxic for me. I moved to Nashville not knowing a soul after I finished treatment. I met Matt and Will through an ad in the paper. They were looking for a lead guitarist for their band. We hit it off and then we picked up Tatum after our lead singer quit, and the rest is history."

"Do you still have feelings for her?" she asks, biting her thumbnail.

"I feel an obligation to make sure she's okay while on this tour with us." I look out over the water and listen to the waves crashing. "My brother doesn't get it. She turned pretty ugly after we broke up and I can't forget that," I muse. "I have nostalgic feelings for the way we were before I found out she cheated on me, because those were happy memories for me." I look over at Sarah. "But I don't have romantic feelings for her…no."

"But you were kissing her."

"Aye, and I'm so sorry you saw that. She pretty much threw herself at me. I'm actually glad it happened because it made me realize how much I didn't want her, and how much I longed for someone else."

"Oh." She swallows. "And what about all the other women…"

"What about them?"

"Do you have feelings for any of them?"

I snort. "No, Sarah, they were just a distraction for me, a stress reliever. I don't do relationships anymore."

"I see."

I shake my head as I put my heart on the line despite my head telling me not to. "I want to try with you."

"Oh."

"I'm not making promises, but I'll try. Would you be willing to take that step with me?"

She nods, her chin quivering.

I stand up and reach my hand toward her as Kane Brown's "Live Forever" starts to play on my phone. She puts her hand in mine, looking up at me quizzically. I bring her to her feet.

"Dance with me, *Mo Ghrá*?" I ask gruffly. She arches an eyebrow. "It means my love."

This song speaks directly to my heart as I hold her in my arms. I sing along as I stare into her whiskey-amber eyes, our bodies moving together. The breeze whips around us. It's just her and I in this moment together; no one can butt in or interrupt us. I breathe in her light strawberry scent and all my problems melt away.

The song ends but I still hold her. I can no longer hold my feelings for her at bay, nor do I want to. I tuck a lock of hair behind her ear. "I'm going to kiss you."

"Okay," she breathes out.

I dip down and brush my lips along hers. She parts hers allowing me entrance and I greedily accept her invite. I hold her in place as I devour her, hungry for all the times I've wanted to do this since that first day I saw her in the coffee shop.

She moans and the sound completely undoes me. I groan as I take from her, our tongues clashing as her body melts against mine. Her fingers thread through my hair as I drag my hands down her side causing her to shiver as I palm her ass. I'm so hard for her I'm aching. I lift her up and her legs wrap around my waist. I move her against the French doors as we frantically grope and kiss each other. I lift her top up and gently graze my fingers over her breast, thumbing her nipple. She moans and arches into me.

"Yes." She sighs as I lower her delicate lacy bra cup. She's sweet as strawberries as I bend down to suckle her nipple.

She grips my hair hard. "Jesus."

"Sunshine, can we take this inside?"

"Hell yes…no…I mean yes…gah."

I pull back and look at her in confusion. "So that's a…yes?" My lip cocks up in an unsure smile.

She takes a deep breath and looks into my eyes. "You're clean, right?"

"Yes, Love. I've never not worn a condom and I get tested regularly." I kiss her nose.

"Okay, me too." She lifts her chin up. "One more thing. I swear to God, Lex, if you stop and tell me you aren't the right guy for me, or wake up and decide you made a huge mistake, I will smother you with a pillow in your sleep. Are we clear?"

I huff out a laugh. "We're clear. We'll go at your pace, Princess, and I won't stop until you tell me to. I'm tired of denying myself. I just can't do it anymore."

"There is a God," she mumbles into my neck as I carry her into her room. I lay her down on the soft cloud-like comforter and she looks like a fucking angel spread out against the white duvet. I hover over her as I drink her in. Her lips are swollen from my kisses, her neck red from where my cheek scraped against her delicate skin. She's perfect, and just for this moment, she's mine.

I gently kiss her, but she pushes against me as she sits up to quickly pull her shirt off and then pulls off her leggings. She's wearing a black lace demi cup and matching panties. I can't help but stare like a total creeper. She's stunning.

"Lex?"

"Yeah?"

"Touch me?"

"Shit, yeah." I almost come in my pants at her request. She makes me feel like a teenager crushing on my first girl.

I slowly lower her bra cups so her perky full breasts are on display. I lean down and nibble on one tender bud as she cries out, arching into me. My other hand massages the other breast, begging for my attention. I move my hand down to her panties, pushing the silky material aside, and glide a finger into her. She's so wet and warm and it's just for me. She moans and cries out my name as I curl my finger dragging it slowly in and out as I rub her clit with my thumb. I can feel her building as I pump in and out.

"I need to taste you, Princess." My voice sounds ragged to my own ears. I gently lay kisses along her body as I move south and slowly peel down her lace. She's wet and glistening just for me.

I put my lips on her and tenderly suck as she writhes and pants my name. I lap her up while her fingers sift through my hair and yank hard. She screams my name as she crests her wave and comes into my mouth. It's the fucking hottest thing I have ever experienced. Who knew my sweet girl was a screamer?

I hastily remove my jeans as she comes down off her high and sheathe myself with a condom I grab from my back pocket. Once again I position myself over her and look into her glassy eyes. Nothing is more intoxicating to me than a thoroughly orgasmed Sarah. "Is this okay?" I ask, hoping to

God it is, but understanding if she's not ready. She trails her fingers down my abdomen, her touch igniting my skin with lust and desire.

"Jesus, yes, hurry up!"

I chuckle as I slowly lower down onto one elbow and guide myself into her. Her tight warmth and wetness feels like heaven. Like the present I've always wanted on Christmas day, cozy nights in front of a fire…coming home. I'm not going to lie, I've been with a lot of women, but this feels different. I try not to dwell on that last thought as I pump in and out of her. I can feel her orgasm building again as she tightens around me.

"You feel so fucking good, Sarah. You're fucking everything I've ever wanted." I lean down and suck on her nipple because I can't get enough of her as I feel her tightening around my dick. "Oh god, I'm going to come, Princess. Come with me. *Ceann álainn,*"—so beautiful.

She comes hard just as I release into her. "*A Thaisce, Mo Cuishle,*" I murmur as I bury my face in her neck. *So fucking beautiful, my treasure, my pulse.*

Coming with her is like free-falling out of an airplane. Helpless, out of control, a high I don't want to come down from. And when I hit the ground, I want to get right back up there and do it again.

Chapter 24

Sarah

I SLOWLY OPEN my eyes as morning light streams through the open window. I'm having a déjà vu moment as I leisurely stretch. I turn away from the bright light reflecting off the water and come face to face with the most beautiful man on the planet. His broad chest rises up and down as he slowly breathes in and out. His lips are slightly apart and his five o'clock shadow no longer a shadow, but more of a scruff. I want to reach out and trace my fingers along his beautiful lips, but I don't want to wake him just yet. I want to stare at him like a total stalker in case last night wasn't real.

Was last night real? I lift the comforter up and sure enough I'm naked, and yep…pretty tender down there. It's the best feeling in the world. A huge smile overtakes my face as I inwardly sigh thinking about the hot sex we had last night. Hands down, Lex Ryan is the best lover I've ever had. Not that I've had a ton, but he puts my past boyfriends to shame. I've never had multiple orgasms before. Hell, I've never had sex multiple times in one night! It's like he's insatiable, and I'm totally onboard with trying to satisfy his voracious appetite.

And did he really say he wanted to try a relationship with me? I almost burst into tears last night when he said that. I'm not sure what that entails, but I'm willing to put my heart on the line for him.

"Are you going to stare at me all morning, Princess?" he says gruffly, his eyes remaining closed.

"How did you… I wasn't staring."

He grins. "As long as you aren't plotting my death, I'm okay with it."

"Okay, you got me. I was deciding which pillow would be the fluffiest to smother you with."

His grin turns into a full-wattage smile—bright white straight teeth and that cute little dimple. His black hair sticking up in all directions makes me want to run my fingers through it. He's so damn handsome he should have been a model. He hums in pleasure when I trace the Celtic cross on his shoulder.

"Do you always wake up this pretty?" I'm ninety-nine percent sure my hair has turned into a rat's nest and I have raccoon eyes since I never washed my face last night, not to mention morning breath.

"Always."

I gently shove him and laugh. "Jerk."

I run my hand down his washboard abs and follow his sexy little happy trail, and oh my, *hello*, he's super hard. I wrap my hand around his impressive length and he hisses out a breath. He feels like silk and steel. How the hell did this thing fit inside me last night? I look back up at him and grin as I run my hand up and down again and squeeze him. His breathing is shallow and his eyes are hooded.

"Jesus woman, you're going to be the death of me."

Feeling empowered by his reaction, I move the comforter down and slowly lick him from base to tip.

"Christ." He clenches the covers and thrusts up toward my mouth. I take him into my mouth as he growls in pleasure, his reaction spurring me on. He wraps his fist around my hair. "I'm not going to last long."

I continue to pump his base with my hand while I suck and swirl my tongue around him faster.

"Shit, I'm coming," he grunts as he comes into my mouth and I take it all until he stops. His fist lets my hair go and I gingerly get out of bed as I wink at him and go to the bathroom to clean up and brush my teeth.

Suddenly I feel his warmth behind me as I put my toothbrush in my mouth. He wraps his arms around me and kisses the crook of my neck. He pulls me back into his chest and my eyes widen in the mirror as I stare at him.

"Already?" I say around a mouthful of toothpaste. "That has to be a record."

He grins devilishly. "It's been two years that I've been wantin' to do this to ye, I'm making up for lost time."

"You've been wanting to do this to me for two years?" I ask, completely dumfounded.

"From the moment I saw you." He licks up the side of my neck and my thighs clench.

"I'm not going to be able to walk." I chuckle as I rinse my mouth.

"Good." He runs a hand down my spine, gently pushing

me toward the vanity.

"Um, what's…oh…okay." His other hand reaches around and he strums his fingers back and forth over my clit. He dips two fingers in.

"So wet and ready, just for me," he rasps in my ear, turning me on even more.

He rubs the slickness over me, teasing me until my legs shake. "Bend over, Princess."

I hold on to the vanity as he tears a condom wrapper and quickly sheathes himself, but he doesn't fill me quite yet. He continues to finger me as his other hand tweaks my nipple. I'm panting as I meet his gaze in the mirror. "Please, Lex."

He runs a palm over my ass as his other hand grips my side. He slowly enters me from behind, and Jesus, it feels incredible. He rubs my clit in tight little circles as he moves in and out of me, watching our reflections. His dark against my light.

"Look at me, Love," he rasps as my eyes meet his piercing blues. I watch him pump in and out of me, watch him possess me, making my body his. His eyes are like a kaleidoscope of blues as they turn from light to dark. I smile at him in the mirror because I see the affect I have on him. In this moment, I own him completely. It is the hottest thing I have ever witnessed.

"Oh god, you feel so good, so tight," he says through clenched teeth.

I moan as he moves in and out slowly. "Faster, Lex. I want it fast and hard."

"Shit, Sarah, I'll fuck you fast and hard if that's what you want." He growls. "Grab the sink."

"Yes!" I moan as he slams into me faster.

And he makes good on his promise, so much so that I'm seeing black and blue stars as my orgasm unravels. I yell out his name as I come. He holds me up as he continues to slam into me, my purchase on the sink slipping as he thrusts. He comes hard quickly after me. I'm left feeling completely spent as he holds me up against him, his dick still pulsing inside me. He pulls out slowly and removes the condom. I miss the feeling of him immediately.

He lifts me up and I squeal as he brings us into the large stone shower. He turns the taps on making me shriek again as cold water shoots out.

"Geez Lex, now there's a mood-killer." I laugh as the water quickly heats up. He smiles, pulling me into his embrace. Standing naked against Lex's body, I quickly melt into him as we kiss.

"Who knew my little ray of sunshine was a dirty-talking screamer?" He grins.

"I didn't scream." I bashfully duck my head. He takes my chin and lifts my face until my eyes meet his.

"I liked it. No, I fucking loved it."

I feel my cheeks heat and I smile. "Okay."

"Okay." He gently kisses my lips.

"Lex?"

"Yes, Sunshine?"

"I think I need an ice pack."

His laughter rumbles against my chest as he releases me and we rinse off. "I'll get Maggie to pack you one."

"Good god, no!" I shudder at the thought. "Oh, top of the mornin' to ya, Mrs. Ryan. Can I have an ice pack? Your son and I did dirty things *all* night long, and now my vajayjay needs a cooldown."

Lex laughs as he shampoos my hair. "She probably heard us anyway, so she wouldn't even blink an eye."

"Wait, what?"

"Well, you're not exactly quiet, *mo álainn*."

"Oh great. Top of the mornin' to ya, Mrs. Ryan. What's that? Oh you heard me last night? Yes, your son and I fucked hard and dirty *all* night long. Hope we didn't keep you up! Thanks for the ice pack."

He chuckles. "First of all, we're not Leprechauns. We don't start off each sentence with top of the morning." He smirks as he massages shampoo into his hair while I rinse off. "Second, my mum is an adult. She knows I have sex."

I can't stop staring at him. I pinch myself to make sure I'm really watching Lex Ryan taking a shower, naked, in front of me…on purpose. Water beads down his magnificent sculpted chest and my legs quiver. For two years I've longed for this moment. Yearned for it, fantasized about it, and it's everything and more than I thought it would be. You'd think I would have this realization the four times we had sex, but nope, it hits me like a ton of bricks watching him shower.

He rubs soap under his arms and gives me a goofy smile. "What?"

I quickly avert my gaze and rub soap along my arms. "Uh, nothing." Heat crawls up my neck and cheeks knowing I just made this weird, but my anxiety only lasts about two seconds.

"Can you do my back?"

"Sure."

Hell yes I can wash your back! Lex and I are *finally* together and I'm washing his back! *Yes!*

"It's not a big deal, Sunshine. Don't look so shell-shocked. Like I said, we're adults."

I shake myself out of my stupor. Am I really that obvious that I'm freaking excited to wash his back? "Erm, what's not a big deal?"

"You being loud."

Oh right, me being loud during sex, because that's not humiliating. "Oh…um, right, but still mortifying if your mom and dad heard me." I shudder at the thought. "You must bring out the beast in me…I mean *best!* The *best* in me."

Jesus, where's the duct tape when you need it? Lex smiles as he rinses off and I furiously lather soap over my legs hoping it will wash away my humiliation.

We finish showering and Lex grabs his clothes and heads for the door leading to the deck to get back to his room. He quickly turns around and kisses my tender lips. "See you at breakfast, Princess."

What's that term everyone uses in romance novels? *Swoon?* I am fucking hard-core swooning right now as I flop down on my unmade bed. I can still smell him on the sheets and I roll around happily kicking my feet. I have sex sheets, and they belong to Lex Ryan! I giggle as I do snow angels on my newly christened sheets. I want to shout it from the rooftops, but let's be honest, no one really wants to hear that, especially his mom.

I sigh as I look up at the ceiling. "Lex Ryan is a sex god."

"Is he now?"

"Do tell!"

"Agh!" I quickly try and cover myself with the thin sheet. "Shit, you guys, you scared me!" TJ and Kiki jump on the bed next to me. "How did you get in here?"

"Um, opened the door and walked in? What are sex sheets?" Kiki looks down and then up at TJ. "Oh my god, gross, Sarah!" They both bounce as quickly as possible off the bed and fight over the chair in the corner of my room.

"Move your big ass over," Kiki growls as TJ pushes her off the chair.

"You guys!" I shout, restoring order. "Jesus, you're worse than toddlers. You're going to wake everyone up!"

"It's nine AM and we're heading out soon, so we thought we'd come wake up Sleeping Beauty."

"Yeah, who knew we were waking up Jenna Jameson?" TJ wags his eyebrows.

"She's not a porn star, Tammy Jean. Oh My God, can you imagine if we would have walked in on them?" Kiki looks aghast.

"I would have taken pictures," TJ says. They high-five each other.

I growl, growing more irritated with them with each second that ticks by. "Okay guys, give me five minutes and I'll meet you in the kitchen."

The both stare at me blankly and then start laughing. "As if! We're not leaving until we get the 411," TJ says saucily as he gets up to shut the door.

Kiki rolls her eyes. "Seriously Sare, this isn't something you keep to yourself. You know we won't stop until you give us some golden nuggets of info."

I look at them calmly and shrug knowing I won't get rid

of the nosy pests. "Okay, I'll tell you." I get up and grab a t-shirt from my bag and pull it over my head. "His dick is really small and disappointing. Like a shriveled-up snap pea. He grunts like a pig when we make love and then makes this weird hyena sound when he comes. He's kinky too. He asked if he could pee on me in the shower."

I turn my back as I slide on a pair of skinny jeans, smiling to myself as they take it all in. Suddenly a pillow whizzes by my head causing me to lose my balance and fall to the floor.

"Fine, don't tell us," Kiki pouts. "But tell me one thing, is he like monster-truck big? Where that thing just runs over anything that gets in its way? I feel like he would be."

"Does size really matter?" I bite back a smile as I sit up and locate my shoes.

"Oh my god!" TJ whispers dramatically. "He's more like a Prius isn't he? The dull blue kind that only gets up to 55 mph on the highway and needs a plug-in to recharge."

"What on earth are you talking about and why are we comparing Lex's dick to cars?" I laugh and smile to myself as I sit down on the bed and slip on my Converse.

"More like a Bugatti. Sexy, luxurious, but still a sleek beast."

Silence hangs in the air as Lex leans in the doorframe with his arms crossed over his chest. He looks incredibly sexy in just a black t-shirt and jeans. I'm pretty sure my face is purple as I die from embarrassment.

I steal a quick glance over at TJ and Kiki, and I might need a crane to pick their jaws up off the floor.

"Ready for breakfast, Princess?" Lex winks at me.

I jump off the bed. "Yup! Let's go!" I can hear Kiki and TJ try to smother their laughter as they trail behind us.

"So, Lex, how much of that conversation did you hear?" Kiki pipes up.

Lex looks down at me and smirks. "Pee on you in the shower? Really? That's some nasty shit there, Sunshine." I groan in embarrassment as Kiki and TJ die laughing all over again as we walk into the kitchen.

"What's so funny?" Lex's mom is swinging her ample bottom to the beat of Def Leppard's "Pour Some Sugar On Me" as she flips a pancake.

"Oh geez, Ma, do we really have to listen to this crap in the morning?"

"Take a seat, my little starkeeper. You know I've got to get my sugar on." She sets a plate down on the table as she winks at me.

Oh Jesus, did she really hear me?

"You okay, Sarah? You look like a tomato," Kiki observes as she shovels bacon onto her plate. I kick her under the table. "Owe! No reason to get violent. Just a concerned friend asking."

"Don't let her fool you, she's only concerned about herself," TJ interjects as he pours orange juice. "Owe!"

"Ma, do you have any coffee?" Lex gets up and kisses his mom's cheek as he reaches for the French press.

"What? No tea? You've become too Americanized," she gripes as she passes him the cream.

"Aye, I know. Coffee, Love?" He pours me some coffee before kissing the top of my head. I'm not used to this soft affectionate side of Lex and it's throwing me for a loop.

Kiki grins at me from across the table. Feeling self-conscious, I steal a glance at his mom but she's by the stove smiling to herself as she hums along with the music. Matt and Will roll into the kitchen next, bright and cheery.

"Hey everyone. Looks good, Mrs. R!" Will sits down at the table and grabs the sausage platter.

Matt slides onto the bench across from me. "Morning, Sunshine." He spoons fruit onto his plate and passes the bowl to me.

"Morning, Matt." I smile, feeling a little weird that he's just singling me out. I catch him looking at me as I shove a strawberry in my mouth. "What?"

"Nothing." He shrugs looking suddenly constipated. His gaze flickers over to Lex and back to me.

"What, Matt? You're weirding me out." Oh crap, did he hear me too? I feel like if I blush any more my cheeks will remain permanently red. Lex is staring at Matt like he wants to rip his head off. His jaw visibly ticking.

"Pissant, stop staring at her," Lex growls.

Matt puts his hands up in surrender. "I'm not."

Tatum walks into the kitchen breaking the weird tension at the table. "So I think if we head out in an hour we should make it there by three." He checks his phone totally unaware of everything that's happening at the table. "Lee, Jess, and Jimmie will meet us in Glasgow at the hotel. TJ, Jimmie was able to secure you and Connor rooms at the hotel."

"Why is Connor coming?" Lex looks confused as he looks up from his food.

"Uh…" Tatum shifts uncomfortably in his seat and looks over at TJ.

Lex follows his eyes and you can actually see him snapping the puzzle pieces together by the astonishment on his face. "Connor and TJ?"

"Surprise!" TJ does jazz hands.

"You've got to be fucking kidding me… *TJ?*"

Lex's mom comes over and places her hands on TJ's shoulders. "Oh Lex, *ná bí i do leanbh.*[4] I think he's perfect for Connor."

"Awe, thank you, Maggie." TJ smiles up at her as he pats her hand.

"And you know that in the three hours you talked to him last night?" he questions. "Am I in a fucking *Twilight Zone* episode? What the fuck is going on? Does everyone know but me?"

Everyone avoids Lex's gaze except Matt and Will. "Uh, I didn't even know your brother was gay, dude," Will says innocently.

"Tatum, even *you* knew?"

"Ah shit, Kiki might have mentioned it last night."

TJ glares at Kiki. "You've been demoted as best friend."

"Hey everyone, what's going on? Oh no, Ma has Def Leppard on again…" Connor enters the kitchen and bends to kiss his mom on the cheek.

"Oh just filling Lex in on your new boyfriend, *A Pheata*[5]," Maggie says cheerfully as she starts collecting plates.

Connor looks aghast at everyone around the table, his gaze finally landing on his brother.

---

[4] Irish for Don't be a child.

[5] Irish for darling.

He shrugs. "Well, guess the cat's out of the bag now." He sits down next to TJ and smiles.

"But it's been like two days!" Lex sputters.

Connor levels Lex with a stony look. "Well, when you know, you know."

"So does this mean you're openly gay now?"

"Lex Finlay Ryan! Watch yourself," Maggie admonishes him.

"It seems so. Got a problem with that?" Connor's angry expression mirrors Lex.

Lex blanches. "No, I don't have a fucking problem with that. I can't believe you'd even think that. What I have a problem with is that everyone at this fucking table knows you're all of a sudden 'in a relationship' except for your goddamn fucking twin brother! Fucking Facebook probably knows before me!" Lex yells as he gets up from the table and stalks toward the kitchen door. He slams the door as he heads outside.

"I didn't know," Will says quietly.

Connor sighs and gets up from the table. "I'll go talk to him."

I fold my napkin and stand up. "You eat your breakfast. I'll go see if he's okay."

Connor stares at me for a beat, then nods. "Thanks, Sare."

"What bee stung his butt?" Kiki asks the table as I take my plate.

"He's always moody like that," Matt says around a mouthful of pancake.

I bring my plate over to Maggie who's washing the dishes

to give Lex a little more time to calm down. "Can I help you, Maggie?"

"Oh no, my love, I only get to do this once in a blue moon."

"Wash dishes?" I smile.

She laughs. "No, clean up after my boys and their friends…and their loved ones." She winks at me.

"Can I ask, why do you call him starkeeper?"

"Ah, when Lex was a boy, he loved to go fishing with Finn. He learned the constellations before he learned his alphabet. He had a fascination with the stars. Any good sailor does. Finn and I always knew he was going to become famous someday. He just had that drive in him. He was our little starkeeper, figuratively and literally."

She winks at me as she washes. "Some nights I sit out on our back deck and look at the stars and I like to think he's looking at them too, wherever he is. Makes me feel closer to him."

My heart feels happy and sad for Maggie all at once. I feel her love for her son, but I also feel her sorrow that he's so far from them. She smiles at me as I dry her finished dishes.

"Go slowly with that one and have lots of patience. You're gonna need it, *Mo ghrá beag,* my little love."

"How did you know…"

"I know everything." She winks at me as she turns back to the sink.

I FIND LEX sitting on a teak wooden bench on the backside of the house in a beautiful colorful garden overlooking the ocean. Butterflies flit and swirl around, bees buzzing from one flower to the next. The ocean's waves break on the craggy cliffs below. It's incredibly peaceful.

"Can I join you?" I ask cautiously.

"I'm not good company right now, Sunshine."

I hesitate, knowing he doesn't mince words, but I also know right now he just needs a quiet hand to hold. "It's okay, we don't have to talk."

He sighs and pats the seat next to him. I sit down and breathe in the salty air, closing my eyes. A couple minutes go by in companionable silence, just the waves crashing on the rocky cliffs below and the sound of Lex flipping a guitar pick through his fingers.

"I'm his brother, for fuck's sake. I should've been the first one he told."

"You're hurt."

"Hell yes, I'm hurt." He sighs running his fingers through his hair as he bends forward and puts his elbows on his knees. "We used to tell each other everything."

"What changed that?"

"When I moved away, we became distant...after my overdose."

"I'm sorry, Lex."

He shakes his head dismissing old memories, giving me a crooked smile. "I mean, TJ? No offense, but he's totally opposite of my brother."

"Well, I know TJ is a lot to take." He lifts one eyebrow and I laugh. "But on the inside he's a super sweet caring guy.

I'd want him in my corner if I had to choose. He flew all the way to Ireland because I needed him. He's pretty special."

"Why did you need him?" He peers over at me.

"Let's just say there was this Irish guy and he was confusing the hell out of me. I needed my friends to get me through."

He sends me a guilty smile as he nods. "Aye, that's a good friend."

"Maybe your opinion matters most to your brother and he didn't want to say anything until he was sure TJ was someone worth telling you about."

"Yeah, I guess." He rubs his scruffy jawline. "I just wish I hadn't been blindsided. I hate being blindsided."

"Yeah, I get that." I pull his hand into mine and thread my fingers with his. "But he's your brother and now you've got to embrace it."

"God, I'm a fucking mess. Are you sure you want to get involved with me?" He smiles ruefully at me.

I return his smile. "I like a good challenge. Life gets boring without them." I lean into his side and he kisses the top of my head.

"Thanks, Sunshine." He pulls me closer and softly kisses my lips as I look up at him. His nose dips into my neck and he kisses me right below my ear. He takes a deep breath and his whole body relaxes against me. "You always smell like strawberries and cream," he murmurs against my neck.

I laugh. "It's my body wash and shampoo. Strawberries wild."

"That's the perfect name. It makes me so hard," he groans. His lips find mine again. "And I'm really sorry I confused you. You weren't the only one. Are you still feeling muddled?" He nibbles my ear as I sigh, raking my fingers up into his hair.

"No. Are you?"

"Not one bit."

"Eh-hem." Kiki loudly clears her throat, making me jump. I push back from Lex. "I knew you two would be having sex. Leaving in five."

"We weren't having se—" but she's already disappeared behind the hedge.

Lex smirks at me. "Too bad we're leaving, it would be a great place for sex."

I playfully shove him. "Yeah, at least the waves crashing would drown me out. Come on, Romeo, I've got to finish packing."

"Hey, Sunshine?"

"Yeah?"

"Thanks, Love."

I smile at him as I freaking swoon. "Always, Lex."

Chapter 25

Sarah

"Okay so I've been doing some thinking…like different ways we could spice up the blog."

I arch my eyebrow at Kiki as she shoves a chip into her mouth. We're in Tate's dressing room waiting while the guys are at a meet-and-greet in the Glasgow venue. I reach across the coffee table and grab a celery stick from the veggie platter.

"Wait, where is Jess?"

"I think she's backstage."

"Okay, good. So, these thoughts kind of popped in my head, and I thought these would make great first-date conversation starters, but they're kind of…I don't know, different."

"Okay, let's hear one."

She claps her hands giddily. "Okay, like, why is it when you taste something really bad you want someone else to try it? Or have you ever been super gassy during sex and scared you might let one escape? It's the worst! I mean here you are trying to be all intimate and sexy and you have this bubbling feeling that needs to—"

"*These* are the thoughts you're having?" I just stare at her wondering what alien abducted my friend Kiki.

"Yeah, or the merits of waxing down there or not—"

I hold up my hand cutting her off. "No question. Always wax."

"But what if you can't afford to wax?"

"Then you shave."

"But what if you get bumps from shaving. Then what?"

"Then you forgo the sixty-dollar weekly purchase at Target or give up your daily lattes and go get a damn wax, or you do it yourself."

"Don't shop at Target and no lattes? That's a travesty. I'm just saying, studies have shown—"

"Nope. This discussion is over. The term 'bush' only belongs down in Australia."

Kiki chews on her pen top. "So, these are good, right? You know sometimes it's hard to start a convo if the guy is a total dud and can't form a sentence. I should totally put them on the blog."

"Uh no, you shouldn't. You should keep these little *thoughts* between us."

"Awe, really? Too weird?"

I nod my head slowly. "Too weird and gross. I don't know what guy on a first date would want to know about your gas issues during sex and whether you prefer waxing or not."

"Well damn." Kiki chews on her lip as she contemplates God-knows-what else and then dives in for another chip.

"These chips are *so* good."

Someone knocks on the door. "Seriously, have you been smoking pot?"

"Who me? I don't do that stuff."

"Well, yeah I know, but you're acting weird."

"I'm PMSing. Why do I feel like I could inhale this whole bag of chips? There's another one! Why do you want to inhale every salty and chocolatey thing when you're PMSing?"

"It's called hormones, and I'm pretty sure your date doesn't want to hear about your PMS cravings or your gas. Keep it between us, Socrates."

Kiki shrugs as I open the door. Four giggling scantily clad women greet me.

"Is this Tatum's room?" a busty blonde asks.

"And Lex?" the brunette behind her pipes up.

I flash them a plastic smile. "No, sorry." I close the door in their faces. Usually I'm a lot nicer to eager fans looking for the guys, but now that Lex and I have gotten together, I'm not feeling as helpful.

"Oh, hell no." Kiki gets up and charges the door. "Were those girls looking for our men?"

"Kiki, I wouldn—"

Kiki flings open the door and the girls are still milling about outside. They look at her with excited smiles. "Are you looking for Tatum Reed?"

"Yes!" they shout and giggle.

"Tatum James Reed, *my husband*, Tatum Reed? That one?"

The blonde has the decency to look ashamed. "We just

want an autograph."

"I'm sure you do," Kiki says drolly. "How did you get back here?"

"Is Lex in there?"

"No, Lex isn't in there, but *his girlfriend* is!"

"Kiki, I'm not his girlfriend," I pipe up from behind her shoulder. I don't want word getting back to Lex that I'm going around calling myself his girlfriend. I don't even know what I am to him. I'm taking this fragile thing we've found with each other and holding it with kid gloves.

"Who told you this was Tatum's dressing room? How did you get past security anyway?" Kiki folds her arms over her chest.

The blonde holds up her hands. "It was a woman, light brown hair, she said she was with the band. She told us to go to the dressing room and wait for the boys."

"Alana," Kiki says icily.

"We don't want any trouble." The blonde continues to back away, grabbing her giggling idiot friends.

"Wait!" The blonde looks at Kiki cautiously. Jimmie, Tatum's personal assistant, turns the corner walking down the cinderblock hallway toward us. "Jimmie, hey! Can you give these lovely ladies some pit passes for tonight? They are huge fans. Thanks!"

The girls start to squeal again. "Oh my god, that's deadly!"

Jimmie squints at Kiki and nods, escorting them down to the pit. "Here ladies, you'll need these badges."

Kiki shuts the door and leans against it. "That *bitch*!"

"Who, the blonde?"

"No, fucking Alana! She sent those girls back here to ambush our men."

"Ambush?"

"Sarah, get your head out of your ass, they *wanted* to have sex with Tatum and Lex! Alana let them in!"

"Why would she do that?"

Kiki stomps her foot in frustration. "To fuck with us!"

"Really?" I look at her dubiously. "That's pretty petty."

"Hellooo? She's pissed you're Lex's girlfriend now."

"I'm not Lex's girlfriend. It's been like two days of amazing sex, but he doesn't do relationships…I don't know what we are."

Kiki chews on her thumbnail as she flings herself onto the couch. "Okay, as much as I want to bang my head against the wall over that statement, I can't think about that right now. First thing we need to take care of is Skanklana."

The door swings open and Tatum strides in with a big smile on his face. "Ladies, care to tell me why Jimmie had to finagle four pit passes for some boisterous fans?"

I point my index finger at Kiki.

"Have I told you how hot you look in those jeans, Tater Tot?"

He arches his eyebrow at her and folds his arms over his chest.

"Ugh, okay fine. Alana sent slutty fans to your dressing room and I may or may not have gotten a little territorial. I asked Jimmie to give them the passes because Kimberly always tells me to soothe a crazy fan with something that will make them happy."

Tatum nods. "Next time come find me or Lee. I don't

want anyone getting hurt, especially you." He kisses the tip of her nose as they gaze lovingly into each other's eyes. "Sarah, do you mind…"

"Yup! I'm out!" I laugh as I leave the two love birds alone in the dressing room.

I close the door and head down the hallway toward Lex, Matt, and Will's dressing room. I can hear laughter and voices. I knock on the door and then gently push it open when no one responds. I walk in and my smile slides off my face. A crowd of scantily dressed women and a few men are buzzing all around the room. My attention goes to the women, sloshing their drinks and fawning over the three members of the band. Kiki would have a stroke if she saw this. Alana is on the couch with a cocktail chatting with a fan sitting on Matt's lap. I spot Lex on the other side of the room cornered by two women while he drinks a beer, smiling at something they say. One of them trails her fingernail down his chest, while the other leans up on his shoulder. I want to rip that cheap press-on nail right off her finger. I quickly step back toward the door hoping to escape before anyone notices me.

"Leaving so soon, Sarah?" Alana sneers.

Lex's eyes collide with mine. He smiles when he sees me, but it quickly slips as he excuses himself. I turn to leave, but he catches my arm before I can grasp the handle. I don't want him to see the hurt in my eyes.

"Sunshine…let's go outside." He opens the door and gently propels me to the wall outside the door. It's quieter out here in the hallway, but there are still a lot of people milling about waiting for the concert to start. He leans his forehead to mine and breathes in deeply. "Say something."

"What do you want me to say?" I quickly blink back the glaze of tears I feel advancing, my nose prickling.

He tilts my chin up and wipes away a traitorous lone tear that escapes. "Hey, what's wrong? Did someone upset you?"

I huff out a bitter laugh. "No, Lex, no one has upset me."

"Are you unhappy because you saw me talking to those women? I was just talking, Sarah." I nod as his thumbs gently rub back and forth along my cheeks. "They're just fans and they've paid a lot of money for a private meet-and-greet. I promise they mean nothing to me, Love. It's like a fucking knife to my heart that I made you sad."

I press my palms to his chest. "It's not you, it's just…I was caught off guard. I'm okay."

He kisses my forehead and I die a little inside. "*Mo chailín milis*, my sweet girl. I've got to get ready. Stay with me tonight?"

"Okay…yes." I concentrate on the open buttons of his shirt. If I look him in the eyes, he'll see that I'm falling apart. I can't fall apart. If I do, whatever it is that has started between us will go up in flames.

"Do you want to come back in with me?"

I shake my head. *Hell no I don't want to witness women fawning all over him right in front of me.* He kisses me softly on my temple and pushes away from the wall.

"Listen, I have to go back in there to wrap things up, but I promise you, you're the only one I'm thinking about. Come watch from my side of the stage, okay? I love knowing you're there for me."

I nod and smile as he goes back into the dressing room from hell. I collapse against the wall as tears leak out. I can't handle these feelings. I'm in love with him, I think I have been for the last two years…but his past is like a ghost that keeps haunting me. It's not a secret that he's a womanizer. Can I trust him? I want to…but then I see a woman flirting with him and my heart breaks apart allowing all the self-doubt to creep back in.

We haven't talked about monogamy or where this is going, it's all so new and incredible. All I know is he doesn't do relationships, and I don't know if my heart can survive that. I know he's trying for me, but at what point will he feel that it's not worth it? That I'm not worth it?

I mentally shake myself. I can't freak out every time an overzealous fan fawns all over him, because it's going to happen again. At the same time I want to put a tattoo on him that says, *Property of Sarah Bowen.* Kind of like Kiki just did with those fans.

Why can't I be more outspoken like her? I'm going to have to learn to trust him, otherwise this will never work. But it's going to be hard after two years of seeing him with different women hanging on him after every show.

I push off the wall in frustration and go look for Jess to see if she needs help, knowing I'm going to have to have this talk with him sooner or later.

Chapter 26

Lex

GLASGOW WAS A blast and now we are headed to England tomorrow for two shows before we head back to the States. As much as I loved seeing my brother and parents, I'm ready to get back home. My phone dings with a text from my brother.

Connor: *Fancy a few scoops downstairs before I head back?*

Me: *Always. Meet you in five.*

I grab my wallet and phone and head downstairs. My brother is already at the bar with two pints of beer. I slide onto the stool next to him and elbow him in the side.

"How are ye, ye feckin' donkey?" He slides me a tentative smile.

"Better than you since I'm the better-looking brother."

Connor smiles and takes a sip of his beer. "I'm Ma's favorite."

I laugh because it's true. She's always taken up for Connor, the more "sensitive" one. But I don't begrudge him for it. I was our dad's favorite which meant I spent less time being coddled in the kitchen and more time on the boat fishing with him.

"You guys sounded really good last night. I wish I could come to England with ye."

I take a sip of my beer and stare at the rugby game on TV. "Why can't ye?"

"Because I have a bar to run."

"You need to sell that place. It's a headache for ye."

"I'm waiting for ye to come back and help me run it."

I huff out a laugh. "Don't be a fuckin' eejit. You know that's not happenin'."

"I like Sarah."

I side-eye him. "That was a quick change of topic."

"Not really. I'm sure she's one of the reasons you won't come back home."

"Nashville's been my home for a while, ye know that."

"I miss ye, brother. Don't stay away so long this time."

"I miss ye too."

We sit in silence contemplating our lives. I hate that I live so far from my family.

I clear my throat. "I'm sorry I overreacted about TJ. He's a cool dude. A little weird, but cool."

Connor smirks. "He is weird, isn't he? He makes me laugh though. I know it's been quick and this will sound cliché, but there's something about him that just feels like my missing puzzle piece."

I grunt knowing exactly what he means because that's how I feel about Sarah. I haven't had a nightmare in the past three nights she's been with me. I feel at peace with her, and dammit if I'm not attracted to her even more than before, she's sexy as hell and smart and beyond beautiful.

"I get it bro. It's like all the chaos in your head stops when they're around and you just feel safe."

"Exactly." He arches an eyebrow. "Is that Sarah for you?"

I stare blankly back at the TV. Of all people in my life I should be able to tell my brother everything, but I'm tongue-tied. "I don't know what Sarah is. I'm feckin' scared. I don't wanna hurt her. These feelings I'm having terrify the living shite out of me. Love feels like a death grip on my balls. I don't know which way to turn, and it's making my feckin' vision blur."

"It does do that, doesn't it." Connor chuckles as he clinks his beer glass to mine.

"I'm just not sure she can handle my lifestyle and I don't want to break her. She's just so feckin' innocent, d'yaknow-whatimeanlike? Last night she walked into our dressing room and saw me talking to two female fans. She looked like she was going to fall apart. It killed me."

"Hm, that's tough. If you want it bad enough, you'll make it work. Communication and trust are key."

"The question is, does she want it bad enough? Love is feckin' complicated."

"Oye. Is my brother in love?"

I scoff and try to backtrack. "I didn't say love. What's love got to do with it? Pfft, love."

"Taking the Tina Turner route I see, ye feckin' eejit." Connor snorts and shakes his head. "*Sláinte*, ye tosser."

"*Sláinte*, ye spanner."

I'M HEADING TOWARD the plane when Tatum yells for me to wait up.

"Can we have a minute before we board?"

"Yeah mate, what's up?"

"What's going on between you and Sarah?"

Shit, twice in one day I'm being asked to explain my feelings and it irritates me. I run my hands through my hair. "I don't know what you mean."

Tatum gives me a steely look. "Cut the bullshit, Ryan. She's like a sister to me. Just…don't hurt her. She's not a one-night-stand kind of girl. Be honest and upfront with your intentions. Got it man?"

I nod and look over his shoulder as I clench my jaw. "Got it."

I understand where Tatum is coming from, but it still irks me. I'd never intentionally hurt Sarah and it bothers me that he thinks I would just toss her to the side like all the others.

Tatum nods and slaps the back of my head. "Okay. I love you, brother. I don't want to have to beat the shit out of you."

"It's cute you think you could, mate." I sling him into a headlock and give him a noogie. He elbows me in the side and thumps my back hard as we make our way up the stairs of the private jet.

As soon as I step into the galley a pretty flight attendant bats her eyelashes at me as she asks if she can get me anything I might desire. I ignore her eager question as I scan the plane until my eyes find my sunshine curled up on a loveseat with a blanket and a coffee.

"Uh, no, I'm good." I sweep by the dejected attendant and make my way to Sarah.

"Lex! Lexy, sit with me!" Alana pipes up to my left patting the seat next to her. I didn't even notice her on the plane. I internally sigh because I don't want to deal with her right now. Tatum told me about the girls she tried to have come to our dressing room and it pissed me off.

"Um, not right now, Alana. Sarah saved me a seat." I continue on, leaving her with her jaw hanging open. "Is this seat taken?" I dump my bag on the seat next to the loveseat.

Sarah looks up smiling at me. "Nope, unless you're going to snore and tell bad jokes."

I scoff as I sit next to her, pull her into me, and kiss her temple. "First of all, I don't snore. And second, my jokes are Comedy Central worthy."

I hear Kiki snort across the way. "Got something to say, *Coffee Girl?*"

"Nooope." She squirms in her seat as I stare her down. "Just that your jokes suck."

I throw a pillow at her head which makes Sarah giggle. Tatum comes walking down the aisle followed by Lee and Jess. "No gummy bears this trip." He points a finger at Kiki.

"Wait...is that why I had gummy bears stuck in my hair?" Sarah and Kiki suddenly become very quiet. I turn toward Sarah. "Did you put gummy bears in my hair?"

"On my life, I swear I did not." She snickers.

I arch my eyebrow at Kiki as I settle back against the

comfy couch. "Payback's a bitch, Coffee."

"Ooh, I'm scared." Kiki thumbs through her magazine pretending to ignore me.

I look over at Tatum and he smirks. "Every day of my life, dude."

"Where's TJ by the way?" Sarah whispers.

"He stayed back for a few days with Connor. He's going to meet us for the second show."

"Oh…how do you feel about that?"

"I'm good, I'm happy for them. He deserves to find love."

She nods and smiles, squeezing my arm. "I'm happy for them too."

Will and Matt are the last two to board, both wearing sunglasses and looking hungover.

"Jesus fucking Christ dude, did you get jumped last night by a vampire or what?" Tatum laughs at Matt. "Think you can cover that on his neck for tomorrow night's show, Sunshine?"

Matt quickly looks at Sarah like a deer caught in head-lights, his face turning beet-red. "It's nothing…it's just a bruise."

I throw a wolfish smile at Tatum. "With what, dude? Did she use a fucking sledgehammer?"

"I don't know, Matt. I might have to get the heavy-duty tattoo coverup out for that bad boy." Sarah smiles brightly at him as she puts earbuds in.

Matt covers his hickey with his hand mumbling that we're all assholes as he quickly moves to the back of the plane. I squeeze Sarah closer to me and breathe in her strawberry scent. I close my eyes and relax in her heady fragrance.

"Eh-hem. Lex, can I talk to you?"

Her voice is like nails down a fucking chalkboard. I don't bother opening my eyes.

"No."

"Lexy, stop being an ass. I *need* to talk to you," she pouts.

I open one eye, annoyed that she's still standing there with her arms crossed over her chest as she digs her heels in. "So, talk."

She looks over at Sarah who is engrossed in her magazine.

"She has her earbuds in. She can't hear whatever you have to say, so spit it out."

"I need privacy."

"Then whatever you want to say can wait until we get to England."

"Miss? I need you to take your seat and buckle up, please. The plane is taxiing," the stewardess says sternly to Alana.

She huffs and turns on her heel to return to her seat. I rest my head on Sarah's thigh and she smiles down at me as she runs her fingers through my hair. I close my eyes and hum in pleasure. It's so easy with Sarah. *So easy to fall in love with her.* My stomach clenches at the thought, my blood pumping through my veins faster as I realize I am already in love with her.

Chapter 27

Sarah

"Um, Sarah...got a second?"

I smile brightly. "Sure, Matt, come on in."

"Uh...think you can cover this up?"

I smother my laugh as he self-consciously puts a hand over his neck. "Sure thing, come sit down." He sits down in the chair and I peer down at the dark bruise on his neck. "She must have been a wildcat." I laugh.

"Uh yeah." He shifts uncomfortably in his seat. "Listen, um, I need to talk to you about something."

"Shoot."

"I don't really know how to say this."

"Whatever it is, you know you can talk to me."

He inhales deeply. "Okay, I know you feel something, uh...romantic for me...and I really care for you—"

"Whoa, slow your roll. What are you talking about?"

"You have a crush on me."

I snort out a laugh as I start to sponge makeup on his bruise. "I do? And where did you hear this from?" My mind is flipping through conversations like a rolodex as I try to figure out where he got this crazy idea from. Suddenly it dawns on me. *Fucking Kiki, I'm going to kill her.*

"It's not important. Look, you know I love you, but my feelings are more…"

"Like a brother-sister relationship?"

He lets out a relieved sigh. "Exactly, it would feel…"

"Incestuous?"

"Yes!" He smiles appreciatively.

I decide to play with Matt a little. I slide my arm around his neck and lean down to whisper in his ear. "That's a shame, Matt. You and I could have been really good together." I blow in his ear.

He shivers. "Ugh, no Sarah! I can't, you're beautiful and all…but just no! Besides, Lex would kill me."

I smile feeling a small sense of victory as I straighten back up and snap my gum. "I don't have a crush on you, Matt. I'm just messing with you. That would be gross."

"Oh, thank God… Wait, a minute, that's harsh. I'm a hot commodity."

I laugh as I dust powder over his neck. "I'm sure you are, and I love you like my brother, but that's as far as it goes. Whoever told you was mistaken."

He nods and releases his breath. "Good. Can we never speak of this again? And can you please not tell the guys? They'd never let me live it down."

"Yes, let's never speak of this again." I take the towel off from around his neck.

He looks at his hickey in the mirror. "Damn, you're good! Can't even see it."

"Hey, is this why you've been giving me creepy looks?" I arch an eyebrow at him.

"I don't give creepy looks."

"Who's giving who looks?" Lex says darkly from the door.

I smile brightly at him over my shoulder. "Hi babe! Just talking about Matt's hickey." *Did I just call him babe?* Lex strides over to me and wraps his arms around me, lifting me off the ground as he kisses me on the lips.

"Shit, I'm out. No need to mark your territory, Asswipe. We all know she's yours." Matt quickly exits the room as Lex smiles devilishly down at me.

"Do I need to kick Matt's arse, because I'd love to have an excuse."

"Uh, no, he's good."

"Did you call me babe?"

"Um..."

He squeezes me tighter. "I liked it. Makes me want to throw you down on this table and make you scream it." He runs his hand down my backside and cups my ass pulling me against his hard-on. This man can turn me on in zero point six seconds. The door suddenly bangs open.

"My eyes are covered! Please put on all articles of clothing and put a stop to THE SEX!" Kiki shouts as she blindly comes through the door with one hand outstretched in front of her and the other covering her eyes. Tatum follows behind her.

"I think you're safe, CG, they're just standing here."

"Are their clothes on?!"

"Why are you shouting?" I ask her as I start to put away

my makeup.

Kiki drops her hand. "Phew, Matt said you guys were getting your sexy on in here."

"Sorry to disappoint, Love." Lex winks at me. "See you on my side?"

"I'll be there." I smile.

He starts to leave with Tatum but then strides back over to me and whispers, "For Kiki…and also for me." Before I can question what he's talking about, he picks me up and sits me on the counter scattering makeup everywhere. He takes my face in his hands and roughly kisses me, his tongue parting my lips like he wants to devour me. My legs automatically wrap around his waist bringing him closer to me. I feel the kiss all the way to my toes and just as I want more, he gentles the kiss and licks my lips, leaving me panting.

Holy shit that was so hot.

"Seriously? A little warning next time? Are *we* that gross, Tater Tot?"

"You guys are worse." Lex smiles at me as he kisses my nose and leaves the room laughing with Tate.

Kiki looks over at me as I sit dazed on the countertop. "So, things are going good I see?"

I laugh and feel my cheeks heat. "I don't know? I think I'm in over my head, Kiki."

"Sit down and let me do your hair while we talk."

I look at her dubiously.

"Hey! Don't give me that look. I've been watching some YouTube tutorials. I promise it will be okay." I sit down in the chair and she brushes out my long hair. "Your hair is like silk. Hmm, this might be challenging." She pauses and bites her lip as I arch my eyebrow at her in the mirror. "I got this, no problem. Don't worry about what I'm doing. Talk to me goose, why do you feel in over your head?"

"Because I know he doesn't want anything serious, but how can I not be falling for him?"

"Have you talked to him about it?"

"What's the point? He's said it like a hundred times that he doesn't do relationships. If I didn't get the memo then I'm an idiot."

She starts to braid a section of hair as she chews her lip. "Well, maybe he's falling for you too. He seems pretty into you. And you know he never repeats."

"He said he's Mr. Right Now, not Mr. Forever. He's into me right now. I mean our chemistry is off the charts, but maybe it's just lust he's feeling. What will happen when we get back home and back to our regular routines? He'll be touring and the throngs of women throwing themselves at him will make him want to go back to his old ways. Those girls in Glasgow were amateurs compared to the girls back in the States."

"What if you're his forever?"

I shake my head. "You're a romantic, Kiki. I can't let my heart go there."

"I think it already has." She ties the braids up on top of my head and starts sticking bobby pins in. "I think you need to talk to him. Nothing is worse than not knowing where you stand, take it from me." Kiki and Tatum were apart for months because of a miscommunication and misunderstanding.

"You're right, I just need to bite the bullet and ask him where we stand."

"Done!" Kiki steps back and my hair looks like a bird pooped sloppy braids on top of my head. One braid slips out of its hold and falls down in front of my face.

"Uh…"

"Damn, I suck at this. How do you make it look so easy?"

I laugh. "I don't know, but it was a good effort."

"Oh, please Sunshine, it sucks banana balls."

I giggle. "Yeah, it really does. You just stick to the clothes and I'll handle the hair and makeup."

Kiki snorts and starts to undo my hair. "So, we need a plan for Skanklana."

"What do you mean?"

"Have anything in that magic box of yours that will dye her hair green or make her break out?"

"Ooh, you're evil."

"I never said I was a saint. We'll call it *Operation Green*." She tugs a braid out.

"Ow! Easy on the hair, sister. And how do you plan on getting her to use it?"

"I haven't thought that through yet."

"I don't know, Kiki. Maybe we should just let it go. Lex totally ignored her on the plane yesterday, and he's been with me every night. She just seems desperate to me. Besides, we only have two more shows."

"Okaay…if you're sure." She looks at me dubiously.

"I'm sure. She's not worth our time."

Kiki pouts as she brushes out the tangled mess she's

made. "You're too good to be my bestie. You're like the good angel on my shoulder and TJ is the evil one."

I laugh. "Too true, but I love you both."

"We love you too, Sunshine. And just think if you and Lex stay together and get married, we can be one big happy family! Besties with husband besties."

I chew my lip and nod, but I don't share the confidence in my relationship that Kiki does. "Oh, by the way, I just had a very awkward conversation with Matt thanks to you."

"Me? What did I do?"

"Remember when you told Alana I have a little crush on him? Well she delivered the message loud and clear."

"No!" Kiki covers her laugh. "Oh my god, Sare, I'm so sorry. I totally forgot about that. What did he say?"

"We both agreed we are more like brother and sister and the thought of being interested in each other makes us want to hurl, so I'd say it went fairly well. Lex walked in at the tail end of our convo. I can't imagine what would have happened if he heard it, he has a little bit of a jealous streak in him apparently."

"Operation Green. She's playing dirty. That's all I'm sayin'." Kiki lifts her hands in surrender.

"I'll keep that in mind, but we have two more concerts and then we can say Adios Skanklana!"

"Okay, but I'll be ready just in case."

I laugh as I throw my hair into a ponytail. "I never doubted your evil-planning skills for a second."

Chapter 28

Lex

MAC, MY GUITAR tuner, hands me my baby as the stadium starts to fill up. London is just as electric as Dublin with the crowd chanting our names.

"Lexy, can we talk for a moment?" Alana slides up next to me and I give her an irritated look.

"Right now? I'm literally about to go on stage." I look at Mac and he shakes his head.

"Well every time I try to talk to you your little friend is always clinging to you!"

I shake my head. "Jealousy isn't a good look on you, Alana."

She stamps her foot. "Do ye really think she's going to be able to hang with you? That this relationship will go the distance? She cries every fecking time she sees you talking to another woman, for God's sake!"

I glare at her as I pull my guitar strap over my head. "I'm done with this conversation."

"Okay, you're right. But I really do need to talk to you

about something important."

I sigh in frustration. "Fine. Tomorrow morning, meet me at the coffee shop in our hotel."

"Okay! Thanks!" She gushes. "Break a leg, Lexy!"

I ignore her as I walk out on stage behind the screens we use to block the audience from seeing us. I'm so annoyed and pissed off I can't even concentrate; my skin feels itchy and tight. Tomorrow I'm going to have to tell her that we are completely done, I don't want her in my life anymore, not even as an acquaintance.

Will and Matt take their places on stage and Tatum walks out next to me. "You all right, man? I've been trying to get your attention."

I look over to the side of the stage where I just walked from. Instead of Alana I see a smiling Sarah talking to Mac, and my heart rights itself again. "Yeah man, I'm good. Let's kill it."

Tatum fist-bumps me and the screens lift as I start the opening chords for our hit song.

LATER THAT NIGHT I'm wide awake as Sarah and I lay facing each other in my hotel bed. She snuggles next to me placing her hands on my chest as I trace my fingers over her shoulder and down her arm. We can't seem to be next to each other and not touch.

"Lex, do you think we're going too fast?"

I lean up on my arm, resting my head in my hand.

"What do you mean?"

"Well, we've known each other a long time, but we've only started this a few days ago"—she gestures between us—"because I'm not sure what to call this. It just seems fast."

"It is and it isn't. Remember when I first met you?"

"You mean when I was dealing with that asshole business guy at the coffee shop?" Her lips tilt up in a smile. "How could I forget?"

"Yeah, Captain Wanker. It was that moment that you knocked me to my knees. I couldn't stop thinking about you the whole way back to the studio, the girl who had the most beautiful smile. And when you showed up to the dressing room I was floored. How could you show up in my life randomly twice in one day?"

"I know, that was so crazy."

"It wasn't crazy, Love, it was fate."

"Well, then why did you hate me so much that first day?"

I rear my head back in disbelief. "I didn't hate you, Princess. I wanted to drag you out of that room, find a closet and make you scream my name. But I knew you weren't that kind of girl. You were too…"

"Sunshine on crack?"

I laugh, remembering what I called her that day. "Yeah, my sunshine on crack. It pissed me off because I knew once you were part of the band you were not to be messed with. I was pissed at Tatum for hiring you because I wanted you for myself. But I also knew, I wasn't a relationship kind of guy and you would have wanted that." I memorize her features as I trace a finger down her face. "For two years I've wanted ye, but I swore I would leave ye alone and not touch ye. I convinced myself I wasn't good enough." My accent grows thicker with my emotions as I run my fingers through her silky hair.

"Every time I'd see you leave with another girl I wanted to scream in frustration because it wasn't me. I once told a girl who was bugging me about you that your dick was teeny tiny and you itched a lot down there."

I snort out a laugh. "Huh, so I pee on them, have a small dick, and a bad case of the crabs. You've got a real catch on your hands."

She smiles coyly. "Luckiest girl in the world."

I kiss her nose and roll her on top of me. "I'm the lucky one."

She kisses me tenderly. "I could never work up the nerve to get close to you. I was too damn shy to do anything about it. How stupid are we to have both wanted each other for almost two years and not do anything about it?"

"Not stupid, Love, the timing just wasn't right for us."

"And now it is?" She rests her chin on my chest.

"Aye, Princess, now it is."

"And what will happen when we return back home? Will you still want me? Just me?"

This is it, the million-dollar question I've asked myself over and over. I want this. I want a relationship with her. I want to go the distance and see where this goes. I trust Sarah not to hurt me.

"Aye, I'll still want you. I'll always want you, *Ghrá mo chroí*, love of my heart. Just you."

"No more waiting, Lex." She sighs as I roll her back

under me and dip two fingers into her velvety wet heat.

"No more waiting. So wet for me, *mo banphrionsa*."[6]

She runs her thumb over my shaft and wraps her small palm around my dick causing me to groan. I'm so hard I can't see straight. I remove my fingers and guide myself into her as I look down into her amber eyes. I slowly rock into her and she matches my rhythm. I make love to her slowly, tenderly, worshiping her body as I make up for the last two years.

---

[6] Irish for My Princess.

Chapter 29

Lex

I KISS A drowsy Sarah as she snuggles next to me the next morning. I don't want to leave this bed, but I need to get this shit with Alana over with.

"Want to come downstairs with me and see what she wants?"

"Not really…not unless you need me to."

"No, I just don't want to leave you."

"Five more minutes?"

"Yeah."

She burrows against my chest and I kiss the top of her head. I lightly strum my fingers up and down her bare arm that's draped over me. I stare up at the ceiling and swallow. I'm so fucking in love with this girl it catches me off guard. When did she sneak in and steal my heart?

"Sunshine?"

"Mmm?"

"I…" My phone buzzes on the nightstand. I look at it and sigh. It's a text from Alana announcing she's on her way downstairs. "I've got to go. I'll be back in half an hour."

"I'll be here." She smiles drowsily. I want to flip her over and make love to her again, but I don't have time.

"I'm counting on that." I get up and pull a pair of jeans and a t-shirt on after brushing my teeth. I grab my phone as I head out and take the elevator down to the coffee shop. Alana's sitting at a corner table for two sipping a drink. I order a coffee before settling down at the table.

"Mornin', Lexy," she says brightly.

"Mornin'. What's up?" I grumble.

"Your concerts have been going really well. Last night was amazing! The crowd responded so well to you guys."

"Is this an interview for your magazine?"

"No, but—"

"Then cut the crap, Alana. What are you so desperate to talk to me about?"

She sits back and folds her arms over her chest. "We have a long history together, no? We were engaged—"

"That was *ten* years ago. Get. To. The. Point. And tell me what you want!" I bang my fist on the table.

"Fine!" She looks away and fumbles with the spoon next to her cup. "I don't know how to say this." I get up to leave and she desperately grabs my wrist. "Wait! You have a son!"

My whole world tilts on an axis and comes crashing down around me. "I'm sorry, I couldn't have heard you right…"

"You and I have a son together, Lex. He's ten years old and he's bright and handsome just like his da…" she rambles on.

I hold up my hand. "Stop. What the fuck do you mean

we have a son and why am I just learning about this *right now*?!" My voice raises as patrons look over at us.

"Ssh Lexy, calm down."

"Don't tell me to calm the fuck down!"

"Okay, okay…look, he's here in England. I had my mum bring him. They're staying at the Carlisle. Do you want to meet him?"

My head is spinning in a thousand different directions and I can't keep up. I have a son? I have a fucking *son*? "Not to be a dick, but how do I know it's mine? It's not a secret I wasn't the only one you were fucking, and I always wore protection."

She blanches. "He's yours, Lex, trust me. Condoms aren't foolproof."

I scoff. "Trust you? You probably poked a hole in the condom, knowing you." I shake my head in disbelief. "You're the last person I trust. What I can't understand is why I'm just finding out about this now?"

"Well, when I found out I was pregnant you had already left for the States. Then you started using drugs and I didn't want the baby to be around that. I was waiting for you to get better, Lex…"

"I've been fucking clean for *nine years*."

"Well, then this chance at the magazine came up and I convinced my editor that we needed to do this article on you guys. I thought while you're over here, kill two birds with one stone." She shrugs and takes a sip of her coffee.

"You're so fucking selfish, Alana. You've kept this from me for ten years, you manipulate your way back into my life, and just as I'm starting to feel love again, you drop this fucking bomb in my lap."

"He's not a bomb, Lex, he's a child! *Your* child. I thought you'd be happy." She starts to cry and I sit back and look at her in disbelief.

"You thought I'd be happy that I've missed the first ten years of my child's life? That my parents have missed out on their only grandchild? He probably has no fucking clue who I am!"

She swipes at her cheeks. "Oh, he knows! He knows you're his da and he's so excited about it. He's told all the kids at school his da is a famous guitar player."

I just look at her, my mind numb. "You told him I was his da and I haven't even fucking met him yet? What the fuck, Alana? What if I didn't want to meet him? That would crush a kid at his age. What's his living situation been like? Have you had a revolving door of men coming in and out of his life?"

"Jesus Lex, you don't have to be such a gobshite. He lives with my mum during the week and I see him sometimes on the weekends. And I knew you would want to meet him. Why wouldn't you?"

I put my head in my hands in exasperation. I chuckle without any humor. "I can't fucking believe you."

"I mean just think, he'll be so ecstatic to finally have his mum and da together at last. He prays for it every night."

I look up suddenly. "No, I'm not getting back together with you. I live in another fucking country for Christ's sake. I can't *believe* you had the audacity to tell him about me before I even knew. You're setting him up for heartbreak, anger...I don't even know what the fuck else you promised him, because I will never *ever* be getting back together with you."

Alana waves her hand flippantly, ignoring me. "He's so excited. He has all your music on his phone. He tells my mum he's going to be a guitar player just like you."

I grind my teeth as I look down into my coffee cup. I have a son? A ten-year-old *son*?

"So, do you want to meet him or not?"

Her voice brings me back to the present. "Uh, yeah…I just—"

"Great, I'll go get them. Just wait in the lobby, k?" She hurriedly gets up from the table before I can change my mind.

"Alana, wait, I'm not ready!" But she's already gone around the corner and out the door. I could chase after her, but to be honest I'm feeling completely disoriented, like I'm trying to keep my head above water but the waves keep towing me under.

I slowly get up from the table and walk out to the hotel lobby like a zombie awakening for the Apocalypse. I sink down into a leather club chair. I can't believe I have a son! *A ten-year-old son.* I try to remember what I was like at ten years old, but all that comes to mind is playing guitar and going fishing with my da.

I can take him fishing! I have a son that I can take fishing! I can teach him guitar and how to drive. Realization suddenly slams into my chest like a sledgehammer. I can't go back to the States. I've missed the first ten years of his life and I'm not going to miss a minute more.

I'm lost in my own head when Alana reappears with a

little boy in tow. "Lexy? Meet your son, Jax."

I look up at the sound of Alana's voice and then at the gangly timid boy standing next to her. I smile, but it doesn't reach my eyes. I think I'm still in shock. He has black hair and blue eyes, *just like me*, but his mom's delicate features.

I clear my throat and stand up, extending my hand out to him. "Hi, Jax. It's nice to finally meet you."

Chapter 30

Sarah

I LOOK AT my phone on the nightstand. What the heck is taking Lex so long? More than an hour has passed since he left the room. I text him to make sure he's okay. I throw back the covers and decide to take a shower and get dressed. I check my phone when I get out, but still nothing from Lex. I dry my hair and look at my phone again like an obsessed woman. I have two missed calls from Kiki and a text from her telling me to come to the lobby. I put on some light makeup and then grab my phone and a keycard, still perplexed as to where Lex is.

Kiki rushes up to me as I step off the elevator. "Sarah, we've got a situation…"

"What's going on?" I look around worried Lex has been in some kind of an accident. I look toward the seating area in the lobby and see Lex crouched down in front of a black-haired little boy. Alana is standing behind the boy with her hands on his shoulders and she's laughing. My stomach drops and immediately I know.

"Oh my god," I whisper as I grab Kiki's arm.

"I'm not sure what's going on but I told Tatum to get his ass down here ASAP. Do you think that's his—"

"His kid? Seems that way." I know without a doubt it is. Kiki and I slowly walk over to them. Alana gives us an evil smile and winks.

"Oh no she didn't." Kiki squeezes my hand.

"Kiki? Permission granted for *Operation Green*. ASAP."

"Oh, thank God, because I already did it."

Lex looks up as we approach. "Sarah!" He wraps me in a hug and then quickly releases me. "I want you to meet Jax. He's my...my son. Jax, these are my friends, Kiki and Sarah."

Jax smiles shyly at us. My heart is sputtering in my chest. *Lex has a son?* A grown one at that. And it isn't lost on me that he introduced me as his friend. Lex grabs his hand and crouches down next to him. I smile shakily at Jax. Poor guy, it's not his fault. "Hey bud, nice to meet you."

"Your accent is funny," he pipes up and I smile.

"I suppose it is, isn't it?"

"What's going on?" Tatum comes up from behind us and puts an arm around Kiki and me.

"Tatum, meet my son, Jax." Lex looks up at his best friend in wonderment.

Tatum's eyes freeze as he looks from Lex to Jax to Alana. "Wow, uh...wow. I had no idea, man."

"Neither did I."

"That makes four of us." Kiki glares at Alana.

Lex gets up. "Hey little man, can you go for a walk with your mum? I need to talk to my friends in private."

"Come on Jax, let's get some breakfast." Alana cheerfully grabs his hand. As they walk by me, she stops and whispers, "You can't keep him from his son. He has a family now."

I swallow back the tears that threaten to fall. I turn away from her and walk over to Lex. "Can we talk?"

"Yeah, let's go upstairs where we have some privacy. Tatum, I'll be right back." Tatum nods and then looks at me with concern in his eyes.

As we ride up, Lex explains how Alana dropped the bomb on him in the coffee shop.

"I can't believe it," I say weakly as I sit on our bed once we get to our room.

"I can't either. At first, I was super pissed, but he's such a cute kid, how could you not fall in love with him?" He gushes as he paces back and forth in front of me.

"He is a cute kid. I can't believe she's kept him from you all these years." My tone sounds flat to my ears, like muffled voices speaking from behind a wall.

"Yeah, I'm really pissed at her, but I don't want Jax to see that. This has to be just as overwhelming for him as it is for me."

"So, what does this mean, Lex? Are you going to have them move back to Nashville with you? Visit him on holidays? What's your plan?" *Where does this leave us?* I selfishly wonder.

"I don't know. I mean so much has happened in such a short time. I haven't really thought through the details."

I swallow past the lump in my throat. "Are you getting back together with Alana?"

He stops pacing and gently sits down next to me as he

grabs my face in his hands, kissing my lips. "Never." He leans his forehead against mine. "I know this is a lot to take in, Sunshine, but nothing will change for you and I."

I lean my head back so I can look up into his eyes. "I don't even know what we are. I thought you didn't want a relationship…"

He looks intently into my eyes. "I thought I made myself clear last night…I'm falling in love with you, Sarah."

My heart takes a great leap in my chest as my hands wrap around his wrists holding him to me. "I'm falling in love with you too."

He gives me a megawatt smile. "Stay with me in Ireland."

My hands drop. "Wait, what?"

He stands up and starts pacing again threading his fingers through his hair. "I mean I know it's crazy! But I've missed the first ten years of his life, I can't miss another minute!"

"But you just said you weren't sure what you were going to do."

He laughs and turns toward me. "I don't know! I feel kind of manic right now. I'm like on this huge high. We can live in Kinsale. I can work with my brother and you can pursue your photography and sing at the bar on weekends with me. We'll sell your photographs in the bar!" He thumps his fist on his leg in excitement.

"Whoa, wait Lex, I can't do that. I don't *want* to do that. And what about the band? You're just going to leave Tatum, Will, and Matt high and dry?"

"No, I mean I'll stay with them until they can find a

replacement."

"A replacement? You can't be replaced."

"You know what I mean."

"No, I don't think I do," I say, sad beyond words.

He claps his hands and jumps around. "Look, I've gotta go talk to Tatum. Think about what I said. Can you believe it, Sarah?! I have a fucking son!" He grabs my face and kisses me before he rushes out of the room.

"No, I can't believe it," I say helplessly to the empty hotel room.

Chapter 31

Lex

I ARRIVE BACK in the lobby and see Tate talking to Lee. I walk up to them with a plan formulating in my head.

"Hey mates, we need to talk."

Lee gives me a long look as Tatum glances over my shoulder. "Where's Sarah?"

"She's fine. She's in the hotel room."

"Lee, can you give us a minute?" Lee nods and walks toward the coffee shop.

Tatum walks over to two club chairs and we sit down. "What the fuck, man? What's going on?"

I bounce in my chair. With each minute that goes by I get more excited that I'm a dad. "I have a fucking son, bro, can you believe it?"

"You and Alana have a kid together?" he asks incredulously.

"Yeah, I guess she was pregnant when I called off the wedding, and then when I got into drugs, she didn't want me around the baby. Then as the years went by, I dunno…it pisses me off she kept it from me until now, but that's typical Alana."

Tatum shakes his head. "I don't trust her, man."

"I know, but he looks *just* like me. He's mine, I know it."

"All the same, Lee and I think you should do a paternity test." Tatum holds up his hands before I can protest. "Just...do it for me, for legalities with the band. It's the smart thing to do."

I shrug. "If it means that much to you, but it won't change anything."

Tatum nods as he looks down into his coffee. "What are you going to do?"

"I think I'll stay here in Ireland...at least for the summer. I'll come back to the States in time for Fall Fest, but the more I think about it, the more it makes sense. I'll stay with you guys until we can find a replacement for me, but I don't want to miss another minute of his life. I don't want to uproot him and change his life. My family is here, Alana's mum is here..."

"And what about Sarah?"

"I asked her to stay with me." Tatum raises his eyebrows. I chuff, "Don't look so surprised, you know how much I like her."

"And what did she say?"

I rub a soft spot on my jeans. "She didn't. I told her to think about it." I shrug. "I don't know what she'll do."

"And..."

"And fucking what?" I snap. "I can't make her stay."

"But you want her to."

"Yes, I'm fucking in love with her." Tatum leans back in

his chair and smiles. "Don't give me that smug look, you asshole. You've known."

"I have, I just wanted you to say it out loud." He fist-bumps me. "I can't say I'm happy you're leaving the band, but I get it. I'm going to miss you, brother."

I look down at my shoes and feel like another string in my life is being cut. I know this is the right thing to do, but it fucking sucks to leave the guys and my home in Nash-ville…and possibly Sarah. It guts me that she might not choose to stay with me, but I can't make her promises I can't keep. I need to be present for my son. I'm just hoping she'll choose me.

Tatum slaps his thighs. "Well, let's go talk to Lee. The sooner we can get this paternity test going, the sooner we can decide what to do."

I say it again, "It won't change anything."

"I know, bro, I know." He claps me on the back as we walk toward Lee.

Chapter 32

Sarah

KIKI AND I walk down into the hotel lobby as we wait for TJ to arrive. After yesterday's bomb-drop, I haven't seen much of Lex. He's been talking with his parents and his brother about the new turn of events. I tossed and turned all night deliberating what to say to him. I'm happy for him, but I'm scared. I don't know what's going to become of Lex and me. I feel like he's being impulsive and not thinking this through clearly. He could still have the best of both worlds if he would just slow down and take a deep breath. It makes me so sad for him that he would give up the band. I don't trust Alana or what she's capable of. She's like a dark cloud that has settled over us. I just hope Lex can see through her bullshit and still maintain a healthy relationship with his son.

"Have you seen Alana since she announced her Lex trap yesterday?" Kiki asks me.

"No and I hope I don't have to. I still can't believe she told me not to get in the way of her family. I couldn't sleep at all last night."

"I hope she's using that special conditioner I gave her."

I look over at her and smile. "Oh no, what did you do? After all the hoopla yesterday, I forgot to ask."

"I may have given her a conditioner with Nair and peroxide in it."

"No, Kiki!"

"Yes. I told her a fellow blogger had sent it to me and it made my hair super shiny so she asked if I had any more. I told her she had to leave it in for ten minutes."

I chuckle. "This isn't nice to say, but I hope she uses the whole bottle."

"Fuck being nice to her, she's an evil twat."

"She really is. So weird because she seemed so nice in the beginning." I sigh sadly thinking about everything going on with Lex.

"Yeah until she realized you were *numero uno*. That kid probably isn't even hers. She probably hired a child actor just so she could get her hooks in him."

"I wouldn't be surprised, but he sure as hell looks like a combo of them."

"Yeah. Oh my god, speak of the devil! And she's wearing a scarf over her head." Kiki starts giggling uncontrollably as Alana walks through the hotel lobby wearing a headscarf and big sunglasses.

She spots us and quickly makes her way to where we're sitting. She rips the scarf off of her head causing me to gasp. She has patches of hair missing, her once-beautiful hair cut off jaggedly.

"I knew something was up when it started to itch and burn really badly. I can't *believe* you!" she seethes.

"Geez Alana, that looks awful, what happened?" Kiki asks, feigning concern.

TJ walks into the lobby and quickly makes his way over. He does a double-take when he sees Alana. "Snap, crackle, pop!" He wheels his suitcase over as he circles his hand around Alana's head. "Oh honey, that's some sadness right there. Did you accidentally use Nair on your head? And maybe some peroxide? That's an interesting color…like a Tijuana hooker's early morning sunrise."

I can't help but giggle because where the hell does he get this shit from? Alana sends me a scathing glare.

"A friend of mine did that once to his Aussie hair, if you know what I mean. And he had to ice his balls for *two* weeks." TJ shudders. "Ugh, I can't even! Don't worry, Elaine. It will grow back in a year."

Alana's patchy head looks like it's about to blow off from her body as she points a finger at Kiki. "You are going to pay for this, you bitch!" She turns to me. "And as for you, I've had a long talk with Lex. I made it crystal clear that you're going to be in the way of his relationship with me and his son. So whatever you two have going on, expect it to end."

"Skanklana, go find someone else to harass. No one cares about you or your pitiful attempt at trying to get your hooks back in Lex," Kiki bites back.

"I'm going to press charges!" she screams.

"Elaine, do you need a hug? Because I can go find someone to give you one."

Alana points her finger at TJ. "I'm going to sue *all* of you for harassment! Stay away from me and Lex!"

"Geez, someone's a touch grumpy. Are you not liking

your new Sinead O'Connor hairdo? It is a little patchy if we're being honest." TJ clucks his tongue. "I'd ask for my money back."

Alana screams again as she ties the scarf back around her head and stomps off.

The three of us start giggling uncontrollably.

"Thanks, guys." I squeeze their hands. "Can she really press charges?"

"The only thing she can press and charge is her vibrator."

"Don't worry about her." Kiki squeezes my hand back. "She doesn't have any proof."

"Kinky, that has you written all over it." TJ smirks.

"Of course it was me. What on earth is Aussie hair?"

"Aussie hair…hair down under. Hello?"

Kiki and I laugh. "And who do you know that Naired his balls?"

"Um, some guy I knew," he says evasively as he starts to look through his carry-on bag.

"Tammy Jean…"

TJ sighs dramatically as he stands back up fanning himself with a magazine. "Fine! I did…by accident."

"How do you accidentally Nair your balls?" I raise my eyebrows as I tuck my legs underneath myself on the couch.

"Okay fine, it wasn't an accident. Let's not relive it. It was awful. Road rash and dangly things just don't mix."

Kiki and I both cringe. "That's TMI and disgusting."

"So was your farting-during-sex story, but you still shared it with me!"

"Oh no, she told you about her crazy first-date conversation starters too?" I giggle.

"It's a miracle she got a second date with Tatum." TJ plunks down next to me on the couch.

"It's a miracle she's married." I smile.

"I thought the same thing."

"Yoo-hoo, I am sitting right here." Kiki lifts her hand waving at us.

"I can't believe she wanted to put them on the blog as ten first-date convo starters." I giggle.

"More like how to lose your date in ten seconds."

"Okay, okay guys, I get it. They sucked. Geesh, tough crowd."

My phone buzzes with an incoming text from Lex asking me to meet him up in his room. "That's Lex, I've got to go tell him I'm not staying," I say sadly. "Wish me luck."

"Awe, Sare Bear, it will be just fine. Distance makes the heart grow fonder." TJ hugs me to him. "You guys will make it work."

"Shit Sare, I'm sorry I made Alana so mad, I hope she doesn't run crying to Lex."

I shrug. "Lex isn't going to listen to her. We'll be fine. That was worth seeing her so pissed, I really needed that laugh." I smile at Kiki, but my heart is beating hard in my chest. I'm putting on a brave face for my friends, but the truth is, I don't know what Lex will say when I tell him I'm not moving to Ireland. I'm hoping we can somehow make it still work if he's not willing to leave here. I used to think the unknown was an exciting adventure, but right now it's the scariest shit in the world.

Chapter 33

Sarah

LEX SLAMS HIS dresser drawers closed as he throws more clothes on the bed. I look at him in disbelief, my fists clenched. "I'm sorry, what did you just say?"

"I said I'm not going to let you make me feel bad about this! I'm not going to choose between the two of you."

"I never said you had to choose!" I scream back in disbelief. "I'd never ask you to choose me over your son. I grew up without my parents—I know how important family is, Lex."

"Unbelievable. Alana said you would try to guilt-trip me," he mumbles to himself.

My vision goes red. "So now you're listening to Alana? Get your head out of your ass for two seconds and hear what *I* have to say!" I pace our hotel room as Lex throws the rest of his clothes in his bag. I take a deep breath as my hands shake. "I'm not asking you to choose. I would *never* ask you to choose. I'm not asking anything of you. I'm just telling you I can't stay. That would be a huge risk for me to put my heart on the line thousands of miles away from my friends and my home. What if we didn't work out? My life is in Nashville, not here in Ireland."

He looks at me over his shoulder and his eyes narrow. "Then go."

"Lex...please don't...." I start to cry. I'm embarrassed I can't keep my emotions in check but I'm also feeling desperate and scared. He's not even giving us a chance. I can feel him pulling away, slipping through my fingers like fine silk.

He curses as he stands with his back to me. I watch his shoulders rise and fall as he takes a deep breath. He runs his fingers through his hair and then drops them heavily to his side. He turns around placing my hand over his heart, his eyes shining with regret.

"Sunshine, you're right, it's better this way. Clean slate. Go find a nice guy that will give you what you want, that can make you promises and keep them, that can give you forever." He gently wipes the tears with his other hand. "I'm not that guy. My son needs me here, and I need to build that foundation with him that I never got a chance to do. I understand you can't stay; I get it. You're a strong girl, Sarah. You'll be just fine. You'll always be right here in my heart."

"Lex..." Tears stream down, blurring my vision as he drops my hand and grabs his bag. He stops and kisses my forehead. He closes his eyes and breathes me in before he lets go.

"You'll always be my Sunshine," he says gruffly before he closes the hotel door on us.

"Come back to me," I whisper as I crumple to the floor, but he's already gone.

Chapter 34

Lex

"THANKS FOR BEING here, man." I shake Tatum's hand as we meet at my brother's bar. As promised, I finished the European tour with the guys. Matt and Will flew back home with Jess, Lee, TJ, and the girls. It's been a little over a week since I left Sarah and my heart is still hurting that she didn't stay, but I understood. I was asking a lot of her, and she was right, what would happen if we didn't work out?

"Is Alana meeting us here?"

"Yeah, she'll have her lawyer with her to read the results."

Tatum nods as we head to a back booth. Connor sets down three pints and joins us. He's been very quiet upon hearing the news about my newfound son. I can't blame him, he doesn't trust Alana, but it irks me that he can't be happy for me. He hasn't even asked to meet Jax. My parents have been extremely closed-mouth on the subject as well. They are understandably upset that they've missed out on Jax's first ten years, as am I. After we get this silly paternity test out of the way we'll have a party at my parents' house so the whole family can meet him, and I pray to God everyone's attitude will change and they'll accept him with open arms.

Alana balked when I asked her to take the test, but when Lee threatened to get lawyers involved, she immediately complied. I was annoyed with Tate when he first mentioned it, but Lee assured me for legalities, it was best.

And I'm glad we're doing it now so my brother and parents can stop griping about the mother of my child. Despite the hints she's dropped, the truth of it is, Alana and I will never be getting back together. But she will be a part of our lives from here on out whether my family likes it or not.

"You nervous?" Connor eyes me over his beer.

I shrug. "I just want this over with."

"Aye, me too."

A tall lanky man dressed in a charcoal pinstriped suit steps into the bar and looks around. He's carrying a black leather briefcase. I wave at him as he heads toward us.

"Mr. Ryan?"

"Yes."

"May I?" He points to the seat next to Connor and slides in. "I'm Edward Ashbury, Alana McKenna's barrister."

"Where's Alana?"

Mr. Ashbury pauses before he clears his throat and lifts his briefcase onto the table. "She should be here shortly. I'm here to read the results of the paternity test between Lex Finlay Ryan and Alana Walsh McKenna. May I see your passport, Mr. Ryan?"

"Of course." I dig out my passport and pass it to Mr. Ashbury. "Don't we need to wait for Alana?"

"No, she's asked me to go ahead without her."

My brother looks at me strangely across the table. "She doesn't want to be here? Hmph." He leans back and crosses his arms over his chest as he eyes Mr. Ashbury suspiciously.

Tatum turns to the lawyer. "You're allowed to read the results without the mother present?"

"There's no law that says both parents have to be present. I could have mailed this to Mr. Ryan, but I know he wanted the results immediately." The lawyer clears his throat and looks at me. "Are you okay with these two gentlemen to bear witness?"

"Yes, sir."

He nods and pulls a manila envelope from his case. He removes a thin file from it and starts talking about the test results broken down into four parts. There's a Genetic System Table, a combined paternity index, the probability of paternity, and then the final results. I start to zone out from all the legal talk. *Just get to the point already!*

"Lex Finley Ryan, in conclusion from the DNA results, you are excluded as the biological father. In other words, the data gathered does not support a relationship of paternity. I'm sorry, Mr. Ryan, for any grievances this may cause you."

A rush of air leaves my chest and I feel like I've been sucker-punched. Connor and Tatum are talking but I can't hear anything. There's just a loud buzzing noise in my head. I get up from the table and stumble into another table and chairs. I hear the guys calling my name but they sound miles away. I take a step forward and everything goes black.

Chapter 35

Lex

One Week Later

"HOW ARE YOU doing, brother?" Tatum sits down in the Adirondack chair next to mine on my parents' back dock.

"Not much biting. I thought you left already?"

Tatum looks at my fishing pole that's set in its holder, the line bobbing up and down with the waves. He eyes the six-pack of empty beer bottles as I open a fresh one from the cooler next to me.

"Tonight. Have you even checked it?"

"Nah. Just sitting here thinking."

"Man, I don't even know what to say."

"There's nothing to say. I'm a fucking fool who fell for her antics all over again. Hook, line, and sinker."

"You okay?"

"No. I'm Embarrassed. Pissed. Angry. Those are just my top three."

"What are you going to do from here?" Tatum rests his arms on his legs as he looks at me.

"I dunno. I need some time to process this. I just...I dunno." I sigh heavily. "I've fucked everything up...with you guys, with Sarah..." My voice cracks on her name and I feel like I'm about to break down. Tatum rescues me before I start bawling like a baby.

"I talked to Will and Matt last night. When you're ready, we want you back playing as our lead guitarist. But I want your heart to be in it. I don't want you to come back because you're running away from here. I want you to come back to the band because it's where you want to be." He sighs, leaning back in his chair as he runs his hands through his hair. "As for Sarah, give her time, brother."

I scoff as I stare out at the ocean. I take a sip of the iced beer, but I don't even taste it. "Time. I broke her fucking heart. I told her to go live her life without me and to go find a nice guy. I shoved her away from me when she was begging for me to not give up on us. I let Alana manipulate me once again. She told me Sarah would try to guilt-trip me and convince me to leave my family here. I let her words taint my heart. I swore to myself I would never let a woman manipulate me, and I fell for it all over again. Sarah was a casualty in Alana's fucked-up mess."

"Man...I don't even know what to say. Sarah is strong though, and she loves you. She's also really good at forgiving. The heart always circles back to what it wants. Hers will too."

"Not this time, mate," I say grimly as I pick up my beer and take another sip.

Tatum stares at the horizon. "I hate to ask, but have you heard from Alana?"

I huff out a humorless laugh. "She's fuckin' gone, man.

She left Jax with her mum and just vanished. Her mum said she signed her legal rights of him over to her before she left and she's gone. I left her a not-so-pleasant voicemail which she hasn't returned. She fucking knew the whole time Jax wasn't mine. I've hired a private investigator to find her so I can get some goddamn answers and end this once and for all."

"What's going to happen with Jax?"

"I dunno yet, but I'm not going to let that poor kid suffer because his mom is a deadbeat. When I told him I wasn't his dad he broke down into tears. Jesus it was fuckin' hard. Alana's mum called me today and said he's devastated, apparently he's started acting out. I can't blame the kid. I would too if my mom kept up and leavin' and I have no clue who my da is. I told him he could always count on me even if I'm not his biological father. I'm going to help him, I just haven't figured out how yet."

"That's…wow man, that's cool of you. And we have no idea who his dad is?"

I get up to check the fishing line. "The PI is digging into that as well."

Tatum nods as I sit back down. "Well, I've got to leave to catch my flight for tonight. Take some time with your parents and Connor. Find out what the hell the PI knows. Come back when you're ready, we'll be waiting for you." He gets up to leave.

"Hey, Tatum? Thanks, mate."

"Take care of yourself, Lex. Get your answers and then come home and get your girl. You deserve some happiness."

I nod as he heads back up to the house. "I don't think my girl will be there waiting for me, bro."

Chapter 36

Sarah

Three Months Later

I LINK ARMS with TJ and Kiki as we leave work. We're headed to the No. 308 bar in Nashville to meet up with my new boyfriend Sandy and some of his friends. I met Sandy not long after I returned from Europe one night when Kiki, Heather, and I had a girls' night out at a small bar near the university. I literally bumped into him as I was coming out of the bathroom. He's cute in a nerdy-preppy kind of way. I was immediately attracted to his nice brown eyes, blond hair, and pale skin. He's polite, thoughtful, reliable, and kind of boring. *The exact opposite of Lex.*

We hit it off and when he asked me out on a date I immediately jumped at the chance.

Anything to take my mind off of *you know who*. Has he swept me off my feet? Not exactly, but I know he's not going to break my heart either and I'm good with that. We've been going out for a month now. A boring, lackluster, uneventful month.

"Do you think his friends will be fun?" Kiki asks as she checks her phone.

"Sandy's fun, so I'm sure his friends will be."

Kiki and TJ exchange a glance.

"What? I saw that. You guys did a look…"

"Sare Bear, I hate to break it to you, but Sandy is about as fun as Kirk Cameron at a gay bar on beers-and-bears night."

"What the heck does that even mean?" I laugh as I poke TJ in the side.

"Sandy is the opposite of fun," Kiki explains.

"You guys haven't even given him a chance. You'll see, tonight will be fun!"

We arrive at the cute hipster bar and I immediately see Sandy sitting with two girls and a guy at a table in the back. He whispers something to the woman sitting next to him as we approach. Sandy stands and gives me a perfunctory kiss on the cheek and then greets TJ and Kiki as we all grab chairs and sit down.

"Sarah, Kiki, TJ, these are my friends, William, Amelia, and Marjorie."

"Classic names, I don't think I've ever met a Marjorie," TJ says as he shakes hands with everyone.

"It's pronounced Ma-jorie. The R is silent."

"Right…hey Madge, can you pass me the drink menu?"

Marjorie frowns at TJ as she hands him the drink menu. "They have specialty craft drinks here."

"Fab. Ooh! Check it out, Kinks! It's SCHWING to-night!"

"What's that?"

"It's an all-nineties dance party starting at ten PM." TJ does a little shake of his hips in his chair.

"I'm in! Sare?"

"Sure! Sounds fun."

"Um, we probably won't stay for that. It gets super loud in here." Sandy puts his hand over mine on the table. My first instinct is to pull away. It's not a romantic gesture where we thread our fingers together, it's a possessive one and it's making me kind of uneasy. Amelia frowns as she zones in on our hands. I quickly pull mine away feeling as if I've done something wrong to her. I grab my purse and distractedly look for some lip balm.

"Oh, come on Sandy. When was the last time you shook your Calvins to some Spice Girls?" TJ teases.

William smirks. "Yeah, Sandy?"

"That would be uh…nevuary."

"Oh my god, I think Sandy just tried to make a funny," Kiki whispers loudly across me to TJ.

"Totes." They both snicker as I pinch them under the table.

"So, Sarah, Sandy tells us you're a makeup artist. I can't imagine that's a very lucrative profession in Nashville. Don't you think you should be moving to Los Angeles for that?"

"Are you trying to get rid of me, Amelia?" I laugh as I put my purse down and peruse the menu.

"Oh! Ha ha ha!" She looks around the table nervously and then leans in closer. "No, but seriously, Nashville isn't exactly a hotbed for celebrities."

"*Au contraire*, Amelia Bedelia." TJ holds up his finger. "Nashville is the Southern mecca for celebrities. They are coming here in droves now more than ever for the music scene and special events. And don't forget all the country music stars that live here."

Amelia looks at TJ doubtfully. "I'm just saying you would be a lot busier in LA."

"Oh my gosh, this is *so* embarrassing. I didn't realize you worked for us? TJ when did you hire Amelia to be our schedule coordinator at Nashville Style Studio?" Kiki leans over and quirks a smile.

"Uh, that would be nevuary," TJ mimics Sandy's words as Amelia turns bright red. William, Sandy, and Marjorie frown at us.

Oh shit this is getting uncomfortable.

"You guys, behave," I whisper. "So, Amelia, what do you do?" I ask sweetly to defuse the tension.

"I'm a tax lawyer."

"Is that as boring as it sounds?" Kiki whispers next to me. I elbow her as I stifle a giggle.

"Ooh! Does that mean you get to bust big-time gangsters and celebrities like Al Capone?" TJ asks excitedly.

"Um, no, very rarely. Usually I settle back taxes, undoing property liens, halting wage garnishments, helping with unfiled ret…is he snoring?"

I look over at TJ who looks conked out in his chair, slightly snoring. I elbow him sharply in the ribs. "TJ!" I hiss.

"Oh, sorry, must have dozed. Where were we? Oh right, Amelia and her dreadfully bor…owe! I mean her fascinating day at the tax shop. Madge, what do you do?"

Marjorie narrows her eyes at TJ. "I work in banking with Sandy."

"Wow, this is all so exciting! And Will, let me guess…um, you are a docent for the natural history museum."

William assesses TJ coolly over his handcrafted Saturday Night Special. "Actually, TJ, I'm an IT director."

"That doesn't mean Identical Twin," Kiki whispers loudly as she leans across me.

"Well snaps, I was hoping for one exciting job out of this group," TJ mumbles.

My heart suddenly deflates at Kiki's mention of a joke made in Ireland over Lex and Connor being twins and my mood plummets. "Where's the waitress? I need a cocktail ASAP," I gripe as I look around the bar.

"I'll go get her." Sandy stands to go find the waitress. "I'd like to finish our drinks here and go to another place for a nightcap."

"That's a great idea, Sandy." Amelia beams at him.

"A nightcap? But it's only eight PM, right?" Kiki double-checks her watch.

"Guess we're not getting our nineties on," TJ grumbles.

Sandy approaches our table a minute later with an exasperated-looking waitress in tow. We quickly order our drinks, and then sit in awkward silence.

"Has anyone read that new book called the *Propaganda of the Misfortunate*?" William pipes up.

"Not yet, but I can't wait to get my hands on it!" Amelia wags her eyebrows up and down in excitement.

"Oh, I love new book suggestions, what's it about?" I ask trying to throw a bone in this conversation.

"It's about the decline of Chinese politics in the seventeenth century regarding the Qing dynasty."

"Sounds like a real barn-burner," Kiki mumbles.

The waitress brings our drinks and I thirstily gulp mine. *Geesh it's strong, that was a mistake.* My eyes water as I try to get past the burning sensation in my throat. Once again, I'm thrown back into a memory of Lex and I drinking whiskey and my heart aches for him.

"Oh! Did you all see the last episode of *Game of Thrones*? It was insane!" TJ squeals at Marjorie.

"What's *Game of Thrones*?"

TJ gasps. "Madge, do you live under a rock? It's only the best series on!"

Marjorie looks perplexed and grumpy. "Is it a political show?"

TJ shrugs. "Um, sure yeah…there's a political vibe to it. You'll have to watch it."

"Isn't that the show with dragons?" William asks with a note of confusion in his voice.

"Sandy, do you want to dance?" I ask before TJ can launch into a full-blown description of GoT, because this definitely isn't the crowd to understand it.

"I don't really dance, Sarah, and besides, there's no dancefloor."

"Oh geez, I'll dance with you, Sare Bear. Come on Amelia, you look like you could use a good dance partner. Madge I would ask you, but you kind of scare me."

TJ grabs a shell-shocked Amelia out of her chair before she can utter a word and Kiki grabs my hand. Pharrell's song "Blurred Lines" starts playing and TJ, Kiki, and I start dancing in the middle of the bar floor. Amelia is standing next to us, against her will, looking like she took a handful of laxatives and they just kicked in. She tries to escape and run back to her chair, but TJ refuses to let her go, making her twirl back into the group.

The song ends and we all return to our chairs laughing…well all of us except Amelia. She looks like she's about to cry.

"You guys were the only one's dancing," Sandy acutely observes.

"I didn't see a *no dancing* sign out there, did you, Sare?"

"Nope." I giggle as Kiki and I clink our drinks together.

"Sarah, can I speak with you privately for a moment?" Sandy gives me a stern look as he gets up from the table. I feel like I'm in trouble with my dad as I reluctantly put my drink down.

"Uh, sure."

Sandy leads me away from the table to the bathroom hallway. "Why are you acting like this?" he hisses.

"Like what?"

"You're acting crazy. You downed half your drink in one gulp, you're dancing, your friends are acting like lunatics."

"No, we're not. We're having fun." I look back down the hallway to our table and see Kiki chatting with William, and TJ is showing the girls something on his phone. "If anything, you're being a fun-sucker."

"What does that mean?"

Uh exactly what it sounds like… I sigh, tired and not really wanting to start a fight with Sandy right now. "This is supposed to be easy"—I gesture between us—"so let's keep it that way. I'm not here to fight, I'm here to have a good time."

Sandy's features soften as he smiles. "You're right, let's go have a good time. Let's head to our next destination." He grabs my hand and pulls me down the hallway.

"But we haven't finished our drinks…"

"I think this location has gotten…tired. You can get a drink at our next stop, although you may want to switch to water or soda." He squeezes my hand and smiles lovingly at me. It leaves me feeling confused. His smile says he adores me and is just looking out for me, while his words leave me feeling trapped like I can't breathe.

"Okay kiddos, let's head to the Tin Roof."

TJ and Kiki groan. "We haven't finished our drinks."

Sandy looks at his watch. "Well, we need to get there by twenty-one hundred."

"What happens at twenty-one hundred?" TJ whispers as everyone gets up from the table leaving the three of us to down our drinks.

"Sandy turns into a vampire," Kiki deadpans.

"Ooh, I bet Marjorie is one too. She's definitely putting off that *only drinks blood* kind of vibe."

"I heard that," I say dryly as I grab my purse from the table and take a big 'fuck you Sandy' gulp of my drink. "Try to be nice, it's just one night." Kiki links her arms with me and TJ as we follow the other four out. "All I'm going to say is I've had more fun getting a cavity filled than hanging out with Sandy and his besties."

"Amen to that, sister."

Chapter 37

Sarah

"ARE YOU SURE about this?" Kiki asks as she pulls a tank over her head.

"Yes, Kiki, I'll be fine! Besides, Sandy will be with me and it's a festival! It's not like an intimate one-on-one session with him." I quickly braid a small section of my hair and gently loosen the braid using it to pin up half my hair as I curl the bottom.

Okay, so I'm lying through my teeth to my best friend right now. We're heading over to the Fall Fest to watch Tatum and the boys play and I'm totally nervous to see Lex again. It's been three and a half months since he received the news that must have devastated him.

When I heard what happened, I wanted to be there for him, the guilt of leaving Ireland and him behind eating me alive. I wanted to call and text, but I was weak. I was afraid he wouldn't answer or return them and that would have been like a boot-kick to my already-pummeled heart.

We left things like shit between us.

The morning he left me completely devastated on his hotel floor, he texted Kiki and told her to go get me. She and TJ arrived minutes later and they just sat with me while I cried, my heart completely wrenched. Eventually, TJ lifted me into his arms and carried me to the car where we left on an evening flight out of London. I never saw or spoke to Lex again.

According to Tatum, after Lex received the news that Jax was not his child, he stayed with his parents and did a lot of fishing with his dad and some soul-searching. I heard he even spent time with Jax, which just breaks my heart all over again for him. Everyone, including me, was worried he'd fall back down that rabbit hole and get into drugs again, but under watchful eyes, he's remained sober. *Thank God.*

I had a hard time coping when I came back. I was consumed with guilt, feeling like I should have stayed with Lex and supported the life he wanted with his son. While the other part of me felt like he was being so selfish for not asking me what I wanted, just assuming we'd live this happy little life in Ireland. He didn't even blink an eye when he asked me to give up everything I had built for myself in Nashville.

When we got the news that he wasn't Jax's father, I just felt really sad for him, for us, for what could have been. Time has allowed my wounds to partially heal, the guilt and anger festering beneath flimsy Band-Aids.

I pull on my black skinny jeans with a white tank top and grab a lightweight army-green jacket from the hall closet. I look in the mirror and take a deep breath. I can do this. I can see him again and be okay. I've moved on.

"Ready, Kiki?" I yell down the hallway.

"Ready Freddy. I'll text TJ when we get there."

I nod just as the doorbell rings. I bounce over to my front door and fling it open, because I know it's Sandy. He's right on time, punctual as always.

"Whoa! What did you do to your hair?"

"Oh, I forgot you haven't seen it." I chuckle as I self-consciously touch a curl. "I dyed it. Do you like it?"

"It's…it's pink and purple…"

"Yep, it's actually a purple to magenta to light-pink ombre. It took me awhile, but I'm pretty happy with it. Come on, Kiki!" I shout over my shoulder. I turn back to Sandy who still has his mouth slightly agape and I quickly survey what he's wearing. "Are you sure you want to wear loafers? There's going to be a lot of walking."

He's wearing a starched Vineyard Vines button-down with pleated khaki pants and loafers without socks. A sweater is loosely slung over his shoulders. His outfit screams watching fireworks out on the country club greens, not going to a country music festival.

"I'm comfortable in these. We really need to get a move on if we are going to make it there by thirteen hundred hours."

"Got it. Kiki! Let's go!"

Kiki runs into the hallway with a scowl on her face. "Keep your thong on, I'm here! Oh, hi Sand."

Sandy clears his throat. "It's Sandy. How are you, Kiki?"

"Great! Let's go!" She grabs my arm and we scoot past Sandy.

"Don't you need to lock your door, Sarah? Ugh, never

mind, I've got it."

I know Sandy isn't too fond of my friends. He always gets this irritated, exasperated look whenever Kiki and TJ are with us. The feeling is mutual. Kiki repeatedly asks me why I'm dating such a snoozer, but I just shrug. She doesn't understand that Sandy is like my security blanket. He's filling a void that Lex left in my heart and I'm not quite ready to let him go.

Kiki comes to a stop and puts her arm across my chest as if we're about to get in a car wreck. "*Oh my god, he drives a Prius.*" She hisses.

I shrug. "So?"

"It's blue!" She stamps her foot.

"Yeah…a lot of people drive blue cars. Come on, you're being ridiculous." I push her toward his car knowing where she's going with this.

"Maybe we can take my car?" Kiki pipes up.

"I've got it." Sandy walks up behind us. "My car is energy efficient. It doesn't go as fast as your car, but it gets the job done."

"That's what *she* said," Kiki mumbles as she gets into the back seat.

Sandy eyes her in the rearview mirror as he gets behind the wheel.

"What? I'm just saying, it's not a Bugatti—"

"And we're off!" I say lightly as I try to diffuse the sudden tension in the car. Heaven knows I'm already a ball of nerves, I don't need anything else added to the mix.

MY NERVES SIZZLE at an all-time high as we meet TJ and Connor in the parking lot at the Fall Fest. Seeing Connor makes my heart lurch because he is so identical to Lex, but it's a good test of sorts, hopefully subduing my initial reaction. At least I'm not standing here staring at him bawling. I introduce him to Sandy after he gives me a long hug and kisses my cheek.

"When did you get in town?" I ask as he releases me.

"I've been here for about two weeks."

"Oh…did you come before Lex?"

"No, we flew together." He quickly glances over to TJ and then back to me. His expression turns to worry as I swallow past the growing lump in my throat.

Two weeks? Lex has been home for two weeks and this is the first I'm hearing about it? I can't believe TJ or Kiki hasn't said anything! I mentally shake myself. It doesn't matter, Lex doesn't have any reason to contact me, and I'm sure my friends are just trying to protect me. Besides, what business is it of mine? I'm with Sandy now. *Good ol' dependable country-club Sandy.*

I paste on a bright smile. "Well, this explains why I haven't seen much of TJ."

TJ wraps me into a hug. "I wanted to tell you, Sare Bear. I just…"

"No, no it's okay. I'm good."

"Where are we going to first?" Kiki hands out our VIP passes as she bounces around excitedly diffusing the somber mood I'm suddenly in.

"What time do the guys go on again?" Connor asks her as he pulls a hat low over his face and pulls out a pair of sunglasses. The chance of him being confused with his brother at an event like this is high.

"In an hour, so maybe we catch a few other acts on the smaller stages first."

"I think we should head to the big stage." Connor checks his watch. "It will be really crowded."

Sandy tugs on my hand. "I agree."

"Big stage it is!" TJ links his arm with mine and I can feel Sandy bristle next to me. We follow Kiki and Connor inside the festival grounds after passing through security.

On the big stage I hear one of my favorite songs playing.

"Oh my god! Old Dominion is singing!" I scream as I drag everyone toward the music.

"Isn't Old Dominion a university in Virginia?" Sandy asks the group.

"It's Sarah's favorite band. How do you not know that?" Kiki playfully elbows him and he rubs the spot on his arm as he not-so-subtly moves away from her. TJ and Connor push their way through the crowd up to the pit where security lets us through.

"Oh my god, Kiki! I'm like arm's reach from Matthew Ramsey and Trevor Rosen!" I'm fan-girling big time and I don't care. Kiki and I hold onto each other and sing along with the chorus to "Break Up with Him". Sandy stands behind us next to Connor, his arms folded over his chest, looking bored.

"Thank you so much, Nashville! Before we leave the

stage tonight, we've asked our friends to join us." The crowd roars with approval in anticipation of who will be joining them. "Give it up for…Tatum Reed and Lex Ryan!"

The crowd goes crazy and my heart stills. I'm not prepared to see him yet—I thought I had at least an hour to compose myself. Who am I kidding? I need months to compose myself as I see him walk out on stage. I cling to Kiki a little tighter. TJ and Connor are shouting and hooting as Sandy politely claps as if he were watching a tennis match. I never told Sandy that Lex and I used to be together.

Seeing Lex again after all these months is like seeing a ghost. He's right here in front of me but I refuse to believe he's real, his image growing fuzzy as tears glaze my eyes. Even though it hurts, I can't tear my eyes from him as he thanks the crowd.

His hair is shorter on the sides and styled sexily on top. I had asked Heather to step in for me for this gig because I knew it would be too soon for me to see Lex and help out the band. He looks happy and on top of the world as he smiles at the crowd, making my heart hurt a little that he's doing so well without me. A girl next to us screams his name and he looks down in her direction, but his eyes immediately find mine. His smile widens, but his eyes look sad, the damage from his past reflecting in them.

He nods at us as he waves to the crowd. "Thanks for letting us share the stage with you guys!" The crowd goes wild and I'm swept up in the energy.

He's electric up on stage—a star, like his mom predicted. He's wearing black jeans, black boots, a black fitted button-down with the sleeves rolled up showing his colorful tattoos.

The shirt is unbuttoned enough to show his silver necklaces dangling from his neck. The epitome of sexy rocker bad boy.

The crowd cheers as three stools are brought onto the stage jutting out over the pits, right in front of us. He sits down on one with his guitar and Tatum and Trevor sit on the other two.

Trevor speaks into his mic first. "We're gonna take it down a notch, Nashville, if you're all right with that."

The crowd screams their approval. There's a few 'Marry me, Trevor, Tatum, and Lex!' coming from some overzealous female fans, but for the most part the crowd quiets. Lex laughs as he adjusts his guitar against him. There's an appealing magnetism to him up on that stage and I want to fling myself at his feet and beg him to make me his too.

"Have you ever wanted something so bad, but it's just out of reach?" Lex asks into the mic. The crowd goes nuts again. It's the same question he asked me when we were sitting on the rocks at Kiki's wedding.

Tatum smiles. "Oh man, so many times."

"Do you ever just go for it?" Lex's voice turns husky and the crowd goes wild.

Trevor chuckles. "I always go for it, but I don't always get it." The crowd roars with approval.

"Sounds like a heartbreak song to me." Tatum smirks at Trevor and Lex.

"Let's sing one then." Trevor strums his guitar as Lex leans up to his mic, closing his eyes.

I'm expecting an Old Dominion song, but when he sings the first note, I'm mentally knocked on my ass.

"Ain't no sunshine when she's gone…" he croons and

strums his guitar.

Whistles and hoots echo around us, but the crowd starts to sway and sing with him. He smiles over at Trevor and Tatum as they join in with him and it's pure magic.

And I know without a doubt in my heart, he's singing this song for me, to me. I've always been his sunshine on crack, and I always will be no matter what happens between us. That kernel of knowledge nestles its way into my heart.

A tear slips down that I quickly and discreetly swipe away. I can feel Sandy's arms encircle my waist and my body wants to revolt as he tries to sway with me. I tell myself to accept the arms that want to be there and not push him away like my instinct wants to do. Lex puts his heart into the song and by the end the whole crowd is singing with them and it's electric.

He strums the last chord and smiles at Trevor, then grins at the crowd. "Thank you for indulging me, Nashville! Old Dominion! Tatum Reed!"

The crowd roars. Lex looks down at us in the crowd and his eyes burn into mine. He winks at me and gives me a dimpled lopsided smile before he looks back over the sea of people. The girl next to us starts screaming to her friend that Lex Ryan just winked at her. She crowds against us, pushing to get closer as Matt Ramsey comes back out and Old Dominion thanks Lex and Tatum again before they start playing their final song.

The crowd in the pit surges forward against our group and I start to feel panicky. I scoot back against Sandy and elbow him to get out of his arms. I feel like I'm drowning, unable to voice my fears or catch my breath as I struggle for space. Lex looks down at us, concerned, and shakes his head at his brother to get us out of there.

Connor grabs Kiki and my hand and leads us back past security to behind the stages. TJ and Sandy trail behind us.

"God, that was crazy!" Kiki looks just as panicked as I feel.

Lex suddenly appears with Tatum from behind the stage. Kiki lets go of my hand and runs and leaps into Tatum's arms, kissing him.

"You guys okay? That crowd is getting rowdy." Tatum looks over at us.

Connor nods and gives Lex a hug. "We'll just watch you guys from backstage."

Lex looks over at Sandy and I standing off to the side and walks toward us. "Sarah, how are you?"

Before I can take a step back, he engulfs me in a hug, lifting me off my feet. "I've missed ye so much, *mo banphrionsa*," he whispers in my ear as he gently squeezes me.

I breathe in his familiar mint, leather, and woodsy scent, missing his touch more than I'll ever care to admit. Damn him and his sexy accent, speaking to me in Irish, and damn him for saying he's missed me, because I've missed him more.

Before I can even form a sentence, he sets me back down and turns to Sandy. "Hi, I'm Lex." Lex reaches out and shakes his hand.

"Sandy Sanderson. Nice to meet you."

Lex lifts an eyebrow at me, trying to suppress a smile, but I can see his cute little dimple popping out. I cross my arms over my chest and look away. Stupid cute smile and stupid dimple.

"Are you a friend of Sarah's or—"

"I'm her boyfriend," Sandy cuts off Lex a little too hastily for my liking.

Lex's teasing smile grows wider. "Ah, her boyfriend."

"Oh, for Pete's sake," I grumble, getting flustered by Lex's presence and the awkwardness of the situation. "Don't you have a show you need to do?"

"Uh, Sam, can you give Sarah and I a minute alone, please?"

"It's *Sandy*. Only if Sarah wants a minute with you." He steps back from us and folds his arms over his chest watching Lex warily.

Lex doesn't take his eyes off of me as he murmurs, "Right, how could I forget, same first and last name. Sarah, can I have a minute with you?"

"I—"

"Good, that's settled." Lex takes my hand in his and guides me to a private corner. I smile nervously at Sandy over my shoulder and almost laugh at the scowl he's sporting. I fidget as I look around for Kiki and TJ, but they're standing over with Connor and Tatum talking to some people I don't know.

"Sunshine…I like the purple and pink, it suits you and it's sexy as hell." He tucks my hair behind my ear as he stares at the magenta and purple locks mixed with light pink. He tosses a look back to Sandy. "So, what's the story with yer man? He's all wrong for you. He's a…Muppet."

"Lex, don't…please. What do you want?"

He smiles ruefully. "You."

I huff out a sarcastic laugh. "No, you don't. What do you really want? It's been three months without a word from you." My voice quivers, betraying my mask of indifference.

"I'm so sorry, Love," he says gently, squeezing my hand. "I wasn't in a good place. There's so much I want to tell you. But first I need to say how sorry I am. For everything." He runs his finger down my cheek and exhales. "For Alana, for not listening to what you wanted, for not standing behind you. I was a fucking mess. I—"

"Okay." I take a step back from him and shake my head. I'm mentally breaking down at his words and his touch and I just can't handle it. Not here, not right now.

"Okay?" he says. "That's it?"

I look up into his anguished eyes and my guard slips a little. "What do you want me to say? I forgive you? Of course, I understand what you were going through. It was a lot and I hope you're doing okay." I gently slide my fingers down his arm and my pinkie hooks with his, just wanting to feel him one last time, even though it tears at my heart. "But I've moved on." Lex scoffs as he looks away and I tug on his pinkie. "*Remember,* you told me to? I'll always be your friend, no matter what."

"Sarah—"

"Lex, man, we need to go!" Tatum shouts.

"Sunshine, I have more to say."

"Yeah, but I'm not sure I'm ready to listen." I look away from him before I break down and start bawling.

"Sarah, are you ready?" Sandy appears from behind me as I step back from Lex. I nod and paste on a fake smile as I turn to him.

"I'm ready to go," I whisper to Sandy as we walk away from the group.

"I thought you wanted to stay for the show. Are you friends with Lex Ryan? I thought you just knew Tatum through Kiki, but you seem pretty chummy with Lex." Sandy continues to talk as I rub my head, feeling confused and sad.

"I'm not feeling great all of a sudden. Do you mind taking me home?"

"I guess, I mean we just got here."

"Sandy, please? I can get you tickets to whatever concert you want, anytime you want."

He looks over at me dubiously. "Seriously? What did you do, sleep with the band?" he jokes, but I don't find anything remotely funny about it. He sees my expression and his smile slips. "Okay, let's go, my loafers are giving me blisters anyway."

I look back one last time to see Lex and Tatum grab their guitars and walk on stage, the crowd roars, and a tear slips down my face. I thought my heart could survive seeing Lex again, but in one simple apology, he's managed to open up those freshly sealed wounds, his words a salty sting instead of a soothing balm. Every word cut deep because I know we are never going to get back together.

Chapter 38

Sarah

THE NEXT DAY I'm back at Nashville Style Studio waiting on my last appointment for the day and I'm feeling totally discombobulated. I can't stop thinking about *him*. He texted me last night to see if we could talk, but I ignored him. I've been wallowing in a Lex-induced funk all day and according to TJ I have a really difficult client coming in for her makeup to be done this afternoon. I need my A-game on, but I'm feeling more like the last one picked for the dodgeball game in gym class. *Just my luck.*

"Sarah, your appointment is here." Kiki pops her head into my workspace. "Good luck with this one," she whispers loudly.

I smile big and mentally shake myself to get it together. Be professional and courteous. Your clients don't need to know that your whole world feels like it's falling apart. Your focus needs to be one hundred percent on them.

I walk out to our main studio after my pep talk and see two tall stylishly dressed women who could be models standing by the elevator. I'm trying to wrack my brain to place where I've seen them before but I can't come up with anything.

"Hi, are you Sonja?" I ask as I hold out my hand to the blonde that's not hovering by the elevator.

"Who else would I be? You do have me down for a three o' clock, right?" she says coolly, arching an eyebrow as she continues to look down at her phone.

"I, er, right…yes, it's nice to meet you. I'm Sarah Bowen."

She looks down at my outstretched hand, but ignores it. I quickly wipe it down the side of my thigh as her friend smirks at me.

Why is the universe putting me through this today of all days?

"Uh, is that a *cat*?"

I follow her hostile glare and look over to the large windows where Oreo is snoozing in the late-afternoon sun.

"Oh, that's just Oreo. He's kind of a celebrity around here. Ready to head on back?"

"Well, I'm allergic to cats." She crossly folds her arms over her chest.

Her friend smirks. "Me too."

This ship is starting to sink fast. "Oh, he's hypoallergenic."

She eyes me suspiciously. "I've never heard of a hypoallergenic cat before, except for the hairless kind."

I smile and wave nonchalantly. "Oh, he's a designer breed. Follow me and we'll get started. Can I get you ladies anything to drink?"

"Uh, I had my PA call ahead of time and give you a list of my likes and dislikes. She said she spoke to a guy."

I inwardly groan. *I'm going to kill TJ.*

"Um, right, I will check on that. Could you remind me what you would like to drink?" I walk them into my studio space and her friend plops down on the couch while I gesture for Sonja to take the chair in front of the mirror.

"Ugh, this is wasting my time! This already should have been set up. Where is the charcuterie board I requested? And the Veuve Clicquot?"

"Okay, let me check on that really quick. I'm so sorry this wasn't set up ahead of time. Excuse me for one minute. Please make yourselves comfortable."

Sonja gives me an evil glare and huffs before speaking slowly. "Well, why are you standing there? Hurry up. I've only got so much time and you're wasting it." She rolls her eyes at her friend like I'm a complete dimwit.

Biscuits and gravy, this lady makes Savannah Edwards look like a Disney princess. I quickly run and grab Kiki from her office and drag her into our little kitchenette.

"What's going on?"

"Ssh! Apparently, TJ promised this lady that we would offer her champagne and a charcuterie board."

Kiki starts to giggle. "That's pretty funny."

"Not when she's super pissed! She's someone in the industry, I just haven't figured out who yet."

"Yeah, she does look familiar…"

"Just help me out and look for stuff we can give them." I reach up into one of the cupboards and grab a white porcelain square platter. Kiki bends down into the mini fridge and starts moving stuff around.

"I don't know, Sare, it looks pretty dismal in here."

"Do we have any good champagne? She requested Veuve Clicquot."

"We have an old bottle of Andre Brut…definitely not Veuve, not even close."

"Do you think she'll notice? I've never had Andre."

"I mean, it's like a five-dollar bottle of champagne versus a sixty-dollar bottle…I think someone brought it to our grand opening last year."

"I'll take it! Put whatever you can together on this plate and bring it in. Also call downstairs to your brother's bar and see if they can deliver anything up."

"Ooh! Found a box of saltwater table crackers." She bites into one and then immediately spits it out. "Ugh, they're stale."

"Doesn't matter, just throw them on there."

"Oh! TJ has an old tuna fish sandwich in here from when we went to that deli on Fifth three weeks ago."

"Better not, we don't want to poison our clients."

"You sure? If anyone deserves a good spoiled mayo cleanse, that girl would be it."

"Kiki…tempting, but no."

"Okay, okay, I'm on it, don't you worry."

I walk back in to find both ladies on their phones. Sonja is furiously typing away on hers.

"*Finally.*"

"Sorry Sonja, my partner is getting your drinks and food."

"I told you they were a couple." The friend on the couch

snickers as she types slowly with one finger on her phone.

"I'm not…she's my business partner…" She's not even listening. I take a deep breath, praying I can get through this next hour. "Shall we start? Tell me what kind of event you're going to and what you'll be wearing."

"*Once again*, this should have been in the notes my PA left with your assistant."

I paste on a big smile. "Okay, well, I don't have an assistant or notes, so if you could just quickly give me the details for tonight, that would be really great. I want you to leave here feeling happy and beautiful."

She scowls and pulls up a picture on her phone. "I'm already *not* happy and I'm always beautiful, right, Amanda?" she titters as she smiles over at her friend on the couch. "I'm wearing this white sheathe dress. I want my hair in my signature look. I want heavy smoky eyes like I had for the *Harpers Bizarre* party."

Shit, I have no clue who this woman is! How the hell am I supposed to know what her signature look is? "Okay, I'll do my best." I quickly turn and discreetly text TJ.

Me: *I have never wanted to strangle someone as much as I want to strangle you.*

TJ: *Awe, sweets, I'm not feelin' the love today. Gettin' kind of a Ted Bundy vibe from you which is a little creepy. Did you finally get a look at Sandy's goods? That would make me super grumps too.*

Me: *TJ, who the hell is this Sonja lady and why does she keep telling me her personal assistant requested a bunch of shit from you?!*

TJ: *Oh no, that lady is there?*

Me: *Yes!!!*

TJ: *She's a hot potato. Some reality TV Paris Hilton that got kicked off of Paradise and U after three weeks. She thinks she's hot shit, but no one can stand her.*

Me: *Me included. You need to send me her "signature look". I'm expected to do it and I have no idea what she's talking about, oh and find me a pic of her at some Harpers Bizarre event.*

TJ: *K, I'm on it.*

Just then Kiki walks into the room with a tray and two flutes of bubbly.

"Hi ladies, here you go. If you need anything else, we can get the bar downstairs to bring something up."

"Ugh, like I'd eat *bar* food," Sonja's friend Amanda says from the couch.

"Suit yourself!" Kiki says cheerfully as she quickly exits.

Amanda looks down at the platter and quickly stuffs something orange in her mouth. *Are those cheeseballs? Oh Jesus, Kiki.* There's something that looks like cut-up hot dogs, a dollop of strawberry yogurt, the stale crackers next to some string cheese, and I don't even know what that green stuff is…

Sonja sips her champagne and runs her tongue over her lips. *Oh crap, here it comes.* I hold my breath.

"I just love Veuve. I refuse to drink anything else. Don't you, Amanda?" She raises her glass to her friend who pops two more cheeseballs into her mouth and takes a big sip of the five-dollar champagne.

"Me too! Sooo good."

I have to bite down hard on my lip to keep from laughing. My phone dings and it's a picture of Sonja with heavy eye makeup and her hair slicked back into a high ponytail on top of her head. I get to work on her hair first, spraying it down and then putting a crapload of product into it to get it to stay slick without flyaways. It's so tight it pulls her face back in a pseudo-facelift.

As I start on her makeup her friend Amanda pipes up. "I'm so excited for tonight's party! I wonder who's going to be there!"

"I don't know. I'm hoping I'll bump into the Jonas Brothers so I can say hi to Joe and Nick. I haven't seen them since Vegas."

"Where are you all going?"

Sonja sniffs. "Taylor Swift's party for her new album."

"That sounds fun! Taylor's super nice."

"Oh, you know her? How come *you're* not going?"

"Oh no, I've only met her one time, but she was genuine and friendly."

"I heard Tatum Reed and Lex Ryan are going to be there! Lex is so smoking hot," Amanda gushes.

"Didn't you used to work with him?" Sonja looks up at me as I shape her brows.

"Uh, yes, I tour with the band."

"Like a groupie?" Amanda pipes up excitedly from the couch.

"No, like a makeup artist."

"Oh." Amanda deflates and chomps on a cheese stick.

"I'm going to get my hands on him tonight. He's single you know. And I've heard he's an amazing lover," Sonja declares and my hand slips while filling in her eyebrows.

Jealousy zips through my body and drags me down like quicksand and I can't pull myself out of it. The more I struggle with it, the deeper I go.

"What's he like, Sarah?"

"Yeah, what do we need to know to get into Lex Ryan's pants!" Amanda gleefully claps.

I'm seriously in my worst nightmare right now. I can't seem to escape Lex no matter where I turn. If he's not in my head, he's being talked about, or photographed, or certain words trigger a memory. Is this how the rest of my life is going to play out?

"Um, he's a really nice guy."

"He's kinky as fuck."

I look up to see Kiki leaning against the doorjamb with her arms crossed in front of her, her lips pursed in a frown. Sonja turns to look at her as I'm trying to fix her brow. I grumble in annoyance as I turn her head back to me.

"What do you mean he's kinky? Good kind or bad kind?"

Kiki rolls her eyes and bites into a carrot. "He likes to pee on girls in the shower."

"Eew," Sonja mutters as I try to hide my smile.

"I could get on board with that." Amanda shrugs as she drains her glass. Sonja glares at her friend. "What? It's Lex *freakin' gorgeous* Ryan we're talking about. He's *so* mysterious."

"He also likes to pump and dump during sex leaving his lover totally unsatisfied," Kiki says casually.

"What the hell is pump and dump?"

"You know, where he goes at it like a jackrabbit and

comes within thirty seconds. You don't even realize what's happened before he's in the bathroom throwing his condom away. Pump it and dump it. That's if he can even get it up."

I have to bite down hard on my lip to keep from laughing.

"Well, *that's* disappointing," Sonja mumbles.

"So disappointing," Amanda echoes.

"Tell me about it," Kiki says glumly as she sits down next to Amanda and puts her feet up on the coffee table. "The rumors aren't true, he's a complete dud."

"Maybe Liam Hemsworth will be there! I could hit that." Amanda looks at Sonja for approval.

"Why should we believe *you?*" Sonja asks Kiki snidely, ignoring Amanda.

Kiki looks over at me and smiles, shrugging her shoulders. "Because my best friend used to date him."

I wink at her, grateful to her for always having my back when I need her the most.

Chapter 39

Sarah

A KNOCK ON my door has me groaning as I get up from the couch. Today has been the longest day I've had in the history of ever. Despite Kiki squashing the women's hopes of jumping into bed with Lex at first meet, it still bugged me that they wanted a piece of him. And even though I did Sonja's hair and makeup just like she asked, she still complained, asking me to redo her shadow twice, causing me to spend twice as long with her than I would a normal client. I left our studio at seven and immediately came home to put up my feet, zone out, and watch Netflix.

I shuffle toward my door in my pjs and slippers wondering who it could be at eight PM. I open the door, keeping the security chain still in place, because I've watched too many scary *Missing* shows with Kiki. Surprise has my eyes widening. "Lex?"

"Can I come in?"

I close the door and take the chain off of it and open it back up. I step aside and motion for him to come in. I close the door and take a deep breath. *What on earth is he doing here?*

"Is Sam here?"

"Who?"

"Your boyfriend."

"It's Sandy, and no, it's just me."

"I brought you Chinese." He holds up two paper bags like a peace offering.

"Oh, um, thanks. I'm not really that hungry right now."

He shrugs. "Yeah, me neither. I'll just put it in your kitchen."

I nod and point him in the right direction. He comes back to my living room and stands with his hands in the pockets of his jeans. My living room is a pretty reasonable size, but having him standing in it makes it feel tiny and claustrophobic. I gesture toward my sectional couch.

"Weren't you supposed to be at a party?"

He shrugs. "Not really feelin' it."

I inwardly smile knowing Sonja and Amanda won't get the chance to get their claws in him tonight.

"Want something to drink?"

"No thanks, I'm good."

"So, what's up?"

"Were you going to bed? Cute slippers."

His stare is equivalent to a match being struck to gasoline. It travels from my head to my feet in a *woosh* leaving me burning up in its wake. I look down at my bunny slippers and want to die. I'm suddenly feeling very self-conscious in my tank and super-short sleep shorts. I quickly kick off my slippers as I fold my arms over my chest.

"Uh, just watching TV."

He takes a seat and I notice a new tattoo on the inside of his left wrist.

"Does that say *Sunshine*?" I want to reach over and trace my lips over it, it's so beautiful.

Lex looks down and smirks. "Got it over in Ireland."

My heart feels like it stops in my chest as I will myself to breathe.

He sighs. "I want to talk to you, and before you send me packing, I just want you to hear me out."

I nod as I sit on the other end of the couch and hug a throw pillow to my chest. The pillow acts as a barrier keeping me from launching myself at him and begging him to give us another chance. I need to stay strong because I promised myself I wouldn't go through this heartbreak with him again.

"Sarah, I had a lot of time to think about my life when I was in Ireland." He leans forward and puts his arms on his legs, clasping his hands together. "I've done a lot of things wrong, and I've made a lot of mistakes that I can't take back, but I sure as hell wish I could."

"Lex, you don't have to—"

"No, please, I need to say this." He sighs heavily. "My biggest mistake was trusting that *sleevan* again. I've banged my head against the wall a thousand times wondering why I let her back in when I swore I never would. I just thought...*Jesus*, I don't know what I thought. If we really did have a son together, I didn't want to miss one more minute. I have the best da and wonderful memories with him and it killed me that I missed ten years of Jax's life already. I wasn't thinking it through and I wasn't fair to you. I mean we had just connected and I was in…" He rubs his head. "I thought if I could throw us all together it would work."

"But then when I didn't want that…"

"Right, when you didn't want that I felt rejected, and I protected my heart the best way I knew how. I pushed you away."

I nod, holding my breath to keep the tears at bay. Lex leans back and rests his head on the cushions as he looks up at the ceiling.

I slowly exhale. "I would have tried to make it work, Lex. You didn't even give me a chance."

He turns his head to look at me. "It wouldn't have worked, Love. Deep down I think ye know that."

"I would have at least tried."

"And what? Drag out the inevitable for months? Fly back and forth, and then what?"

We both sit in silence for a moment lost in our own heads.

"When I found out he wasn't mine it was like my whole world was upended. I didn't know which way to turn, I felt like I was drowning. Imagine being told you have a child, connecting with that child and then discover it's all a lie. On top of that, I threw the band away, you away…"

I wince in pain for him. "I can't."

He places his hand on my foot and a thousand nerve endings ignite. "I'm not gonna lie, I got to a real low point where I wanted to do drugs and just escape the whole world. Luckily, I had the presence of mind to tell my brother that. He and my parents helped me through it. I couldn't come back here…I wasn't well."

"You could have called me, Lex. I would have understood. I could have helped you." Tears slide down my cheeks. I want to wrap my arms around him and hold onto him, he's so vulnerable right now. But I can't. He's not mine anymore.

He slowly rubs his thumb along the inside of my foot. "I was protecting myself. I couldn't chance having you reject me. It would have been the final nail in the coffin."

I quickly swipe the tears from my cheeks. "Lex…it wasn't that I didn't want you. You wanted this life and I wasn't sure where I would have fit into it. You wanted me to sing and…"

"I wanted *you, mo ghrá*. It didn't matter what you did. You made me so happy, Sunshine."

"But you never even asked me what I wanted. You never gave me a chance. What about my happiness?"

Lex swallows. "I thought it was the same. Did I not make you happy?"

I huff out a breath trying to collect my thoughts. "Yes, you made me happy, but we were together only for about two weeks. It was so new! It would have been insane for me to stay in Ireland with you."

"Aye, I get it, Love, I see that now. Like I said, I've made a lot of mistakes in my life. I don't want to make any more. I love you, Sunshine. Is there any way we can work this out? Can we try again?"

I squeeze the pillow tighter and pull my knees up to my chest breaking our physical connection. "I'm with Sandy now. How many times have you told me you can't give me what I want? To find someone safe. I'm scared to trust you again, that when the going gets tough you're going to tell me to leave because you're scared."

Lex groans and runs his fingers through his hair, but I push on. "It's my turn to say I'm not ready. I'm sorry, but I can't give you what you want."

"What can I do to earn your trust again?"

"I don't know. I need more time. I need to see where this thing with Sandy goes. We can still be friends though."

Lex scoffs and mutters, "Fucking unbelievable. Sarah, that guy is all wrong for you."

"And you're the right guy?"

He pulls his hair in frustration. "Yes! That's why I'm here, with my heart in my hands beggin' for ye to choose me!"

"I don't know who the right guy for me is, but Sandy makes me feel safe. I don't have to worry if he's going to go home with some hussy at the end of the night or throw the towel in when he gets bored with me."

Lex blanches and stares intently at a spot on the floor, nodding once. *Shit, that was cruel of me to say.*

"I guess wild hearts can be broken, eh?" He quietly stands up, leans over me, and drops a kiss to the top of my head. "I'm not giving up on you. *On us.* Take your time to figure it out, but hurry up, Love."

He walks to the front door without looking back and quietly lets himself out. I hop off the couch and grab my phone. I ask Alexa to play the song that has gotten me through the last four months. It makes me cry, but it's so beautiful I can't help myself. I head to the kitchen and grab a bottle of wine and uncork it, drinking straight from the bottle. Then I call Kiki.

"Hey Sare, what's up?"

"Kiki..." I sob into the phone.

"Oh shit, what's wrong?"

"Le...Lex just came by."

"Do I hear...Are you listening to 'Could You Love Me Anyway' by Pink again? Because you know TJ and I banned you from playing that."

I look around my living room. "How can you hear that?"

"Because you're blasting it."

"I love this song, it makes me sad." I hiccup.

"What did Lex say?"

"He got a sunshine tattoo," I wail.

"He stopped by to tell you that?"

I turn down the music. "No, I just happened to notice it. He got it after I left Ireland. It was so intense. He said he loves me and wants me back and I said no because I'm with Sandy now and I can't trust him, but we can be friends." I cry. "Why can't I let him back in? I'm so confused. My heart wants him, but my head just pushed him away."

"Dammit, I'm on my way and I'm bringing my friend Jack with me."

"Who's Jack? I don't want a stranger in my house right now, I'm wearing bunny slippers!" I wail into the phone.

"Jesus, Sarah, I meant I'm bringing a bottle of Jack. Turn the music off. I'll be there in ten."

"Oh okay. I have Chinese. Lex brought it," I bawl.

"I'm going to kill him. Be there in a minute."

I get up chugging the bottle of wine and unlock my door for Kiki.

Chapter 40

Lex

I PACE BACK and forth in front of Tatum, running my fingers through my hair in frustration. "I fucked up, mate. Shit, I fucked up and she won't let me fix it. In her mind we're just friends."

"Well, mayb—"

"Just friends my ass. Did you see that boring arsehole she was with? Is that what she's attracted to? Don't answer that."

"She just nee—"

"Fuck him, I mean seriously who has a name like Sam Samson?"

"It's not Sa—"

"Seriously, the wanker looked like a fucking banker in khakis and a button-down at the Fall Fest. TJ says he's a total dud and drives a Prius. A fucking Prius! Is that what she wants? A khaki-wearing Prius-driving gobshite?" I stop pacing and look at Tatum. "Why the fuck aren't you talking?"

Tatum throws his hands up. "Dude, if you would shut

the fuck up and take a breath, I could get a word in."

I sit back down on my couch and grab the beer I opened up. "I just don't know what to do," I say miserably as I take a sip.

"Just give her time. Kiki says she's not into her boy-friend, and your talk the other night really affected her. Kiki ended up going over there after and slept over. They were both pretty hungover the next day."

"Not really the effect I wanted to have on her." I shake my head in misery. "I wrote something. You want to hear it?" I get up and grab my guitar.

Tatum perks up and turns the volume down on the game. "Yeah man! I know you've been stuck on this melody. Is this it?"

I nod as I strum the tune I've been struggling with for months now and begin to sing.

Heartbreaks aren't for heroes.
Love is just a big fat zero.
You left me alone and now I'm sinking
Wasting away sleeping and drinking.
Your love bites, your love claws
Leaving tattoos on my walls.
Your love teases and displeases.
I'm sitting here down on my fucking knees…es.

"Stop. Just please fucking stop." Tatum grabs the guitar out of my hands.

"Mate, what the fuck? I was in the middle of my song."

"That wasn't a song. That was shit." Tatum sits back

down and pinches the bridge of his nose.

"I worked hard on that!"

He arches an eyebrow at me. "Kneeses? You know you shouldn't write songs after drinking."

"I…okay, you're right. It's complete shite. I feel like I can't feel anything without her now. I can't write love songs the way you do."

"Then don't. Write from your heart, Lex. You've written some of our best stuff. You can do this. Listen, if it helps, we'll call Joe Donnelly up later and the three of us can sit down and hash out a song to go with your melody. Okay? And as for Sarah, don't give up on her. She'll come around, give her time."

"I feel like time is all I've been giving her. I just want to bang down her door and force her to talk to me."

"Well that's definitely not going to win you any points."

I grab my guitar back and strum a few chords.

He wears button-downs and khaki
Every girl's dream come true
He drives a puss Prius that's lacking
But she wants him still and that makes me blue…

"Dude, stick to your fucking day job." Tatum gets up to leave.

"This is my day job."

"God help the band." He laughs and slaps me on the head as he leaves. "I've got to go check on Kiki. She's not feeling well. I'll call you later."

"Later, man."

Write from the heart. I turn off the football game and

head out to the open patio that overlooks the horse pasture, the same one where Sarah and I sat all those months ago at the wedding. So much has changed since then. So many highs and lows. I shake the ghosted memories from my past as I play and the words start to come.

Wishing on a starless night
Missing you and it don't feel right.
It hurts I can't get through to you
My heart can't take much more, I'm losing too.
Why can't the sunshine clear away my day
Why does the heartbreak never go away
Why can't I just be myself, just be myself with you
Why can't I get over this heartache too?
Changes happenin' all around
I can't find you and I'm feeling down
Give me your hand and we'll get through
Don't lose sight, baby, my heart will beat for two.
Why can't the sunshine clear away my day
Why does the heartbreak never seem to go away
Why can't I just be myself, just be myself with you
Why can't I get over this heartache too?
Love me 'til the end of time
Is that too much to ask, I'll make you mine.
Take my heart if you do
I swear I'll never stop loving you.
Why can't the sunshine clear away my day
Why does the heartbreak never seem to go away

Why can't I just be myself, just be myself with you
Why can't I get over this heartache too
Why can't I ever stop loving you?
Wishing on a starless night
Missing you and it don't feel right.
I'm trying to get through to you
My heart can't take much more, I'm losing too.
Why can't I get over this heartache too?
Why can't I ever stop loving you?
Wishing on a starless night.

Chapter 41

Sarah

I SWING OPEN the coffee shop door as I hurry in and glance around. I'm fifteen minutes late and I know it's going to annoy him. I spot him as he stands to wave and then he checks his watch, as if I don't know how late I already am. I rush over to his table.

"I'm so sorry. I got behind with a client."

"My time is precious too, Sarah."

I grind my teeth. "I'm really sorry, Sandy. Let me get a tea really quick."

"The line is really long. I don't have time to wait for you to get a tea."

"Oh, okay then. I'll just wait until after, I guess." *Geez, what crawled up his ass?*

He smiles at me across the table and it makes my skin prickle with annoyance.

"I wanted to talk about the next step in our relationship."

"Oh! Okay, um, what's up?" I look through my large

hobo bag for my phone that I quickly threw in there when I left the office.

"I'd like to give you my condo key. We've been going out a couple months now, and I think it's time to take the next step."

My hands still and I look up, my phone forgotten. "I uh…wow, this is kind of sudden. I'm not so sure."

"Sudden? Sudden would be me asking you this after a week. What's not to be sure about? We could save a lot of money by moving in together."

"But we haven't even slept together!" I blurt out, my face heating up.

Sandy sputters and turns bright red. "Not for lack of trying." He quickly looks around the coffee shop to make sure no one is listening.

It's true. Poor Sandy has been trying to take it to the next level and I just can't go there. We've been taking it super slow, so slow in fact I'm surprised he hasn't said to hell with this.

Sandy grabs my hands across the table. "Sarah, look, I don't know what guy spooked you in the past, but I'm not him. I think you are kind and respectful. I think you would make a great partner for me. We could have separate rooms if that makes you more comfortable. Studies actually show it's better for couples." He squeezes my hand.

My throat starts to itch and my hand feels sweaty in his. His words sound sweet and sincere, but there's something missing. There's no passion, no desire in his expression, just apathy, and it's confusing me. This sounds more like a roommate proposal, than his confession of undying love for me. I can't do this. I can't lie to myself anymore. *He's not Lex.*

Sandy takes my silence as encouragement and continues, "My place is bigger than yours and closer to my work, so it wouldn't be a question of whose condo. I'd prefer it if your friends didn't come over though. They seem like a messy group. I can just imagine Kiki snooping through my things." He laughs lightly and it grates on my nerves.

Is he serious right now? "My friends can't come over to my place…are you for real?"

He laughs nervously. "*Our* place. I mean come on, Sarah, Kiki and TJ are a bit much don't you think? Our home is our sanctuary, not a place for them to trash with their dance parties and boozing. They make you drink way too much and too often. TJ told me it was his idea for you to do that to your hair." He waves a hand dismissively at my ombre. "Besides that, they don't mesh well with my friends when we go out. I mean, sure I know you still have to see them because you work with them, but I think it would be better if we just hung out with my friends outside of work."

I can't say anything because I can't believe this bullshit coming out of his mouth. My head is about to explode. I just sit and stare at him in stony silence which makes him nervous.

"Sarah, come on. Remember the time TJ tried to dance with my friend Amelia at the bar? He was twerking with her from behind? She was so embarrassed."

"Yes, I remember, because it was a couple weeks ago, and it was funny as hell. Amelia could stand to loosen up a little and get that stick out of her ass. She dresses like a fucking librarian."

Sandy looks like I just slapped him across the face. "Wow, that's pretty harsh of you to judge someone you don't really know. She graduated *cum laude* from Vanderbilt with a degree in sociology and then went on to get her law degree."

"Well, that's fine and dandy for her." I fold my arms across my chest. I know I'm being an asshole, but he's bringing out the worst in me.

"See? This is exactly what I'm talking about. They are bad influences on you. What's wrong with you?" Sandy shakes his head looking disappointed in me.

RaeLynn's song "Bra Off" starts to play over the coffee shop sound system and it's like fate played it just for me at this moment. I gather my purse and take a deep breath. "Nothing is wrong with me, Sandy. This is who I am. I've been kidding myself for the last two months that I want this relationship to work because it's not going to. My friends are my family and if you can't accept them then you can't accept me. I'm not going to change myself to fit into your world. So, you can pocket that little key of yours because this relationship has run its course."

He sits back in his chair looking bewildered.

"You're a nice guy, Sandy. Maybe a little controlling, but nice. I think you should ask Amelia out. She couldn't take her eyes off of you the other night."

"Sarah, wait. I'm sorry."

I stand up. "No, no apologies necessary. This was a long time coming for me, I just couldn't see it. Maybe I'll see you around…" I take a few steps to leave but quickly turn back.

"And by the way, everyone loves my fucking hair color." I flash him a brilliant smile as I flip my hair over my shoulder, turn on my heel, and quickly dash out of the coffee shop.

I soak in the October sunshine and practically skip down the street. I feel like a huge weight has been lifted off of me that I didn't even realize I was carrying.

Lex was wrong, I don't need a nice guy. I need a bad-boy musician with issues, who loves me just the way I am. Now I just need to find the courage to let him back into my heart.

Chapter 42

Lex

"The dreams are back again, Doc."

"Why do you think that is?"

"I don't know. They went away when I got to Ireland. I thought the woman in them was Alana. I thought she needed me back because of Jax."

"And now?"

"I know who she is."

"How does that make you feel?"

"Confused, excited, worried, elated."

"That's a lot of conflicting emotions."

"No shit, Doc." I huff out a laugh.

"Trust yourself, Lex."

"She says she needs time."

"Then respect her wishes."

"I don't want to fuck this up again."

"You won't."

"But what if I do?"

"Trust your heart. It's been talking to you for some time now."

Chapter 43

Sarah

I GINGERLY PICK up my phone and stare at his number. Just do it. *Call him already.* It's been two weeks since I broke off things with Sandy, a month since Lex came to my house. I honestly thought he would have been hounding me every day to get back together but he's been radio silent. I don't know if that pisses me off or I'm grateful he's given me the time I asked for to figure my shit out. I've thrown myself back into work and we've been busy with the holidays coming up.

TJ and Kiki are thrilled I ended things with Sandy. They thought he was mind-numbingly dull. I can't blame them, he kind of was. He hasn't tried to contact me, so I guess my message got through to him. I really do hope he takes my advice and asks Amelia out. She seems like a Prius kind of girl.

I throw my phone down and then quickly pick it back up. Instead of calling him I tap open my text messages. I take a deep breath. Here goes nothing.

Me: Hey Lex, it's Sarah. How have you been?

Little gray dots appear below my text. Then they disappear. Nothing happens. I wallow in despair as I wait, but nothing appears. He doesn't want to talk to me. I fling myself back onto my bed as I chastise myself for texting him.

My phone dings suddenly with a new text. I quickly grapple with my phone and open up the message.

Lex: Hey Love. Good, busy. Been in the recording studio every day with the guys.

I quickly text him back. I don't want to seem eager, but I don't want to lose the thread of conversation either.

Me: Oh, that's awesome! Are you guys working on a new album already?

Lex: Yeah, Tatum and I have been writing a lot.

Me: That's cool. I can't wait to hear it.

Lex: Anytime Sunshine.

Me: Hey, can we meet sometime to talk?

Lex: Sure. I can meet now. Meet me at my house?

A punch of relief floods my veins, followed by panicky nerves. *Now?* I was hoping for next week, but I guess now will work. It's just talking. I can do this. I take a deep breath and respond.

Me: Yes, I'll be there in twenty.

Lex: Gate code is #6822. Front door is unlocked. I'll be on the back-upstairs patio outside the kitchen. See you in twenty.

Me: *ok.*

I hurriedly run a brush through my hair and check my makeup. I add a little gloss to my lips and then grab my purse mustering up whatever courage I have left to stop my hands from shaking as I slide behind the wheel of my car. I'm scared he's not going to want me back. I'm scared to trust that he won't discard me like he so easily did in Ireland.

I'm scared that if I don't lay my heart out on the line, I'll regret it for the rest of my life.

I arrive at Lex's black gates and punch his number in twice before my finger is steady enough to punch in the correct code. The sound of thunder rumbling in the distance has my nerves on edge. *Calm down, Sarah. You can do this.*

Doubt starts to creep in. What if he wants me out of his life for good? Could I go back to being just friends? Could I stand by and watch as annoying girls like Sonja hang on his arm and pretend like it doesn't bother me? Yeah, no way is that happening. If he refuses what I want to give him, then we're finished for good. That terrifies me to my core.

I let myself into the front door of his stunning Tuscan-inspired house. I walk into his massive Spanish cream-colored marble and tile kitchen and look around. Through the floor-to-ceiling windows I can see him sitting out on his covered outdoor patio watching a soccer game. He looks so normal in black joggers with a gray t-shirt that molds to his body perfectly. His bare feet are propped up on an ottoman. He looks so relaxed compared to my frazzled edgy state.

I steal a minute to watch him, memorizing his profile, afraid it will be a long time before I'll get to see him up close and personal again. I slowly make my way to the glass doors and slide one open. Lex looks up and smiles at me.

"Hey Love, want a beer or water?" He starts to get up from his chair.

"Don't get up, I'll get it." I walk over to his bar area as I try to calm my nerves and slip a water out of the mini fridge. "Do you want one?"

"Sure."

I grab two and sit down on the chair perpendicular to his and hand him his water.

"Thanks, Princess."

The endearment hurts my heart. I don't know where we stand and I'm scared and confused. What if I took too long? What if he's already moved on?

He clicks off the game and takes a sip from his bottle. The wind starts picking up and I shiver, tucking my legs underneath me. Without a word he gets up and wraps a cream-colored chenille blanket around me.

"Thanks."

"Mmm."

We sit in awkward silence. He hasn't taken his eyes off of me since I sat down and it's making me edgy. I'm the one that requested this meeting, yet I can't get my tongue to work, my thoughts flying all over the place. He breaks the silence for me as he leans forward and looks out at the trees bending in the wind.

"I love it right before a storm blows in. The dark clouds roll in, the wind picks up warning you something big is about to happen. You can feel the electricity of it hanging in the air."

Goosebumps break out along my skin, not because I'm

cold, but because of his words.

"I love it when the thunder rumbles so loud you can feel it in your bones," he says. "The horses run for cover sensing the danger we can't yet see. Then all of a sudden, the clouds break open and it starts to pour, the smell of fresh rain drowning your senses."

I'm silent for a moment, absorbing his words as the wind lifts my hair in the breeze. Thunder rumbles in the distance. I tuck my hair over my shoulder, gathering my courage. "Lex, I..."

He gets up as the words die on my tongue and walks to the balcony overlooking the pastures as the dark clouds roll in. "The horses are running. It'll start raining soon."

I'm silent, not sure what's happening, not sure where he's going with this. I'm afraid to show my heart to him, fearful that what he's going to say will trample it.

He continues to look out over the balcony. "I'm fucking lost without you, Sarah." Lightning strikes across the sky in a zigzag pattern. "And I don't know how to fix this."

"I'm not sure you can."

He whirls to face me. "Why the fuck can't I? Why can't you trust me?"

I can't find my voice to answer him as my heart dissolves in my chest. I want this, but I need to know he won't throw us away again. Thunder rumbles again in the distance.

"I lied," he whispers. The raindrops start plopping down like big fat tears.

My head whips up at his admission. "What do you mean?"

He walks over to me, takes the bottle from me and sets it

on the table. He pulls me out of my seat and into his arms. "I lied when I said I didn't want this, that I don't want a relationship. I want it more than anything I've ever needed in my whole life. And I only want it with you."

I chew on my lip and shake my head. My heart is beating frantically. This is everything I'd hoped he would feel and yet, I'm so scared to go down this road again.

He tips my chin up. "Sarah, look at me, Love." My eyes find his and drown in his oceans of blue. "I thought I couldn't be what you wanted me to be, but I can. You're worth every piece of my heart. Please, Love, give me another chance."

I nervously wet my lips, his eyes following my movement. I need to know his truths. "Lex, I've moved on—"

"So, move back."

"What about dating nice guys?"

He snorts and tightens his grip on me. "We both know he's not the right guy for you."

Damn his mesmerizing eyes and that sexy dimple.

"And you are?" I repeat our thread of conversation from a month ago.

"Despite my past and all the drama that seems to follow me, *yes*, I'm without a doubt the right guy for you."

I sigh as his arms tighten a fraction. "I'm tired, Lex. I don't think I can survive you rejecting me again."

He shakes his head and gently kisses my lips. "*Trust me*, Sarah, with all my heart, no matter who or what comes into my life I will never turn my back on you again. It's just you and me." He dips his nose and nuzzles my neck. "Let me hold you to get us through the rain."

"Lex..." I sigh as he kisses my neck. It's everything I

wanted to hear and more. He gently places soft kisses on my lips, sucking on my bottom lip which he knows drives me crazy. I return his kiss, wanting more. Thunder rumbles overhead.

"*Is ceol mo chroí thú,*" he says against my lips. "You're the music of my heart. I love you so much, Sunshine."

I sigh into his mouth, my heart finally home. "I love you, Lex." I break the kiss and smile back at him as I run my fingers up his neck into his hair. "I guess you need a little rain so the sunshine can break back through."

"I'm counting on it." He kisses me hard, making my knees buckle. He picks me up and walks toward the glass doors. The torrential rain continues to pelt down outside. "I can't wait another minute, Sarah. I need to feel every inch of you, be inside you. I need to erase any memories you might have made with that other guy."

"I never slept with Sandy, Lex. I couldn't."

"Oh, thank fuck." He kisses me hard as he opens the door leading me down a hallway to his bedroom. "I haven't been with anyone since you. You've destroyed me. *Shilo rum do*, Sunshine."

He wipes the tears I didn't realize were falling down my cheeks. I quirk my lips into a smile. "Is that Irish?"

"I dunno. You said it to me in your sleep one night. I like to think that in your language you're saying, I'm yours forever."

I throw my head back and laugh.

"Forever, *mo chroí.*"[7]

"*Shilo rum do*, Lex. Forever."

---

[7] Irish for my heart.

Epilogue

✦

Sarah

Ten Months Later

I STEADY MYSELF against Kiki as I apply eyeliner to her left eye. "Quit bumping your belly into me. You're going to get makeup on my white dress...did you just shove some chocolate into your mouth?"

"No," she mumbles around something.

"Liar, I just saw you chew!"

"But I'm sooo hungry! Why aren't we allowed to eat again?" Kiki whines as she chews the chocolate square.

"Hold still! Because you'll get stains on your dress, that's why. You could have shared it, jerk," I pout as I swipe under her eye with tissue. Kiki's enormous nine-month belly bumps into me as she readjusts in her chair.

"Are we almost done? I need to pee."

I roll my eyes. "Of course you do."

"Hey! It's not my fault this baby likes to step on my bladder. You just wait."

I quickly do her other eye and apply mascara to her lash-es. "Okay, done. Don't touch your face!"

She gets up and her belly bounces into mine. "I have to wake up three times in the night to pee," she says grumpily.

"There are my preggo bitches!" TJ claps his hands giddily as he glides into the bridal suite.

Kiki makes a beeline for the bathroom as I rub my five-month belly and arch my back.

"Hellooo in there, babies! It's Uncle TJ! Who's your favorite? I am! Only me, no one else, just me."

I lean down and shove TJ's head away from my stomach and giggle. "Don't listen to that creepy Uncle TJ voice, babies. You only listen to Daddy's voice." I look up at TJ. "Speaking of, have you seen Lex? Is he nervous?"

"Cool as a coconut."

"You mean cucumber."

"No, I mean coconut. Slightly hairy on the outside, smooth, creamy, milky-cool on the inside."

"Cool as a coconut is not a thing!" Kiki shouts from the bathroom.

"It is too a thing! Just mind your bees and pee!" TJ shouts back in exasperation.

"It really isn't a thing. In fact, your description sounds really gross." I smile as I straighten his bowtie. "Is Heather with the guys?"

"Yep, she's helping them get ready. She'll be here in a few."

"Hey guys? I need help in here!" Kiki whines from the bathroom.

"Oh Jesus, I knew a long dress would be a bad idea. I should have sent Heather over here and stayed with the guys." TJ rolls his eyes. "You better not have peed on yourself! I did not bring a backup dress for you!" TJ leans into me and whispers loudly, "I totally brought a backup dress. I don't trust her at all."

I giggle as we open the bathroom door to find Kiki crying, sitting on the toilet, her dress bunched around her.

"Oh my god, what's wrong?" I rush toward her.

"I can't..." she sobs. "I can't get myself up off the toilet!"

TJ and I look at each other and burst out laughing.

"It's not funny, assholes! You try gaining sixty-five pounds with swollen cankles and having to pee every ten minutes! How would you feel looking like this when your husband has size-zero sluts throwing their bras at him on stage! And my stupid sister keeps sending me pictures of when she was pregnant and she looks perfect with a cute little beach ball, and she won't stop with the nutritional guides and the dangers of eating ice cream while pregnant. I fucking love ice cream. God, she sucks. You try feeling beautiful when you actually look like a beached whale!" She sniffles.

"Awe, Kinky, it's not that bad. We all know Brooke is a desperate attention-seeking whore, and that her kids are total asshats, so there's that. And that's a lie about ice cream, she's just jelly you can have it and she'll gain ten pounds if she looks at it." Kiki sniffles as TJ hands her a tissue. "And Tate loves you so much he wouldn't even give those girls the time of day. Besides, you look more like a walru—"

"Okay, okay, no need to compare her to any more marine life, let's get her up," I interrupt TJ before Kiki rips his head off and messes up his perfectly coiffed hair that I spent an hour on.

I put my arm under her right side and TJ is on her left as we hoist her to her feet.

"Mary mother of Joseph, you are heavy," TJ moans. Kiki glares at him. "Maybe only one scoop a day instead of three, okay?"

"Let's bring her back to the chair, I'll need to fix her makeup."

"I'm sorry Sarah, I didn't mean to cry, don't be mad."

I laugh. "I'm not mad, goof. I'd cry too if I couldn't get off the toilet."

"I promise I'll always get you off the toilet. Awe, I love you guys!" She sniffles. "Why am I crying? We've got a damn wedding to get to!"

"*Oh, she's sweet but a psycho, a little bit psycho…*" TJ sings under his breath. "Remind me never to get preggers. I knew I shouldn't have gotten that sex swing installed in their house."

Kiki shoves him and then hugs him. "Puhlease, I packaged it up as soon as we got home. I've been waiting for the right time to donate that thing to the perfect couple."

TJ arches an eyebrow at me and I shrug.

"I had it delivered to Sandy and Amelia's house the other day as an early wedding present."

"No, you didn't!" I giggle.

"I did, and I signed all three of our names. You know they've got to be total closet whips-and-chains weirdos."

TJ and I both laugh. "Oh my god Kinky, that's so perfect!"

A month ago, I received a text from my ex Sandy thanking me for breaking up with him, and for my advice on asking Amelia out. They are going to be married this summer. TJ swiped my phone and texted Sandy back asking if he could head up the wedding dance party. Wouldn't it be fabulous if Amelia and Sandy could have a wedding dance-off like at the end of *Footloose*? After never receiving a response, I convinced TJ that our invites must have gotten lost in the mail.

"Okay, okay, sluts, huddle up." TJ makes us form a huddle circle. "I love you girls. You're my family. Kiki, you're amazeballs and I can't wait to meet this little man in less than a month that is making you incredibly cray-cray. But seriously, you're going to be an amazing mommy to the handsomest little stud, besides me."

"Awe, shit, I'm going to start crying again." She sniffs as she kisses TJ's cheek.

"Are you eating chocolate?"

"*No!*"

TJ rolls his eyes. "Liar." He turns to me. "And Sare Bear, you've come a long way, baby. Kinky and I had our doubts"—Kiki elbows him in the ribs as I laugh—"but you held on to that ornery Irish hottie upstairs and now look at you...you put a ring on it and got two muffins in the oven..."

"First of all, why are you talking like Beyoncé? Second of all...why the fuck is she a cute little muffin and I'm a goddamn walrus?"

"Will you stop interrupting me?! I only meant because she's smaller..."

"Oh, so now I'm a fucking giant?"

I giggle as my two best friends squabble. I feel a little flutter-kick. "Oh my god, you guys! You guys! I just felt one of them kick!" They stop arguing and look at me with wondrous smiles.

"Awe, little ones." Kiki rubs my belly. "I hope you can keep little Chase Cameron Reed in line, because the three of you are going to be absolute besties."

"Okay, *as I was saying*, Sare Bear, we are so happy for you and Lex! You're going to be an amazing, patient, loving mama."

I kiss his other cheek, getting misty-eyed as well.

"But the most important thing?"

"What's that?" Kiki and I say in unison.

"I'm getting married, bitches!"

Post Epilogue

"CHEERS MAN, SHE'S beautiful. They both are." Tatum gently squeezes my shoulder leaving me alone with the most beautiful baby girl I have ever laid eyes on as she drowsily sucks on her bottle in my arms.

I look down at her rosy-pink cheeks and run my finger along the softest skin I have ever touched. She's so tiny. I look over across the yard and watch her beautiful mama holding her twin brother, showing him off to our family and friends. Wyatt Finlay Ryan, named after both our dads, was born first with a shock of dark hair screaming like a wild man. Alexis Connor Ryan came thirty seconds behind her brother, quiet as a mouse with a soft patch of blonde fuzz. We were scared something was wrong with her until they laid her on Sarah's chest and she yawned. It was the most magical moment of my life.

The late-afternoon sun dapples the grass as I sit in a chair under the shade tree quietly feeding my daughter. Dusk is quickly fading into night as the twinkle lights hanging in the trees around the yard glow brighter. Sarah catches my eye across the yard and smiles at me.

My forever sunshine.

Shortly after that stormy afternoon at my house when we reconciled, I went out and bought an antique square-cut diamond and proposed to her while we were out riding the horses, with the sun setting over the ranch. It was simple and perfect, just like us.

We decided to get married on a beach in Turks and Caicos. Sarah wanted something beachy with Caribbean-blue waters to match my eyes. I told her it didn't matter where, as long as I had my sunshine. We had our small group of loved ones with us and it was perfect. Kiki put together a *Trolls-*themed rehearsal dinner which she thought was hilarious. I'll never forgive Connor. Tatum, Matt, and Will surprised us with an acoustic version of our wedding song, "Live Forever", the song we danced to the night she stole my heart completely.

She's the best thing that has ever happened to me. And she's a saint for waiting patiently for me to realize that. I haven't had the nightmare once since that rainy November afternoon.

I had some really dark days after I found out Jax wasn't mine. The private investigator finally found Alana living her best life down in Australia with some new rich guy. It turns out she was having an affair with my deadbeat cousin from my dad's side of the family while we were engaged, and he is Jax's real dad. He looks a lot like Connor and me, so Alana thought she could claim the baby as mine and try to milk me for monetary support.

She left for Australia soon after the lawyer read the tests and I haven't heard from her since. Not an apology, nothing.

The article she wrote for the magazine was a fluff piece about a paragraph long and was submitted the same day we had the television interview in Dublin. Her whole ruse of covering our European tour was a total sham. She orchestrated the whole thing just to get back in my life and under my skin. Lee is still kicking himself he didn't vet her better, but I constantly remind him she's a master manipulator. She had us all hoodwinked. Well, everyone except Kiki. Nothing can get past that sneaky one.

I've done a lot of healing this past year and have learned to forgive myself for trusting her again. I've always believed everyone deserves a second chance, but not a third. *Fool me once, shame on you; fool me twice, shame on me.*

I watch Jax as he tosses a football with my brother. He looks over at me with a wide grin and a smile splits my face. He's such an amazing kid. I kept in touch with him after I left Ireland, but I could tell he wasn't happy, and my heart broke for him. He was an innocent bystander in this whole fucking mess. After talking it over with Sarah we asked my cousin and Alana's mother if we could become his parental guardians. He moved to the States to live with us four months ago and we are in the process of adopting him. He's been through a lot, and some days are tougher than others, to be expected, but he has such a tender heart. He's an amazing big brother to the twins and hugs Sarah every chance he gets. It breaks my heart to think he never got hugs from his own mum, and that he wasn't wanted by either of his parents. Sarah and I make sure to tell him how much we love him every single day. He loves fishing and playing the guitar with me, and he's taken a shine to helping out with the horses on our ranch. Broken souls tend to mend each other. They've been good therapy for him, and he for them. We may not be his biological parents, but we're his family, and he is ours.

I did a lot of soul-searching those three months I spent in Ireland after Sarah left. I let the best thing in my life slip through my fingers because I was only thinking about myself. Seems I had lived the last ten years that way. When I returned to the States, I apologized to the guys for letting them down and for how easily I dismissed them because of Alana and her lies. They didn't even question my loyalty, immediately accepting me back into the band. It humbled me to the core.

I've been writing a lot with Tatum. That song, "Wishing on a Starless Night"? Yeah, it went to number one. Some argue it's a heartbreak song, some say it's a love song. I always shrug when I get asked…maybe a little bit of both.

I watch as my mom dances with TJ under the twinkle lights and it makes me smile. "See that wanker over there, Mouse? That's your Uncle TJ. He's crazy, but he loves your Uncle Connor very much and that makes my heart whole. You can go to them for anything. They'll always have you and your brother's backs," I whisper to her as she drowsily sucks on the bottle.

My mum and dad love TJ and his hilarious, somewhat wacky personality. He makes everyone laugh, especially my brother, which makes me so happy that Connor finally found his matching puzzle piece. I am thrilled to have my brother living in Nashville with me now. He sold the bar soon after Alana dropped her bomb and I went into a tailspin.

When TJ left, he realized he didn't want to live the complacent life he had created for himself. He wanted to travel and see the world with sparkles and pizazz. And who better to do it with than TJ? He's now managing the bar that Kiki's brother owns in the building where Sarah, TJ, and Kiki work. He's got more sparkles and pizazz then he knows what to do with.

My dad walks over to where I'm sitting. "Yer mastering parenthood already, lad."

"Yeah? How's that, Da?"

"You've managed to find a quiet corner away from the chaos."

I chuckle as he hands me a beer.

"I'm proud of ye, son. You've done good." He looks down and runs a finger over the velvet-soft top of Alexis's head. "No matter how crazy things get with the twins and Jax, and believe me they will, trust in your love with Sarah. It will get you through the hard times."

I swallow past the lump in my throat and nod at my dad's advice. "I will. You and Mum have been the best role models to follow."

"Finn! 'Pour Some Sugar on Me' is playin'! Get yer tush on the dancefloor!"

My dad smiles. "Some things never change." We both chuckle as he heads toward my crazy mum.

My parents decided to keep their place in Ireland, but bought a little bungalow here as well. I have a feeling now that the twins, Jax, and Connor are here, they won't want to be going back across the pond anytime soon.

I smile as I watch Tatum wrap an arm around Kiki's shoulder as he leans in for a kiss. "And see that little terror making spit bubbles at your brother? That's Chase Cameron

Reed. You stay *far* away from him, little angel. He'll be trouble like his parents—charming like his da and crazy like his mum. If I have to get a restraining order against him, I will."

Chase spits up all over Kiki and I chuckle as she hands him off to Tatum to clean up her dress. "Look, the little dude can't even hold his own milk. What a Muppet."

Alexis pops the bottle out of her mouth and I swear she smiles at me. Sarah slowly dances her way over with a fussy Wyatt as she tries to soothe him and leans down to kiss me.

"Hello, Princess. I think Mouse just smiled at me." I beam as I put her over my shoulder to burp her.

"Eh, probably just gas." She sits on the arm of my chair.

"Way to take the wind out of my sails." My smile turns to my son. "Wyatt, did you hear that? Be on my side, bro—did your sister smile?"

Wyatt cries and pumps his little fist in the air and I smile triumphantly.

"Three against one."

"Hmph, I have a feeling this won't be the first argument where I'll be outnumbered or outvoted." She smiles cheekily at me.

"How's my beautiful wife?"

"Completely happy."

"Me too, Sunshine, me too."

"*Shilo rum do*, Lex."

"*Shilo rum do*, Love."

She leans down and kisses me and I've never felt more at home in someone else's heart than I do in hers.

The End.

Sneak Peek of

The Social Hour

Prologue

Cameron

THE POOL STICK slides easily between my fingers as the quiet click of the cue ball sends the eight ball into its designated pocket. I stand back up and arch my eyebrow at the redhead sitting on the edge of the pool table at the opposite end of me. She giggles and slips the last piece of clothing down her legs. I place the pool stick down on the table and stalk toward her.

"Well, that was quick." She smiles.

"And predictable." My lips tick up into a smirk as I grab her waist and push her back on the green felt. I run my fingers down her chest and over her fake tits as she opens her legs for me. I lean over her and my lips graze against her creamy silky skin following the path my fingers just took.

"Oh god, yes!" she pants as her fingers thread through my hair.

"Is this how you want it?" I murmur against her skin.

"God, yes!" she screams.

"Mom! Are you home? Dad, I think I heard her downstairs in the game room."

I immediately stop kissing her and look up, her wide eyes mirroring my own deer-in-the-headlights frozen stare.

Mom…Dad?

"Are you fucking married?" I seethe as she scrambles out from underneath me.

"Shit, shit, shit!" she whispers. "They weren't supposed to be home until Sunday."

What the fuck?

She shoves my coat into my arms and pushes me toward the French doors leading out to the pool.

"Get out!" she hisses as she turns to quickly find her clothes and put them on. I'm just standing there slack-jawed watching her in disbelief. She growls in irritation as she lunges toward me and grabs the door handle open. "Get out before he catches us!" She violently shoves me out the door. "You're going to have to climb over the back wall. Now go!" She slams the French door in my face, the glass rattling.

My eyes try to adjust to the darkness as I look around the backyard. I'm tempted to barge back in through the door and get some answers from her, but I'm not so sure it's worth it…if she's worth it. Pitiful thing is, five minutes ago I thought she was.

I mentally shake myself and jog toward the back wall. I don't particularly want to meet the fist of a scorned husband right now.

I look up at the eight-foot stone wall. At least I'm used to rock climbing, although not the ideal time to be doing it in the dark, while wearing wing tips, my Dolce & Gabbana suit and Burberry wool coat. I grab the edge of the cold stone as my foot slips on the crusted ice. Dammit, this isn't easy. I get a better purchase on a different stone and heft myself up. I deftly climb up and over the top and jump down into mud.

Are you fucking kidding me right now? My Italian leather custom-made shoes are now ruined. Fucking Jessica. How in the hell did I miss the signs she was married? *With kids?* I wipe my hands off on my wool coat and gather my bearings.

I quickly walk to the sidewalk and spot my silver Audi R8 parked in front of Jessica's neighbor's house. *You're such a fucking idiot, Cam.* Didn't you wonder why she asked you to park across the street from her house? I look at the house in question. It's a sprawling two-story stucco home with a minivan parked in the driveway. I drag my hand down my face in utter disbelief at my stupidity. *Details, Cam, you missed the fucking details tonight.* Like why would a single woman live in such a huge house in an upscale neighborhood? And the fact she always insisted we go to my condo at night, making excuses for why she could never sleep over.

I've been seeing Jessica for the past three weeks, but we always went to my place after our "dates" of her hanging out at the bar while I finished up paperwork. I should have known better. Rule number one: Never get involved with the customers. Jesus, I can't believe I got duped. She probably isn't even an attorney like she said, probably just a bored trophy wife seeking attention.

I shake my head as I get into my car. My pride seriously wounded. I actually liked Jessica, maybe I was even falling in love with her. She was funny and smart, beautiful as hell. I start the car and the engine roars to life. I look over at the house one last time as I pull away from the curb. I can see her in the upstairs window watching me. I grind my teeth and jam my stick into gear, peeling away from the curb.

Never again. I will never let a woman make me feel this way again.

Acknowledgements

A big thank-you to my four biggest fans, Allisson, Lisa, Julie, and AJ. Your support means the world to me. Thank you to all the bookstagrammers and all the readers who fell in love with Kiki and Tatum in *Coffee Girl*. You made *The Makeup Artist* possible! To Sniffy, thank you for being my Irish support, and always answering my questions. To Michelle for having to read and edit this thing a zillion times again, thank you for your support, I couldn't do this without you. I promise to work on my grammar. To my family for their support and insisting on reading *Coffee Girl*, thank you and I love you. To my husband and kids for putting up with my: just give me one more paragraph, one more minute, one more second! Your patience made this book happen. To Josephine and Richard, you make the sun shine through the rain. Thank you from the bottom of my heart for all your love and support.

About the Author

Sophie Sinclair runs on lots of coffee, dark chocolate, and wine. She devours all different genres of books, but romance, especially romantic comedies, are her favorite. If she's not writing, she's reading or out in her garden to keep her sanity. The rest of the time she's a mom to two amazing girls, a husband that has put up with having to read her romance novels, her three rescue dogs, her rescue cat Pickles, and a guinea pig named Fluff.